Where The Heart

Left Off

To JANG
Hope you enjoy the
book. Best wishes!

by Richie Frieman

ISBN 978-1-61392-020-6
First edition: August 2014
Printed in the United States of America

Oaklight Publishing, LLC
4306 Independence Street
Rockville, MD 20853
USA
http://oaklightpublishing.com

CONTENTS

Dedication

This book is for my grandfather,

Howard Smith

for allowing me to use his story.

Acknowledgements

There are many people who made this book possible, and your gratitude and time will forever be appreciated. I couldn't have done it without my grandfather, Howard Smith, who allowed me to borrow his real life for my work of fiction.

Thank you to my amazing publishing team at Oaklight and Heartlight Publishing who believed in my work from the beginning. Matthew Vossler and Rosa Sophia are the dynamic duo who saw my vision and allowed it to shine. I must also thank my hometown of Baltimore for allowing me to use your charm as the backdrop of my story.

As well, to my parents—biological and step—who remain my biggest champions. And as always to the greatest woman in the world, my wife Jamie, and the coolest kids on the planet, Maddy and Cole. No reward or honor can top that of being a husband and a father.

Prologue

Summer 1950

I wish I could cradle you in my arms every morning, and live in that moment forever.

Albert had written those words in a letter to Ella a week before. But in just a few days, everything had changed and all he had were memories to comfort him.

He struggled to climb off his motorcycle, clutching his side as pain lanced through him. He lowered his body in the shade of an old oak tree, alongside the perimeter of Ella's parents' property. The tree was secluded enough that no one could see them while they made love in the fields during hot summer evenings, but close enough they could still hear her parents yell for her to come in for dinner. They'd kissed for the first time beneath that tree, and carved their initials into the trunk. He ran his hands through the soft, tall grass. This was their secret meeting place, and she'd sneak outside to find Albert waiting for her once her parents had gone to sleep.

He leaned against the trunk of the tree, every breath a chore as he gingerly held his hand over his broken ribs. Despite the excruciating pain, he still managed a faint smile while gazing at her house thinking about their first time together.

He would never see her again, or make love to her again, or sit under that tree again. He focused on Ella's bedroom window. He thought about her, now fast asleep, never knowing their dreams would be forgotten by sunrise. Soon, Albert would be far away. Everything he promised her, everything they wished for together, was over.

He reached into his jacket, wincing in pain, and took out the letter he'd written to Ella earlier that day. Blood from his side had soaked through the bandages and his shirt, and onto the corner of the paper.

The letter was a confession, but he knew it would never be enough. His one swollen eye made it difficult to read, and his hand, the fingers bruised and damaged, ached from what had happened earlier that day.

The beating. The warning. He wasn't sure what was worse—the ache from his broken bones, or the throbbing of his shattered heart. His hand trembled and the paper shook. He owed it to her, an explanation—the truth.

He read it to himself for what seemed like the hundredth time, and once again wept uncontrollably on the paper. He balled it in his fists in frustration and rocked back and forth in the grass, focusing on an ant that scurried up the leg of his pants. The insect blurred in and out of his vision as he squeezed his eyes shut, his badly bruised shoulders rising and falling with every wracking sob. The pain of weeping made him grit his teeth in agony, clutching his broken body.

He couldn't understand why this happened. And nothing hurt more than knowing he was seen as an animal—a piece of trash meant to be thrown away.

Everything he and Ella had known for the past two years dissolved like the paper in his hands. Albert couldn't look at her house anymore. He unfolded the letter and tried to read it again, but could only make it through the first two lines.

Maybe they were right. And maybe it would be better if I left.

Before getting back on his motorcycle, he picked a yellow tulip and breathed in the delicate scent. Tulips were her favorite, and the soft yellow petals reminded him of the dress she'd worn on their first date. He took one last look at the house and slipped the flower and letter into his jacket pocket.

In a few hours he would be cruising along the Delaware coast, rethinking his future. The only medicine was time. But Albert knew Ella would remain in his heart for the rest of his life. That was something time could never take away.

1

October Nights

Even if I told her a million times how much I love her, Albert thought, *nothing can compare to how I feel right now.* He'd rehearsed this moment over and over, but Albert's nerves were getting the best of him.

"Albert, why do you keep touching your jacket pocket?" Sophie asked.

"What do you mean?" Albert swiftly placed his hands back on the table.

"I've been watching you all night."

"I'll take that as a compliment." He winked.

"And your watch too."

Albert knew he needed to change the subject. "Sophie, did you enjoy your dinner?"

"I always do. They have the best pasta in the city."

Albert smiled in agreement but noticed Sophie was distracted.

"Is there something wrong, my love?"

"No." She dabbed her lips with the soft silk napkin, avoiding Albert's gaze.

"Are you sure?"

"Albert, everything is very nice, *it is*. But—"

"But what?"

"Why did you take me here tonight?"

"I thought you love it here," Albert said, a lump rising in his throat.

"Oh, I do. I mean it's one of the nicest restaurants in Baltimore. *But* . . ." She took a deep breath and leaned in. "It's so *nice*. Plus, this is our *special occasion place*. It's not my birthday or anything."

"Is that the *only* special occasion we can celebrate?"

"No, I guess not."

"Sophie, we have the rest of our lives to celebrate birthdays together."

"The rest of our lives?"

"Now, if you're done, I have a surprise for you." Albert checked his watch again as he stood up.

"Look, you just did it again!" Sophie exclaimed, pointing at his wrist.

He extended his hand and looked at Sophie. "Trust me, my love." Albert held her chair, then draped Sophie's heavy overcoat onto her delicate shoulders. He placed a soft kiss on the back of her neck.

A crowd of waiters gathered by the door, wishing them goodnight and shaking Albert's hand. The owner even held the door open for them and personally bid them farewell.

"We'll see you again soon I hope, Mr. Abraham?"

"*Very* soon." Albert grinned wide.

Sophie wasn't sure why they were getting the added attention. They weren't regulars, nor were they anyone of importance. "Albert, did you just get elected Mayor and not tell me?"

"I think they're just jealous of me. Look at you."

Sophie rolled her eyes, yet couldn't help but smile at Albert's romantic habits. He always said what was needed at the right times and always made a point to make sure she knew how much he loved her. He left simple notes tucked into her purse that read, *I love you my dear Sophie,* or he stopped by her house in the morning to let her know how much he looked forward to seeing her later that night.

It was rare for Sophie to open her mailbox and not find a drawing from Albert waiting for her, sometimes a simple sketch of a rose, other times a more elaborate portrait of her or a set of hands holding one another. She was always left guessing what he would do next. They headed toward the line of taxis parked outside, but he pulled her along past them.

"What do you say we go for a walk along the pier," he suggested. "It's a great night."

"It's October. It's probably freezing over there."

"More reason for me to hold you close, my love."

My love. Sophie could listen to him say those two words for days.

They hustled across Pratt Street, cutting left toward the piers along Harbor East, where late night diners cuddled together in the cold, hopping in and out of restaurants. Loud cars whipped around one another as they dodged a few speeders.

"Albert, sweetie, wait. I can't run that fast!" Sophie laughed.

"Then I'll have to carry you." And with one clean swoop, he picked her up in his arms as if she was a small child.

Sophie nuzzled her face against his neck.

As they approached the pier the soft wind gently sprayed a haze of bay water against their faces, with a delicate chill that only autumn in Baltimore can provide. The smell of the seafood restaurants around the harbor filled their senses. They could almost taste the famous crab cakes in the smooth, salty air.

When they arrived at the pier, Albert slowly let Sophie down and held her hand close to his chest as he pulled her against him. He kissed her forehead and whispered, "I love you."

Their footsteps echoed on the thick wooden pier as they walked for only a few minutes before coming upon a small bench flanked by a towering light post, casting a gentle glow on the calm Chesapeake Bay. On the bench sat a large rectangular gift filling the entire seating area, wrapped in sparkling red paper, with a bright white bow, along with a bouquet of flowers on its side.

"Look at that." Sophie pointed, amused by the random gift so elegantly propped on the bench.

"Yeah, look-at-that. Why don't you open it?" Albert nudged her gently.

"*Open it? Me?* Albert, that's not mine."

"I think it is."

"What are you talking about?"

Albert looked at the top right of the wrapping and realized his brother Matthew forgot to write Sophie's name on the outside as he had asked him to do before dropping it off while they were at dinner.

"Sophie, please open it. It *is* for you."

"Albert, what is going on?" Sophie asked, giving him a playful push.

Albert raised his eyebrows and grinned coyly. "I guess you'll have to find out."

Sophie looked back at Albert as she cautiously approached the mysterious gift. "This better not be another trick, Albert."

"No trick, my love. I promise."

Sophie began to unwrap the large object, so wide she had to stretch her arms to reach both sides. That didn't stop her as she pulled the paper off with anticipation.

Then, while her back was to Albert, he removed what was in the side of his jacket pocket. Sophie nearly stumbled off her feet as she realized what was going on. The large gift was a black and white oil painting showing a man on one knee proposing to a woman who had just unwrapped a painting of a man proposing to a woman in the same scene. The image went back into the canvas endlessly, forever recreating the scene in which Sophie would always be the main character.

She cupped her mouth, shaking, then turned around to Albert, nearly stumbling over herself. "Al?"

Albert sat on one knee holding a diamond ring in his hand, mirroring the scene in the painting he had been working on for a week.

Now, it was complete.

"Sophie, my love," Albert began.

Sophie shook and bounced on the balls of her feet. "If you're going to ask me to marry you, I'm going to say *no!*" she blurted in a crackled, panicked voice.

"*What?*" Albert felt as if his heart had sunk into his stomach.

"I mean, oh, Al!" She shook her hands uncontrollably as she searched for the right words but was too flustered and shocked to do so. "That's not what I meant, Albert. I can't believe this is happening."

Sophie laughed at her own embarrassment, sniffling through her tears.

"As I was saying," Albert continued, smiling, "Sophie Lynn Golden, I love you and I will always be there for you. Please make me the happiest man alive, and marry me. What do you say?"

Albert kissed her hand, then slid the ring onto her long narrow finger.

"Yes, Albert! Yes, of course!" she shouted.

Albert jumped up and grabbed her close. They kissed again, tears running onto their lips.

"I can't believe the first thing you said was, *If you're going to ask me to marry you, I'm going to say no!*" Albert kidded in a high pitched voice, to mimic Sophie's screeching.

"Oh, stop it, Albert. I was in shock! I had no idea." Sophie leaned her face against his chest. "How did you do this?"

"I've been planning this for a long time."

"How did you get the painting here?"

"Matthew brought it over while we were eating dinner."

"That's why you kept looking at your watch."

"And that's why I kept touching my pocket. I didn't want to lose the ring!"

Sophie couldn't take her eyes off the ring. "It's beautiful."

She looked over at the painting then back at her ring again, still holding onto Albert's face. "How did I get so lucky, Albert?"

"Please. *You?* I've waited for you my entire life, Sophie."

Matthew popped out from behind his car, which was parked on the street alongside the bench, pulling a cigar and a bottle of Champagne out from his long, Army issued winter coat. His hair was still cut close—standard for all soldiers on duty—and he even wore his dress uniform for the special event.

"Can I tell you how nervous I was, thinking you were going to see me?" he said, arms wide. "Come here, you two!"

They all hugged and exchanged kisses on their cheeks.

"*If you're going to ask me to marry you, I'm going to say no!*" Matthew laughed in his newly acquired Boston accent, where he'd been living for the past few years. "What a great line, Sophie! I heard the whole thing." Matthew's olive skin was rosy from sitting out in the cold for the past hour. "I thought for sure you heard me laughing."

"Stop it! I was in shock! Ugh, I'm never going to live that one down, am I?" They pulled each other close and hugged again. Matthew opened the Champagne, and they passed it around, each taking a celebratory sip from the bottle.

Albert wrapped his arm around Matthew. "Thank you, big brother," Albert whispered into his ear.

"I love you, Albert. Thank *you* for allowing me to be a part of this," he said.

Sophie playfully pushed them both. "I can't believe you two."

"Listen, you owe me, Albert. I had to pay off two bums who refused to get off that bench," Matthew said, slapping his back.

"Put it on my tab."

"Okay kids, my job is done here," Matthew said, wiping a last drop of Champagne from his thin black mustache. "Go on, you two. Celebrate. I'm getting out of here."

Matthew hugged Sophie. "Welcome to the family, Sophie." He jumped back in his car and honked his horn repeatedly. "There goes Mr. and Mrs. Albert Abraham, everyone!" Then he sped off into the night, leaning on his horn as he drove away.

Albert raised the bottle. "Cheers to that. Spread the news!"

Albert turned to Sophie and held her face in his hands. As Sophie looked at her ring, she couldn't stop her hands from shaking.

"Do you like it?"

"Of course I do. But Albert, *how* did you ever afford it?"

"This ring has been in my family for generations. It was my grandmother's. She brought it over from Russia. It was one of the only things she had with her when they came over. She gave it to me before she died. There was no diamond, just the setting. They'd sold the stone to get by, but never let go of the setting." Albert paused, thinking about her words that day. "She told me, *Albert, one day you will find someone that will make this ring shine again.* And she was right."

"The diamond, Albert . . . I would never ask for something like this."

"I know you wouldn't. I wish I could afford a bigger stone, Sophie."

"No, Albert, *this* is perfect."

"When I came to pick you up for the first time, the moment you came to the door, I just knew. After our first date I put a little aside each day, pennies, nickels, dollars if at all possible. It took me longer than I liked, but if I had the money that very day, I would have asked you right there on your steps."

Sophie kissed his lips. "And I would have said yes."

***

Albert's alarm clock woke him up at the same time it had for the past twenty years, blaring, *"Good morning Baltimore! Today is going to be a chilly one in Charm City but at least there is no snow, yet that is—give it a couple of months and we'll all be singing a different tune. Speaking of chilly weather, brrrrrrr, here's a classic that fits the temperature, 'Baby It's Cold Outside'."*

After two unsuccessful attempts to get out of bed, followed by an agonizing pain in his lower back and legs, Albert finally rose to his feet. He rolled his neck to loosen the pain and caught the painting from his dream, staring at him from the wall above his dresser, as it had since the day he moved in.

"Good morning, my love."

2

Company

Albert began his routine the same way he had for the past six years. Wake up before sunrise, make a large pot of coffee to nurse throughout the day, call the hospital, open up the *Baltimore Sun* followed by the *New York Times,* then waste away in front of the television. Despite devoting his mornings to reading the paper, the news of today never gave him the feeling it once did when he would rip into a copy of *The Saturday Evening Post* when he was younger. Today everything was crime, tragedy, celebrity gossip—anything *but* what Norman Rockwell used to illustrate. Then again nothing in Albert's life was the same. Still, he would read until he fell back asleep in his recliner with *ESPN* humming in the background.

Albert knew his daily routine was not quite eventful, but at eighty-two he was just happy to wake up, *period*. Today was different. Geoffrey was coming to stay with him, for "just a week or so" as he'd mysteriously claimed. When Geoffrey called out of the blue asking if he could stay with him two weeks prior, Albert was caught off guard, considering his place would be the last house Geoffrey would want to stay for any length of time.

With a massive home only ten minutes from him in Baltimore, as well as a luxury beachfront house on the Delaware shore, Albert's stale townhouse hardly offered the lifestyle Geoffrey had allowed himself over the years. He wanted to inquire more, but he was too eager and excited to say yes. Plus, he figured he was worrying again, and knew that's exactly what Geoffrey would say to him.

But to worry about Geoffrey and his younger brother David was fairly common for Albert and Sophie. They were always worrisome grandparents since day one. Just because their grandkids were grown up, didn't mean they had to stop worrying about them.

"It comes with the gig," Albert always reminded the boys. For Albert, it was more than just being overprotective, it was a promise Albert made to his son, Clark, Geoffrey's father.

Still, the phrase "a week or so" tugged at Albert. Aside from his homes, Geoffrey could also rent the nicest hotel in the city for a month and not see a dent in his wallet. Not to mention he had a wife and daughter to take care of. For a change, it was Geoffrey who was away from his wife, not the other way around. Albert could understand not wanting to be in her presence; he had never liked her.

He hadn't seen the good in Geoffrey marrying someone he'd only known for five months, but his grandson wouldn't listen. Albert still believed Rose only married him for his money. Through it all, he kept his opinions quiet.

No matter who he'd married, the result of Geoffrey's marriage was his daughter Layla, who always brought a smile to Albert's face. Layla had his heart from day one, when Albert first held her in his arms at the hospital and she'd grabbed his nose. Having Geoffrey at his house meant Layla would be over often, which was perfectly fine with Albert.

Of his two grandchildren, Geoffrey was the most attentive. David, two years younger than Geoffrey, was too self-absorbed to be bothered with Albert's slow moving lifestyle. Growing up, the two boys were inseparable, with Geoffrey enjoying his role as the big brother. That was until David passed the bar, joined a top firm in Baltimore, made partner four years later, and became wealthy at a very young age, similar to Geoffrey.

Albert often thought that David felt he needed to live up to Geoffrey's success, and now the result was David wanting to show off what his money could buy. It was a competition that Geoffrey did not like to participate in. David rarely attended holiday events or family get-togethers, preferring to vacation in the south of France, snorkeling in Costa Rica, or skiing in Colorado with any number of women he met along the way. David's only saving quality was that he called to check on Sophie at the hospital throughout the week—a role that all Abraham boys took on.

Albert preferred to see the caring side of David rather than the selfish, so he accepted his faults. It was hard to stay mad at him because every time he saw his face, he saw his son Clark, as if he'd been brought back to life. Knowing he would never see Clark again, he couldn't help but be mesmerized by David's features.

Albert's son Clark and his wife Valerie were killed by a drunk driver while Geoffrey was in college, and David still in high school. Albert and Sophie immediately took over as parents, so fast there was hardly enough time for the impact of losing their only son to sink in. A parent should never have to bury their children, and Albert and Sophie had done it twice. Albert rarely spoke of his first child, Abigail.

When Abigail arrived, there were no tears or screaming, only silence. It was realized right away what the silence meant, and that day changed their lives forever. They held a quiet funeral for her on a warm summer afternoon in September. Abigail received a traditional Hebrew baby naming the day before, *Segula Margalite*, meaning *Treasured Pearl*.

Albert visited her gravestone often, which sat next to Clark and Valerie's. There were two more lots next to them, but Albert hoped he didn't have to fill either of them for a very long while. Every visit he knelt down and kissed their names, and said a prayer in Hebrew as he cleaned their stones with the same care a parent takes when bathing their child. And as Jewish tradition holds, he always left a small rock on top of each of their tombstones. This was all he had left of Clark and Valerie, and all he knew of Abigail. It never got any easier.

***

After they lost Abigail, it took Sophie and Albert another two years to decide on trying again for a baby, and from there they found peace through the birth of Clark. Then, once Geoffrey and David came into the picture, Albert figured their lives were complete. When Layla arrived, however, he knew she was the missing piece, and so he always looked to her as the Abigail he never got to hold. To him, Layla was his own *treasured pearl*.

Albert draped the Sport's page across his thick belly when he heard a car rattle up the driveway. He slipped his glasses up the bridge of his nose as he gathered his strength to swing up out of the recliner. He looked out the open front door and saw Geoffrey's car. Two door slams later, he had company.

Layla burst through the door, yelling for Albert.

"Zaide! Zaide! Zaide!" She had always called him the Hebrew name for Grandfather. As usual, Albert bent forward to accept her leaping bear hug. When she was two and three, he could handle her jump while standing, even though it hurt like hell. Now that she was six years old, she had learned that he was no longer as strong, and she was much gentler on his behalf. His meaty arms, once toned from an active lifestyle of sports and athletics, now sagged on brittle bones—mere remnants of a once well-built man.

Layla collapsed into his chest and burrowed her way to his neck, snuggling her cheek against his rough face like an affectionate kitten. Albert wrapped his arms around her small frame as she bundled herself against him. Whenever Layla visited, it was like a rush of adrenaline to his mind and body.

"I love you, Zaide!" Layla purred, her fingers pulling at the ends of his bristly hair.

"Oh my Layla girl, I love you too! I missed you so much."

Layla reached up and wrapped her arms around his back. "Daddy says we're going to be roommates."

Interesting way of putting it, Albert thought as he tickled her under her arms.

11

Geoffrey walked in a minute later and dropped two large leather duffle bags by the door. The sunlight gave way to Geoffrey's silhouette—tall, thin, and handsome. His good looks made him appear successful; he had a graceful nature that made him stand out in a crowd. His appearance certainly helped to propel his career, allowing him to float in and out of various social circles in countless levels of business. At thirty-eight, he didn't hide the fact he reveled in his twenty-something appearance.

Today he wore a pair of dark jeans, a black cashmere V-neck sweater held tight against his body, showing the fit definition in his chest, under a deep black pea coat. His large sunglasses wrapped around his face, covering his hazel eyes and the tips of his cheekbones. His hair was cut close, but not shaved, and he had a look that seemed effortless, but Albert knew he spent a lot of money on it. Albert smirked at the five o' clock shadow Geoffrey always kept in an effort to appear rugged.

"What's up, Gramps?" Geoffrey said, walking over and picking Layla up, then extending a hand for Albert, pulling him to his feet. The two hugged, slapping one another loudly on their backs as Layla dangled between their legs. They pulled apart, and Layla ran into the living room to watch television.

"Don't sit too close, Layla," Geoffrey reminded her.

"Geoffrey, I couldn't pull you away from the TV when you were her age. That thing isn't going to make her blind."

Geoffrey raised his eyebrows. "Really? Says the man with *quadruple-focals* who watches ten hours of TV a day." He tapped Albert's glasses with his index finger.

"What a smart-ass," Albert said.

"Smells like there's a pot brewing, Gramps."

Albert nodded.

They made their way to the kitchen where Albert had coffee waiting for Geoffrey as usual. Coffee was a famous part of their ritual. Whenever they got together—since Layla was born, it happened more often—they were more likely to share a cup of coffee rather than a bottle of beer. Albert filled a mug for Geoffrey and one for himself, then admired the message on the side of the cup which read *World's Best Zaide*.

"So, we're roommates now, huh?" Albert asked, before sipping.

"What, you don't want company all of sudden?" Geoffrey asked, clearly doing his best to breeze by the subject. "You always ask when I'm going to visit. Come on, this will be great! We can have coffee together, read the paper together. Hell, I'll even get one of those tandem bicycles and you can ride in back." Geoffrey leaned against the small metal kitchen table, a relic from the seventies. He was constantly offering to update his furniture, but Albert wouldn't let him.

Albert grunted, unimpressed at Geoffrey's sarcasm.

"Okay, okay, fine. You can ride in front," Geoffrey teased.

"How are the bakeries doing?"

"Great. Nick and I are thinking about taking *Layla's Cakes* to Chicago in a couple of months. We have a contact there who I know from a real estate deal I made last year." Geoffrey grinned.

"Does he still call you *the Kid* like the rest of those real estate friends of yours?" Albert asked, knowing how much Geoffrey disliked the nickname he earned while a hotshot in college.

Geoffrey rolled his eyes. "That name never goes away. I still remember when I told you I was going to start a bakery."

"I know, I know."

"I believe your exact words were, 'Geoffrey, how on earth do you go from selling homes to selling cakes?'"

"Eh, what do I know?" Albert said, smiling, knowing it was times like that which made being wrong an okay thing.

Geoffrey took a sip of his coffee and his face immediately wrinkled into an expression of distaste. He cocked his head back and jammed out his tongue. "Ugh, Gramps, this is awful! How many scoops did you put in?"

Albert took another sip, and couldn't figure out what Geoffrey was talking about.

"That's it! If I'm staying here, I'm buying you some good coffee." He walked over to the fridge and pulled open the main door. The fridge was bare aside from ketchup, leftover take-out food, and random condiments—all of which were out of date. "*And* I'm buying you some real food!"

"I always order in," Albert admitted, shrugging his shoulders.

Geoffrey poked around the fridge. "Gramps, this mayo says *August*! Are you kidding me? Look, we are getting you some healthier food, ASAP, my friend. You remember what healthy food is, right?" Again, Albert ignored him and took another sip. "Come on, Gramps, like back when you were in your baseball days. Eggs, milk . . . you know, *protein*?"

Albert set his mug aside and crossed his arms. "I haven't thrown a baseball since you were in college."

Geoffrey took two large steps forward, standing only inches from Albert. He tilted his head down and eyed him critically. Without a word, a test of wills had begun. The first one to blink would be mocked for the rest of the day. It was a game they had played since Geoffrey was a child.

At six-foot-three, Geoffrey peered down at Albert's squatty frame. Despite sharing similar facial features, Geoffrey's body couldn't be more different. He could eat anything and not gain a pound. His manicured eyebrows moved up and down as he tried to make Albert flinch, adding his best Clint Eastwood impression for good measure. His build may have come from his mother's side, but Geoffrey's face resembled Albert's. He saw himself in Geoffrey's eyes every time.

"So, you feelin' lucky, *punk!*" Geoffrey hissed.

Albert refused to budge as he stared deep into his grandson's eyes. Just then, Layla came running in and grabbed Geoffrey's leg.

He glances down for a second, and Albert pointed a stubby finger at Geoffrey and snapped *"Gotcha!"* Albert walked out of the kitchen feeling smug.

"Interference! Interference!" Geoffrey exclaimed, while pretending to pull a flag from his pocket like an NFL referee. He followed quickly after him. "Where's the flag, Ref? We all saw it!"

Layla mimicked him, bouncing on her heels. "Where's the flag, huh? Where's the flag, Zaide?"

Geoffrey scooped Layla up with one hand, placing her effortlessly over his shoulder. Much lighter than most kids her age, she had the lean build of her parents, and her hair was a whirlwind of auburn curls like her mother's. Her hair swung down as she reached toward the floor, her cheeks turning rosy.

"Where are we going, Daddy?" Layla asked, now hanging upside down.

Geoffrey grabbed Albert's madras fedora, *another* worn out relic, and tossed it his way.

"*We*," he said, indicating all of them, "are going to the store and getting Zaide some real food, because your Zaide lives like a college kid."

"Whatever, I still got you back there," Albert retorted, swiping his hat from Geoffrey and flopping it on his head.

"*Puh-lease* old man, I *let* you win!" Geoffrey laughed as they made their way out the door.

The three of them piled into Geoffrey's brand new Porsche SUV, with Albert in the passenger seat and Layla in the back. Her father switched on the overhead DVD player, and she slipped on a pair of ear buds. Geoffrey checked himself in the mirror and turned to Albert.

"And . . . we're off!"

3

The Meeting

During their ride, Layla chattered with the rapid vernacular of today's kids. Every other word was "like" or "okay". Albert knew this irritated Geoffrey because he thought it made her sound snotty, when in fact she was the complete opposite. For the daughter of a very wealthy man, this was a rarity.

Layla was well-grounded and never asked for much beyond normal requests for games and the occasional toy. Albert reveled in listening to Layla; in his eyes, she was flawless. She could have been reading the phonebook aloud and he'd listen as if it was Sinatra giving him a personal concert. Albert's lack of regular conversation over the years had increased his ability to listen more intently, even though all Layla talked about were kids in her class, or a pop singer he'd never heard of.

Without his needing to ask, Geoffrey took the country roads Albert preferred, allowing him a chance to take in the landscape. Even though the extended trip would increase the pain of his ailing joints, it was worth it.

Ever since Albert was a child, he'd adored the beauty of this particular stretch of northern Baltimore County's countryside, called Cole Valley, filled with elegant homes that sat in cornfields and horse farms, with long narrow driveways that sank into heavily wooded forests. Where Baltimore City has a reputation for fast paced living, the country is filled with suburban towns, hundreds of years old.

Albert loved Tufton Road for its rustic escape from city life. This place was like no other. The narrow roads wrapped around hundreds of acres of large farmland. It was mesmerizing, almost medicating, for Albert.

The legendary racetrack of Sagamore Farm sat off the main road, and horses could be seen taking laps around the pristine tracks in the distance. Albert and Geoffrey would take Layla to the stables to see the horses, and watch them run for hours. Wooden fences, antiqued from time and weather, snaked along the surface of the mild terrain, outlining each house like a picture frame. When Clark was a baby, Albert would often take this same road with him in the backseat, trying to get him to nap. After a few minutes Clark would be asleep but Albert would drive for another hour or until he woke up. Every time he drove along Tufton, Albert thought of Clark.

During the early mornings around that time of year, when the trees changed and the crisp autumn air blew blankets of leaves across the fields, it was common to see dozens of deer race from the woods and onto the farms. The horses also became an attraction for all who drove by. They'd make their way to the edge of the fences, just feet from the road, and allow people to touch and feed them. Geoffrey and Albert routinely pulled over with Layla after purchasing a basket of fresh apples from the Misty Valley Farms fruit stand to feed the horses.

***

Whenever they drove like this, Geoffrey spent more time watching his grandfather out of the corner of his eye than the road ahead. He'd memorized the turns; they didn't change. Albert, however, changed more and more on a daily basis. As the colors of each season passed across Albert's face through the window, Geoffrey watched time pass with each turn. The Albert of today was not the Albert Geoffrey had grown up with—and they both knew the reason why.

Geoffrey had a harder time accepting it than Albert did. Other than the physical changes, the biggest change was Albert's mannerisms. As much as Albert blamed it on his age, Geoffrey knew the real reason why his zest for life had evaporated. He longed for the days when Albert was considered the life of the party. The only social gatherings he attended now were Layla's birthday parties, and even that took a lot of his energy. Geoffrey always encouraged him to get out and mingle with his friends.

"At my age, all my friends are dead or dying," Albert would retort.

There wasn't much room to argue. It was partly true, and it was clear Albert had made up his mind.

Car rides were a time for Geoffrey and Albert to bond, and Geoffrey enjoyed chauffeuring him anywhere he could—the library, the cemetery, restaurants, and even to Cedarmere Care Center and Hospital to visit Sophie. It took Albert a good hour or so to settle his mind before he left the house for his visits, and afterward he was even more reclusive than before. Geoffrey knew it was hard for him, and he gladly drove as far and as long as Albert needed to come down from each visit. After six years, most days were easier than others but there were some that were too hard for Albert to handle.

On one very bad visit to Cedarmere last spring, Albert was inconsolable as they made their way back to the car. Geoffrey always let Albert have time alone with Sophie, and when Albert emerged that particular day, he was worse than ever. Geoffrey asked, but Albert didn't answer. His only response was his bottom lip trembling. When Albert got into the car, he sat in silence, staring blankly at the hospital through the car window.

"Do you want talk about it, Gramps?" Geoffrey asked, already knowing the answer.

Finally, after fifteen minutes, Albert broke the silence when he told Geoffrey, who hadn't even turned the key in the ignition, "Just drive, son."

Without hesitation, Geoffrey took off with no direction in mind. An hour later after following Albert's points and mumbles, they ended up at Sandy Point State Park, a nearby beach escape on the western end of the Chesapeake Bay Bridge, outside Annapolis, Maryland. All the while, no words were exchanged, only Albert's motions directing him as if some higher power was pulling Albert to the beach, where he found so much comfort in the past.

Where the Heart Left Off

When the car stopped, Albert opened the door, removed his shoes, and walked along the sand until he came to the water's edge. He sat for the entire afternoon, motionless, gazing out at the bay while the water splashed at his feet, slowly burying his ankles in the sand. Geoffrey gave Albert his space, watching from the car, his chin resting on his arm draped over the steering wheel. He only budged to wipe away his own tears.

The cell phone went unanswered.

The radio was off.

When Albert was ready, he would return, and not a minute sooner.

***

It'd been six and a half years since Sophie suffered a stroke that nearly ended her life, and that shattered Albert to pieces. She had not opened her eyes or so much as moved a finger since that day. Despite the doctors' insistence she would never wake up, he was convinced of the opposite. He treated every interaction with her as if she could hear and see him, even though the doctors said she couldn't. Albert visited whenever he could, updating her on everything from the boys, and Layla, to news around the world.

Even when the Baltimore Ravens won the Super Bowl, he stayed in her room rather than with Geoffrey who was hosting a party at his house. Aside from time with Layla, this was the only time Albert was talkative.

Albert was grateful that Geoffrey graciously covered everything the insurance didn't, making sure Sophie was well cared for. It was a secret they kept from David. Since her time in the hospital, Geoffrey had spent well over two million dollars to keep his grandmother alive.

All for Albert.

All for just one more day of hope.

***

They pulled into the closest spot they could find so Albert wouldn't have to walk too far. Geoffrey climbed out and unbuckled Layla, who hadn't stopped singing to songs on her iPod the entire ride. When the doors shut, Albert's eyes popped open, after dozing off during the ride, and he caught his reflection in the window.

"Hustle it up, Al!" Geoffrey said playfully.

Albert clambered out of the car, his steps small as he tried to catch up.

"I'm coming, I'm coming."

Layla ran back and grabbed his hand. "I want to walk with you, Zaide."

Albert blushed. The littlest things Layla did made his entire day. Even going to the grocery store to buy food, which he didn't want or need, felt thrilling as long as Layla was with him. Geoffrey grabbed a cart and lifted her up, placing her in the seat. She sat facing forward and pretended to drive the cart with an imaginary steering wheel.

Despite the luxury of this particular grocery store, the sheer size overwhelmed Albert, so he usually avoided it entirely. Deep down he liked it but he preferred the small market he'd been going to for twenty years. The only other time he'd ever come to the big store was with Geoffrey, to pick up snacks for Layla's birthday party.

It was larger than most, with three restaurants and enough square footage to hold two football fields comfortably—hardly the small grocer Albert was used to that was only a mile from his house. The walls were stacked with every variety of food imaginable, from name brand supplies to a gourmet section that offered everything from sushi to deli meats.

Geoffrey navigated past the frozen dinners and ice cream, heading to the organic section, which immediately annoyed Albert.

Okay, milk, eggs, and coffee I'll do, but there is no way I'm eating some organic tofu crap!

Geoffrey was reading a label on a cereal box that advertised extra fiber. With his grandson distracted, Albert figured he'd wander on his own.

"Geoffrey, I'm going to look around. Maybe pick up some fruit," Albert said. "Grab me when you're ready."

"All right, old man. *Fruit!* Now you're talking. Oh, and pick up some prunes, while you're at it. It's good for what ails ya. They have a great selection," he added with a wink. Geoffrey smiled wide, laughing at his own joke as he placed a box of organic potato chips in the cart. Albert swatted the air in his direction.

What a shmuck.

"Dear Lord, bring me back to life for one day so I can see him when he's my age, peeing ten times a night and praying for a bowel movement. Please Lord, grant me this one thing. *Please!*"

He walked in and out of each row of produce, grimacing at every crowded corner. The sound of loud people in a rush irritated him, and so did the screeching skid of shopping cart wheels. The carts were one thing, but the selection of food bothered him even more. He wished it were simpler.

Apples, oranges, bananas, grapes, and pineapple—the store had ten of each kind. Green apples, red apples, mini apples, apples from Maine, apples from Maryland, apples from Europe.

Whatever happened to just apples from a farm? Albert wondered. As if God were taunting him in a cruel joke, Albert spotted a barrel of prunes. *Eh, what the heck?*

He crept up to the barrel, then glanced around, casing the store for any onlookers, before he placed his hands in his pockets, and rocked on the balls of his feet. He looked around again, noting an elderly woman peeking in his direction, but she turned away when he saw her. Aside from that, everyone else was distracted.

He leaned back against the fat barrel of prunes, then like a frog's tongue chasing a fly, he snatched a prune and shoved it into his mouth. He looked around again. The woman was gone, the coast was clear, and ironically the prune tasted pretty good. He started to walk away to find Geoffrey when someone tapped him hard on the back.

Oh crap! Busted. Layla will see me carried out by ten security guards.

Fearing he'd be accused of shoplifting, he took his time turning around, trying to think of a good excuse for why he snagged a prune. His eyes were shut tight as he turned to the person behind him. He opened his eyes and then began mumbling an explanation, not bothering to look up as he studied the floor instead.

"I'm so sorry, please don't arrest me, it was just *one* prune. One *tiny* prune. Like you guys can't afford one missing prune?" He wrung his hands nervously. "Look, my grandson will buy this entire *barrel* of prunes. I promise! I'll go get him now."

When he realized it wasn't security, but the same elderly woman he'd seen earlier, he began to calm down.

Will she tell on me? I know these stores have some whacky customers who love to rat people out.

The woman simply stared at Albert, not saying a word. She was a bit shorter than him, wearing a rather glamorous gold dress, something most people would wear to a dinner party or a fancy restaurant, not to a grocery store. Her long straight white hair thinned at the bottom, ending right below her shoulder blades. Most women Albert encountered, like at the hospital, wore disgusting, large, hair-sprayed contraptions.

This woman sported three sparkling rings with large stones of different shapes and colors, and an elegant gold charm on her chest, a pair of sunglasses hanging beside it, which Albert thought looked much too stylish for an elderly woman. Her eyes, a thick deep emerald, seemed familiar to Albert, but he wasn't sure why.

She looked at him curiously, as if analyzing every saggy droop on his face. This confused him, and he slowly took a step back. She grabbed his right hand and pressed her other hand on top, cupping his in between. She gently slid her hand down to his fingertips, then released him. Her lips were parted slightly, as if she were about to speak but wasn't sure what to say.

"Can I help you?" Albert asked worriedly.

She continued to focus on him as though he were an abstract painting on display at an art gallery. Then she covered her mouth and gasped deeply, almost to the point of passing out.

Her eyes fluttered.

Albert's widened.

She finally spoke.

"It *can't* be." She lifted her hand to her mouth again. "I thought it was you from a distance, but told myself it wasn't possible. I mean, it must be over sixty some odd years. I thought you were de—" She stopped herself, then pressed both hands against her chest.

Albert was beyond puzzled, and rendered speechless.

The woman opened her mouth again to speak and stopped short, still catching her breath. She shook her head in disbelief.

"Albey?" Her cheeks turned rosy, illuminated beneath her heavy makeup.

"Albey?" Albert repeated. "What? No, no, it can't be."

His fear of being caught shoplifting was overwhelmed by the realization that this person was not just any stranger. In fact, she was not a stranger at all.

4

Once Again

"It *is* you!" the woman cried out. Then she plunged forward, hugging Albert tight, as if clinging for her life. Albert did not hug her back; he was still in shock. No one had called him Albey since high school. There was only one person who *always* referred to him by that nickname, and she was now hugging him for the first time in over six decades. The woman finally stepped back and held his hands once more. She stared at his face, shaking her head from side to side, still in sheer disbelief.

"I can't believe what I am seeing. After all these years. And at *this* grocery store, no less!"

Albert couldn't believe it either. There was no denying who she was. From her soft southern voice, green eyes, and of course the way she said *Albey*, making him tongue-tied and nervous.

"El . . . *Ella?*"

Ella stepped back and playfully smacked the side of his arm. Her southern drawl rang with every word.

"Oh, Albey, like you *don't* know. Of course it's me, hon! Well, I mean, some years later it's me. I'm not as blonde as you remember. Gosh, I haven't seen my blonde hair in quite some time, maybe since you last saw your *dark* hair! But it's me, Albey." She let out a loud girlish laugh, with extra southern added to it—a laugh he hadn't heard in many, *many* years.

"I . . . I can't believe it . . . I, uh . . ." Albert stood motionless, unable to believe his jaw was even moving.

"That's it?" She put one hand on her hip. "We haven't seen each other since Truman was in office and all you can say is *I . . . uh, uh, uh . . . I, uh-uh?*" Ella reached for Albert again. "Hug me, God damn you!"

His limp body slipped into her arms, reminding him of Layla clenching one of her dolls. He didn't hug her back, but Ella couldn't stop smiling. Albert apologized and Ella shook her head in astonishment, letting him go. She talked more—clearly out of excitement to see him—not allowing him to get a word in edgewise. Albert could only observe as she rattled off questions, answering for him, as he remained frozen in shock.

"How's your health, Albey? Well, you look great, so I'd say it's marvelous! Can you drive at night, Albey? What time do you go to bed these days? Me, I don't sleep much, really. Where do you usually eat on the weekends? Do you always shop here? I do. Well, I mean, why wouldn't I? Do you live around here?"

Albert could only watch and listen as Ella rambled on.

"I lived in Florida for most of my adult life, only bouncing back to Baltimore here and there for work and family but never left home really. You remember my parents' old house, Albey? Now I live only five miles away, right here in Cole Valley. I built it a few years back. I can't believe we may have lived in the same town for so long and never saw each other. How have I never seen you here before?"

Question after question went unanswered by Albert. Her enthusiasm was beyond belief, which only added to the incredible difficulty Albert was having trying to comprehend the situation. She touched his arm flirtatiously as she spoke.

This can't be happening! This can't be happening. I can't believe it's really Ella.

***

Geoffrey made his way over to the produce section to find Albert, and saw him talking to a woman he didn't recognize. Most people would assume it was a friend, but Albert didn't have any. The way she was talking to him—so animated, laughing, *touching him*—Geoffrey was shocked Albert had a close friendship like this with anyone.

He walked slowly behind the display of grapes, and parked the cart, watching for a couple minutes longer. Layla was sitting inside the cart, playing on her iPod, not noticing her great-grandfather. Geoffrey couldn't tell what was being said, but saw Albert's mouth move slightly. The only thing he could hear was the woman's infectious laughter. He dipped his head behind the display so Albert wouldn't notice him spying. His eagerness to find out who the woman was, and to encourage Albert to communicate with someone else, finally got the best of him. Geoffrey causally strolled over to the two of them as if he hasn't been watching for the past five minutes.

He didn't want to alarm Albert, so he called out to him.

"Hey, Gramps. We're done over in organics."

The look on Albert's face—his eyes wide and his cheeks flushed—told Geoffrey that he was clearly embarrassed, like a kid caught with his hand in the cookie jar. Geoffrey couldn't help but smirk.

***

I would settle for being carted out by security right now, Albert thought.

He saw Ella's eyes widen, and he quickly ducked his chin into his chest.

"Hi Geoffrey, okay, we can go now," Albert said hurriedly, slamming the words together into a cotton-mouthed mumble. "Nice seeing you again, Ella. Goodbye." He grabbed the cart and started to push it forward, away from Ella. Ella reached for his sleeve as Geoffrey stopped the cart from the front.

Both Geoffrey and Ella blurted out, *"Wait, where are you going?"*

Geoffrey flailed his nostrils and tilted his head in Ella's direction, motioning for an introduction. Ella waited. Albert was trapped between the two of them, helpless.

Albert swallowed the lump in his throat. "Ella, this is my grandson, Geoffrey. And Geoffrey, uh . . . this is . . . this is . . ."

Ella moved to Albert's side and shook Geoffrey's hand, graciously batting her eyes.

"Oh God, Albey, I thought we talked about your mumbling already. Excuse me, Geoffrey, my name is Ella Perlman." Her southern accent turned up a notch, as if Geoffrey was a tourist visiting the deep south for the first time and Ella was the representative.

"Perlman?" Geoffrey said.

"If Albey did not introduce us, I would have sworn *you* were *him* sent from the past. Y'all are identical!"

Geoffrey turned to Albert, a sly smile crossing his face. "*Albey?*"

Albert shook his head. "It's . . . it's nothing."

Ella moved closer to Geoffrey and laced her thin, fragile hand over his right arm, as if they were getting ready to walk down a wedding aisle.

It was clear Geoffrey had immediately taken to her.

She cuddled up to Geoffrey's bicep. "Well, I'd say identical, but Albey, this boy is tall! And from the looks, quite strong too." Ella winked at Geoffrey as he looked down, towering over her. "And a bit more handsome to boot. You know, I have seven grandsons and one fantastically gorgeous granddaughter, Madilyn. She's the only one in my bloodline that stayed here in Baltimore with the family. Everyone else is traveling and working out of state."

Ella leaned her head back in subtle annoyance. "You know, even my five daughters—yes Albey, I said *five*—they don't even live here anymore either. All doing their own thing."

Albert and Geoffrey listened as Ella frantically tried to update them on the history of her life as if any second she'd be whisked away and never have a chance to do so. She hardly stopped for a breath. Neither of them could get a word in, but they didn't try either. Albert was too flustered, and Geoffrey couldn't get enough of her stories.

"Well, let's see, there's Bonetta, my oldest, who we all call Bunny for short. She came out with a little red nose, like a tiny bunny, when she was born and *boom*, the name stuck! Helene, Phyllis, Gayle, and baby Mindy. All over the place, Albey!" Her hands moved fast, like an artist working on a large mural, painting detailed descriptions of her life in vibrant colors.

"Even my grandchildren, *the boys* that is, they're scattered across the globe too." Ella paused for a second, appearing thoughtful. "Two are in Europe, one's in California, another in New York, two in Chicago, and one in Montana. I know, *Montana,* right? Don't ask me. Something about *forestry*? Lord knows. Heck, Maryland has forests too, Albey. That's what I tell that one, I do. In fact, I got nine hundred and twenty-five acres in Western Maryland he could camp out in until he's blue in the face, but oh well, kids are kids, I guess." Ella waved her hands dramatically.

"Unfortunately, I don't get to see them much," Ella said, furrowing her brow. "But my granddaughter, she's right here with her grandmamma." Ella looked up at Geoffrey. "She's single too, you know." She winked and tapped his chest. "I would love for you all to meet her. In fact, I would love for y'all to meet everyone!"

"Of course. Why not? Right, Gramps?" Geoffrey said excitedly.

Albert didn't react.

He couldn't.

He looked away, trying to convince himself Ella wasn't standing in front of him. His life had just gotten a lot more complicated.

Ella noticed Layla, whose eyes were closed as she snapped her fingers and moved her head to her music.

"Well, if that is not the prettiest girl I've seen all year!" Ella exclaimed.

Geoffrey laughed and tapped Layla on her shoulder, motioning with his hands to take out her earphones.

"This is my daughter, Layla," Geoffrey said.

Layla extended a hand to Ella, and Ella unhooked her arm from Geoffrey and placed it on her chest, accepting Layla's hand with her own and dropping her head in a proper gesture to greet her.

"Thank you, Layla. You are very polite. My name is Ella. I'm a friend of your great-grandfather."

"I like your necklace."

"Well, thank you. It's always nice to receive compliments from someone as pretty as you. And you know what, how about this: next time I see you, I'll give you one just like it. Would you like that?"

"Oh, no, you don't have to do that, Ella," Geoffrey said. He must have noticed the necklace Ella was wearing was more expensive than anything a normal six-year-old would wear. Between the gold, emeralds, and pearls, Albert guessed she was wearing close to what Geoffrey made last month—which was a lot.

"I know I *don't*, but I *will*," Ella said, ending the discussion. "She will look even more beautiful in it than I ever could. I love to buy all my grandchildren *and* great-grandchildren presents."

"Really?" Layla exclaimed, her eyes widening. "Thanks! Zaide, when can we see your friend again?"

All three of them turned to Albert, who was still in awe of what had just transpired. In front of him was a lifetime of history—a grandson, a great-granddaughter, and a woman he used to be incredibly close to in a life he had all but left behind.

It was a lot to take in.

He never imagined he would see Ella again, nor did he wish to.

Geoffrey waved his hands in front Albert's face and snapped his fingers. "Gramps, you there?"

Albert blinked fast, coming back to life. "Um, well—"

"Oh Albey, shut your mouth, you're gonna catch flies."

Layla laughed and Ella winked at her.

"We *must* stay in touch, Albey." Ella's smile was so wide it nearly ran off her face.

Albert remained motionless and said nothing.

Ella reached in her purse and pulled out her phone. "Albey, do you text?"

"What?" Albert asked. Geoffrey laughed under his breath, and Albert shot him a glare.

"Okay, I'll take that as a *no*," Ella said. "I guess we'll go the old fashioned way."

Ella reached into her purse and pulled out a tiny piece of paper and pen. She scribbled something on the paper and handed it to Albert. "Albey, that's my home number, cell, and email. You can reach me on any or all of them. You *do* have email at least, don't you Albey?"

"Zaide have email? Yeah right!" Layla shouted.

"Oh Albey, we are going to get you up to date with how us young folk live, ain't that right, Layla-sugar?"

Layla nodded in agreement. There was a short period of silence as Albert stared at the paper in his hand.

Albert knew Ella and Geoffrey both wanted him to talk or say something, at least laugh at Ella's jokes.

Albert just wanted to leave.

"Okay then," Ella said, stepping back. "Well, whenever y'all would like to come over to my house for brunch, some dinner, or heck even a swim, you let me know. It may be chilly outside, but I have an indoor pool everyone loves to hang out in. You just call me, and I will drop everything. Any time of day. You just call and I will be ready."

"You have an indoor pool?" Layla gasped.

"Yes, I do! It's got a big slide I know you'll love. I have a tennis court and a basketball court as well, all on a large wonderful farm filled with animals. You are more than welcome to use any of it at any time."

Geoffrey put his arm around Layla and pulled her close. "Thank you, Ella, that is incredibly generous of you and we *will* take you up on it. *Won't* we, Gramps?"

"Uh, sure," Albert mumbled.

Ella breathed in deep and exhaled heavily as if a large weight had just been removed from her chest. She coughed into a handkerchief, then put it into her purse.

"Okay, you have my contact information and again, the invitation is open whenever you like. As I said, you can call me regardless of the time of day."

It was obvious Ella was waiting for Albert to say something, but he didn't.

"Thank you, Ella, it is very nice to meet you," Geoffrey said, shaking her hand delicately.

"I guess I will let y'all go now." Ella gave Albert a tight hug, then whispered loud enough for everyone to hear, "So great to see you again, Albey. This is truly, *truly* a special day." Her eyes began to water. She quickly wiped them dry with her hand as she stepped back.

"Goodbye everyone," Ella said again, covering her mouth, still trembling as she focused on Albert before finally walking away. "I hope to see you again real soon."

This can't be happening, Albert thought. *This can't be happening!*

***

Geoffrey watched Ella over to a young gentleman in black pants and a maroon button-down shirt, wearing a walkie-talkie on his belt, who listened with intense concentration as she talked to him. The man glanced over in their direction. Geoffrey smiled in amazement at how chatty Ella could be with anyone, including grocery store employees.

"Wow. Well, that was *interesting*." Geoffrey scratched his head, while Albert stared at his feet. "Let's go finish up, Gramps. Sound good?"

"Um, yeah. I need some milk and eggs and . . ." Albert mumbled as he placed his hands in his pockets, his head down and his eyes still wide. He shuffled behind the cart as Geoffrey led him along. Layla grabbed various items within her reach from the shelf, some of which Geoffrey allowed her to keep, as they discussed what to make for dinner, with Albert remaining silent. Geoffrey kept an eye on him, but figured it best not to bother him with questions—yet.

When they were finished, they made their way to the checkout line, and Geoffrey placed the items on the belt. Layla helped from inside the cart. Albert continued to busy himself in his own mind. The teenaged cashier scanned the items, placing bags neatly into the cart around Layla. Geoffrey reached for his wallet just as the young man with the maroon shirt, clipboard, and walkie-talkie approached the register and kindly dismissed the cashier.

"Did you find everything you needed today?" he asked as he checked the bags in the cart to make sure they were safely in place.

"Yes, thank you."

He scanned the rest of the items and placed the remaining bags in the cart.

"Is everything okay?" Geoffrey asked, wondering why a manager had been sent to finish ringing them up.

"Everything is just fine as always, Mr. Abraham. I'm just giving Bradley a break."

"I'm sorry, but how do you know my name?"

The man ignored his question and continued to place the bags in the cart, then stood up straight and placed his hands on his hips, clearly proud of providing good customer service.

"Thank you very much for shopping with us, Mr. Abraham, and might I say, you have a very lovely family. Please feel free to let me know if there is ever anything I can do to make your next shopping experience as enjoyable as possible."

Albert and Geoffrey exchanged curious glances, and Geoffrey shrugged. He started to pull out his credit card, but the manager waved a hand over it.

"No, Mr. Abraham, this one's on the house."

Geoffrey looked down the aisle at the other customers in line, hoping they wouldn't notice the odd and rather *special* treatment he was receiving.

"On the house? *At a grocery store?*" Geoffrey leaned in closer and whispered, "Buddy, there's over four hundred dollars worth of groceries here."

"Yes sir, I know. On the house, sir."

"Did I win something?"

"Um, no sir, not that I'm aware of."

"Do you *always* do this for customers?" Geoffrey asked, still confused.

"No sir, not normally. You three have a lovely afternoon now."

"Okay then. Thanks, I guess." Geoffrey pushed the cart forward, as the man called from behind.

"Goodbye now, thank you again for shopping at Perlmans Grocery," the man added with a wave.

Albert and Geoffrey stopped immediately.

"*That* Perlman!" Geoffrey breathed.

Albert shrugged his shoulders, never one for theatrics. Geoffrey looked to Albert for an answer, but he simply pushed him along.

"Hurry up, Geoffrey, let's go, let's go."

"I *knew* I recognized that name. But I didn't know it was *that* Perlman! Gramps, did you know this?"

"She had a different name when I knew her. Now, come on, let's get out of here."

The manager was still standing at his post smiling as Geoffrey pushed the cart forward. They made their way to the car, where Geoffrey loaded the bags and giggled like a child. He buckled in Layla, and Albert took his seat in the passenger side. Geoffrey didn't start the car right away, he just turned and stared at Albert, open-mouthed.

"What, Geoffrey?" Albert asked tiredly.

"Gramps, I think you just got picked up." Geoffrey patted Albert on the back.

Albert turned away from Geoffrey. He exhaled slowly against the cool window.

"Just drive, son."

5

Past Scars

The last day Albert had seen Ella remained etched in his mind.

He remembered what he said, and what he promised. He didn't know it was the last time he would say goodbye to her, that only a few hours later, he would never kiss, hold, or see Ella again. He remembered why, and that was the hardest part. The scars of that day were deep, and though more than six decades had passed, he could still see those scars today. He never imagined he would see her again and that harsh reality took a long time to form a healthy understanding in his mind, even though it tore at him. He especially did not expect the greeting he received from her. The past was the past, and their past was well buried.

Falling in and out of a deep sleep, Albert tried to get comfortable but was caught off guard by a rapid tapping around his heart, like a snare drum. He tried to breathe slowly, but the tapping continued. It was gentle, yet refused to stop.

Not my heart, not my heart! Not now!

He slapped at his chest, and woke up in a panic. When he opened his eyes, he saw the pressure was only Layla, straddling his belly and poking him with her delicate fingers.

"*Zaideeeeeee, wake uuuuup,*" she whispered, cupping her hands around her mouth.

Albert rubbed his face with his palms, then reached out to kiss Layla's hands. "You are the best alarm clock any Zaide could ask for, Layla-bear."

"I have to go home now, Zaide, but Daddy says I'll be back soon."

Albert pulled himself up to his elbows as Layla struggled playfully to stay on top.

"Leaving? But you just got here."

Geoffrey leaned against the open bedroom door, his arms folded. "Layla is only here a few times a week. She'll be staying at home with Rose while we fix things at the house." Geoffrey's voice was faint and flat, lacking his usual slick confidence.

"That's right. To fix things," Albert said, understanding.

He turned around to get a better view of his grandson. They exchanged nods, another confirmation that the *roommate* situation had more to it than Geoffrey initially admitted.

"Well, in that case!" Albert exclaimed, attacking Layla with kisses as she giggled endlessly. He held her close as she tried to escape his grasp, laughing and kissing him in return.

"All right kiddo, we gotta go," Geoffrey called out.

Layla hopped up and took his hand. He picked up her backpack and they waved goodbye to Albert, who was still stretched out on the bed.

"I hate this part," Albert muttered.

The covers fell around his chest, obscuring the old University of Maryland t-shirt Geoffrey had given him last year, and the gray sweatpants that were almost as old as his grandson. His hair was scattered, his eyes raw and red. Saying goodbye to Layla—even though he knew he'd see her again soon— always made him unhappy. Geoffrey gently petted Layla's bouncy curls and ushered her out the door.

"Should be back after lunch or so."

"Leave the door open, please," Albert said before resting back on his pillow.

He closed his eyes until he heard the sound of Geoffrey's car pull out of the driveway. Then he tugged the sheets off, and urged his vein-speckled feet to find his slippers. He rubbed the back of his neck hard and looked to his nightstand, taking another deep breath.

There, as it has been since the day he was married, was the picture of him and Sophie kissing as they cut the cake on their wedding day. It always made him smile, but it also made him miss her even more. The picture was all he had left of Sophie's beautiful smile. There was a woman in the hospital who resembled his wife, but it was not the woman he'd known for so long.

She was different.

She didn't speak or recognize him.

And as much as he tried to think otherwise, it was so.

Albert walked into the kitchen to begin his routine when he noticed it had already been started for him. Geoffrey had prepared a large pot of coffee with a new high tech coffee maker, much sleeker than his old one. Next to the coffee maker was his favorite mug that read *I love my Zaide*, scrubbed immaculately clean. Albert would usually go a few days without washing it out, letting dark rings of coffee remnants gather at the bottom of the cup. The coffee smelled different too. There was a note next to his mug, left by Geoffrey.

Sorry to split so early. Enjoy the coffee, it's from Venezuela and it's fantastic! P.S. Stop rolling your eyes, old man.

His grandson knew him well.

Geoffrey had left the newspapers on the kitchen table, along with two new additions—*USA Today* and *The Chicago Tribune*. All his papers were neatly stacked on top of one another, and Geoffrey had even put sticky notes in the newspapers, mentioning an article he read and thought Albert might enjoy.

The kid thinks of everything. Albert glanced at the clock on the microwave. It was seven a.m. *What time does he wake up, or did he even go to sleep? I don't even know where they sell the Chicago Tribune around here.* Albert poured the coffee and breathed in the aroma. *Different, but not bad.*

When he took a sip, he was pleasantly surprised at the taste.

Next on his agenda was a call to the hospital, the most strenuous activity of the day. When Albert called, it meant they didn't have to call *him*, meaning Sophie had made it through another night. He often went sleepless, terrified he'd missed a call. Sometimes he woke up every other hour to check his machine just in case.

Every day, he sat down at a small table in front of the kitchen phone and dialed the numbers, each button pressed firmly with frustration. Albert never liked hospitals and could care less for the one his wife lived in now, regardless of how many awards it won or accolades it received from the press. Nothing would ever be good enough for Sophie. There were four nurses who worked on a rotation in Sophie's wing, depending on the week. They all knew his voice and he knew theirs. The calls were never long, merely routine.

"Cedarmere Care Center, this is Hollie." Hollie was a twenty-five-year-old New Yorker with a cheerful Long Island accent, a student at Johns Hopkins University. Albert knew from experience she enjoyed chatting with him.

"Good morning, this is Albert Abraham."

"Hmm, Albert *Abraham,* you say? Can you please spell that for me?"

Again, routine, Albert thought.

"Hi, Hollie."

"Oh, it's *that* Abraham! Why didn't you say so? Great to hear from you, Albert. How are you today? When are we going to see you? Soon, I hope."

Despite his hatred for hospitals, Albert enjoyed her enthusiasm and did his best to keep up.

"I'm fine. I will come in today, if Geoffrey can go."

"How is Geoffrey? I love his cakes so much. I waited for twenty-five minutes at his bakery on York Road. His Chocolate cake, topped with French vanilla icing is unreal! Probably like five thousand calories, but it was worth it."

Albert rolled his eyes, well aware that many women frequented his shops for a chance to see Geoffrey for more than just his baking skills.

"Thank you. I'll let him know. How is Sophie doing?"

"Oh, fine. I just checked in," Hollie replied. Like the other nurses who worked the phones, she knew the answers before the questions were asked. It was as if they read from a script when dealing with Albert. They all liked him, so they worked hard to make each rudimentary answer sound like breaking news.

"How was she through the night?" Albert wondered.

"Great. Perfect night's rest."

"And her feeding tube? Dr. Menning said they were getting a new one in."

"Yes, they did. Works great."

"Her blood pressure?"

"Perfect as always."

"Fevers?"

"Nope. Just right."

Albert paused.

He was protective of his wife and wanted to be able to offer some sort of help or advice they may not have thought of, something to make her day better.

"Can you brush her hair again today? She likes that, she always liked that."

"Absolutely. I'd love to."

"Thank you, Hollie. I appreciate it."

"My pleasure, Mr. Abraham. We'll see you soon."

"Goodbye, Hollie."

He hung up and his chin dropped to his chest.

His eyes watered.

Routine.

His hands begin to shake, still emotional from the call, another part of the routine.

Everything is fine, he told himself. *She is being taken care of, they like her— but who wouldn't?*

"Count back from twenty," Albert said aloud, and he began. By eight, he felt better. He picked up *The Baltimore Sun* and read over the note from Geoffrey.

Check the sports page. The Terps just signed this great forward from Spain.

On each page he turned to, he spotted another note, and another, each one offering a different story for Albert to check out. He was slightly annoyed since reading the paper was the only thing he did that was somewhat productive, and now Geoffrey had shortened his time spent on it. He couldn't shake the thought of how early Geoffrey must have woken up—or if he'd slept at all.

He took the stack of papers under his arm and carried his coffee to the living room. He sat in his recliner with his papers on his lap, placing his coffee on the table next to him, and turned on ESPN.

***

Entering his neighborhood, Geoffrey nodded to the gardener manicuring bushes along the edge of the development's sign that read *Paper Mill Estates*. He had purchased the large *McMansion*—as Albert called it—ten years ago. He fell in love with it from the first minute he pulled into the long road to the house.

The sunlight flickered through the autumn leaves still hanging onto the branches that arched over the street from the sidewalk, casting colorful reflections through his window. Of all thirty some houses in the upscale neighborhood, his was the only one that looked different from the others, thanks to the renovations from the previous owner. Others in the neighborhood wouldn't dare touch the décor. The maroon shutters and large balcony that protruded from the second floor window, overlooking the enormous front yard, immediately caught his eye. He and Layla had spent many nights stargazing, curled up in sleeping bags in a tent.

To him, the house was perfect, but Rose wanted to live in the city, preferably in a two-story condo overlooking the Baltimore Inner Harbor, similar to the homes other successful lawyers in her firm had. She was a city girl, and Geoffrey was not. He always wanted a place for Layla to walk out the house and find friends to play with in every direction. Rose only wanted a city hotspot at her doorstep.

She lost the battle over housing, only because the commute for Layla's preschool—a high-end establishment filled with their friends' kids—would be too long from the city. So she settled, which always bothered him, since their house was more of a dream home than anything less.

When it came to this house, Rose did all she could to rebel. She found the previous owner's taste to be too *eighties,* even though the house had been built in 2005, and she constantly changed the décor to keep up with the rest of the partners in her law firm. She had an obsession with wallpaper, adding a new layer and tearing it down nearly every year.

They argued over this constantly, his opinions falling on deaf ears. The only thing that remained from the previous owner was a small desk Geoffrey kept in his office. When he made his offer on the house, he and the owner sat at that table and agreed to the final number. He saw it as good luck, and thought it would be a fun conversation piece to keep around.

Rose sat on the front porch steps with her arms folded, until Geoffrey came to a stop in the driveway, then she turned her back as she stood. She wore a white tank top that looked painted on, and dark, skintight jeans tucked into large designer snakeskin high heel boots. Her hair matched Layla's—red, curly, and elegantly long. She and Geoffrey were the same height, but she preferred to wear heels or boots at all times to appear taller. She was half English, half Dutch, which gave her luscious, milky white skin, one of the first things Geoffrey had noticed about her. Now she insisted on hitting tanning salons regularly, making her a pumpkin shade. She was hardly the woman Geoffrey first met at a holiday party thrown by his lawyer, who worked in the same firm as Rose.

Even though Geoffrey favored women closer to his age or younger, Rose—ten years older—was different than anyone he'd ever met. She was already well-established in the legal field, and Geoffrey admired her independence. He thought she might look at *him* and not his wallet.

Rose never made an issue of their age difference initially, but now she poked fun at Geoffrey for it, usually after she'd had a few drinks. Only a few months after they'd met, during a whirlwind lifestyle of fantastic dinners and spending every other weekend in a different country, Geoffrey proposed. It was then that Rose flipped a switch, hitting every obnoxious rich stereotype Geoffrey fought to avoid with other women over the years. Now, when she wasn't at the office, she was out with her girlfriends—all of whom were divorced, living off their ex-spouses' money—running up tabs at nightclubs or bars on Geoffrey's credit card.

Geoffrey turned the engine off and Rose shut the door behind her. Layla hopped out and ran inside, but Geoffrey waited for a moment in the car. He gripped the steering wheel tight, his knuckles turning white and his jaw flexing. He let out an elongated sigh before leaving his car, then walked in the house to find the living room walls now a deep crimson floral pattern, rather than the chocolate brown from three days earlier.

The furniture was missing, and the smell of paint seeped through the entire bottom floor. Rose was in the kitchen, leaning against the dishwasher emailing her boss on her BlackBerry. Layla was in the pantry fishing out a box of cereal. Geoffrey approached the long marble island in the middle of the kitchen.

Rose pretended not to notice him.

He watched her for a moment, then dropped his keys on the table making a loud clang, which did not work to grab her attention.

He coughed.

Still nothing.

"Ok, I'll go first," he finally said. "How are you, Rose?"

"Layla's starving." She kept her eyes on the phone. "You couldn't have fed her breakfast? We have riding lessons in fifteen minutes."

Geoffrey bent over on the countertop, resting his elbows against the cool marble. "She was tired, so I let her sleep."

Rose glanced up from her phone to utter a sarcastic response. "What, so now I have to feed her, dress her, *and* take her to riding?"

"I said I would take her."

Rose ignored him as she made her way into the bathroom to fix her hair. "No, Geoffrey. *I'll* do it."

Geoffrey knew Rose was acting unfair, but he hated arguing with her. He followed her into the bathroom, and watched her pull her curls from one side to the other. Being so close to Rose made him lose all control. Her beauty was so gripping that he was helpless, despite any frustration or aggravation she caused him.

"You look great today, Rose."

She glanced quickly at him through the reflection in the mirror. "I'm getting a new car."

"Another one, why?"

"Because it's almost winter and I'm not battling the snow come December in a Corvette convertible."

"Wait a second, so you need a car for every season?"

Rose walked between Geoffrey and the doorway, heading back to the kitchen.

"You don't get it, Geoffrey. What am I supposed to do? Have a car that can't go through the snow and get stuck outside Pazo? That'll be great, *me* broken down in the valet line, like some poor person who can't dig their car out. People will think I live like a bum."

"I seriously doubt people will think someone with a brand new Corvette, at one of the most expensive restaurants in the city, lives like a bum. Plus, I just bought you the Mercedes sedan you *had to have*, which works great in the snow. Why can't you use that?"

"Damn it, Geoffrey, you don't get it, do you? That's *not* how I live my life."

Even though he was annoyed she couldn't be content with having her choice of two cars worth well over most people's condos, he was more focused on her choice of words.

"It's *we*," he said firmly.

"What?"

"Before. You said *I* as in *I live like a bum*, but it's *we* as in *us*. You and I."

"What?" Rose snapped.

"You said *I* not *we*. I'm just saying that—"

"Christ, Geoffrey don't be so dramatic."

Once again, he settled for defeat, then looked around his house, and noticed some pictures were missing. He figured it was part of her recent redesign, but most notably, the ones missing were of *him*. He turned to Layla, who was sitting on the couch looking at a children's cookbook he purchased for her earlier that week. She couldn't read it, but she knew the pictures.

"You like that book, Layla?"

"Look Daddy, cupcakes! Zaide loves cupcakes!" Layla held the book up with both hands.

"That's right, baby, he does. You want to swing by the shop and pick some up for him before we go back to his house? Maybe they can decorate them with some cool designs. You can even help."

"Awesome!"

"Great, Geoffrey, you're teaching our daughter to like fatty foods," Rose chided him. "What's next, you'll show her the liquor cabinet?" She was staring down at her phone again.

"I own bakeries, Rose!" Geoffrey shouted, throwing his hands in the air, even though he knew raising his voice would have no impact on her. "Those cupcakes happen to help buy you those cars."

She ignored him again. "Okay, Layla, let's get going. You'll change at the stables."

Layla grabbed her riding bag, which her mother had prepared, and they made their way to the door. Rose didn't bother to say goodbye, even when Layla blew a kiss to Geoffrey before leaving.

He watched from the kitchen as the front door slammed. The echo from the door bounced off every wall in his giant—and nearly empty—house. His intense headache made for hypersensitivity, and the vibration of the door shot through his body. He'd heard countless doors being slammed in his relationship with Rose, and one more was just a reminder there was something dividing the two of them—something he might not be able to fix.

He walked over to the front window, adjacent to the main entrance of his house, and parted the blinds with his fingers. Layla was buckled in back as Rose fixed her makeup and adjusted her sunglasses in the mirror. Layla turned to the house, and after seeing Geoffrey, waved back to him. He put his hand up and rested it against the cool window as Rose pulled out of the driveway. The car seemed to grow smaller and smaller, until finally disappearing over the hills leading out of the neighborhood.

He kept his hand on the window until it was so cold it was almost numb. Then he balled his hands into fists and began pounding on the front door, so hard his hands hurt more with every blow until his skin was enflamed and sensitive. With each aggressive punch, he cursed and ranted, sweat mingling with unbidden tears. And then, as if cut at the ankles, his body slumped against the hardwood door, and he rested on the floor with his knees bent, supporting his heavily slouched upper body.

Beads of sweat dripped from his forehead.

His hands swelled and his heart beat faster than it had during their last argument.

It keeps getting worse.

Geoffrey reached into his pocket and pulled out a pillbox, emptying one, then two white tablets into his palm. He tossed them into his mouth, swallowed, and then rested his head in his hands. Shame, anger, and frustration all fought for attention. In a few moments, the pain would go away but the truth and the reality of his life would not. No pill could cure that.

***

When Albert awoke from his nap, he saw the *Sports Center* had ended and had been replaced by a European soccer match. He shut the television off and got to his feet. He ached, as he did every day, but with most routines, he got used to them, and today he didn't even bother to groan.

He walked in the kitchen and searched through his now filled refrigerator. Geoffrey had labeled everything with small sticky notes.

What is it with this kid and the frickin' notes?

A note on a pound of turkey meat announced, *Low in fat, great for lunch.*

A side of coleslaw was labeled, *Not so good for you but a small portion for a side is fine.*

The note on the fruits and vegetables said, *Always good to eat any time.*

Geoffrey had even labeled the juices by their sugar content, and on two of his own cakes, he wrote, *Only tiny pieces!*

Albert shook his head in amazement, and prepared himself a lunch despite Geoffrey's health tips—a turkey sandwich with extra mayonnaise, cheese, a side of chips, and a large slice of cake for good measure.

"Honestly, at my age, what is a piece of cake going to do to me?" Albert muttered as he scraped extra icing from the box onto his slice.

He sat in the dining room, where the sun was at its brightest, offering a pleasant amount of light through the parted shades. He ate with one hand, while shuffling through a *Sports Illustrated* Geoffrey left on the table.

Albert rolled his eyes at the note he found on top of the magazine. *Great article about the Ravens on page 82.*

As he flipped though the magazine, he came across another small piece of paper, bookmarking the article. At first he thought it was just another whacky note from Geoffrey letting him know about an article on the next page, but then he looked closer.

The note was Ella's from the other day, with her number and address. Geoffrey had led him right to it. It was crumpled and the edges were damp, since Albert had thrown it away that same day. His nostrils flailed, furious at Geoffrey for fishing it out of the trashcan.

He ripped it three times and trashed it again.

6

Believe In Fate

Between Albert's frequent nightmares, and overactive bladder, the littlest things caused him to wake up throughout the night. This strange flip-flop of sleep patterns sometimes made it difficult to distinguish dreams from reality. So he would force himself to stay in bed, eyes closed, trying to cherish any last chance to sleep. The other month, two fire trucks were blaring their sirens next door to him, which he figured was all a dream, so he tried his hardest to sleep through it. Next thing he knew, his neighbor's kitchen was on fire and she was carted off by a team of EMTs.

Today's dream felt less real. He knew he was dreaming, but he didn't want to leave. He was with Layla, who appeared to be in her twenties, and she was holding his hand as they walked along the shoreline outside Geoffrey's beach house. The sun was just getting ready to set, but it was framed perfectly against the clouds, right on the edge of the water like a postcard. Small waves crashed, lightly brushing their ankles.

"You look a little down, Layla. Is everything okay?" Albert asked.

She pushed back a strand of hair from her face. "Yeah, everything is fine, Zaide."

"Layla, come on now, you can tell me." He patted her hand between both of his.

46

"It's just, I'm a little . . . *lost*, Zaide."

"*Lost?* About what?"

"*Me*, I guess."

"Layla, I need more than that."

She smiled nervously at her own vagueness. "I think I'm falling in love."

"Wow, really?" He hadn't expected that.

"I'm sorry, is this awkward, Zaide?"

"Gosh no! I'm honored you can talk about this to me."

"It's Jack. I think he's going to propose to me."

"Oh Layla, that's fantastic!"

"I'm nervous, Zaide."

"Is this what you mean by feeling *lost?*"

"I'm not sure. Is that wrong?" She laughed at her own reply.

"Not at all. It's very normal. Some people feel nervous, anxious . . . and yes, even lost. You're not the first, my love. Always remember, you can't lie to your heart. The greatest thieves in the world tried to fool the heart, but the heart will always work on its instincts. It will always win, and in the end, when you can make peace with that, only then can you really understand what true love is. And that's when you go after it with all your might."

"How did you know you were ready, Zaide?"

"Me? Well, I knew very early on. And when I say early on, I mean the minute I saw Sophie."

"Really?"

"Can we sit?" Albert asked. They sat down and buried their toes in the cool sand.

"The first day I saw Sophie was July sixteenth. I'll never forget that date. I was on leave from the military for a few months, and taking odd jobs here and there. I had been working in Jamestown, Rhode Island, for several months. I had to get away and find myself too, Layla. So I landed on a lobster boat, and really loved New England, but I missed Baltimore and knew my sea legs were better suited for crabbing. Then, after about four weeks of working the docks by the harbor, my entire life changed. We'd all go to lunch along the piers; it was where all the dock guys hung out back then. The harbor was much different than it is today—cleaner, smoother, and much quieter. We never made it back in time. *Ever.* But that day your great-grandmother walked right past me with a bunch of toddlers behind her."

"She was a teacher, right?"

"The *best one.* That day, she had taken some kids to the harbor to feed the ducks. Back then you could walk right into the shallow end. I was sitting the side of this old tugboat, docked there with my buddy Mark Kayfabe, this loudmouth braggart from up Connecticut. A real tough guy too. He used to wrestle and even box the other guys for side money. I always bet on Mark. But fighting wasn't his only hobby, chasing girls was also tops on his list. He'd spend more time looking at girls and hitting on them than he did working. I mean this guy was dead set on anything that moved!"

Layla giggled.

"It's the truth. But still a great guy nonetheless. So, there we are when Sophie walks by with all the kids. Mark nudges me, 'Albert you see her? Look at her!' And so I did."

"Let me guess, Mark hit on her, right?" Layla asked.

"*Almost.* But fate stepped in."

"Fate?"

"Fate. You believe in fate, don't you?"

"I don't know. I'm one of the few girls who doesn't really believe in fairytales."

"Never stop believing in fairytales, my love."

"I'll work on it, Zaide."

"Okay, well here's how I witnessed fate and you can tell me if it's real or not. All of a sudden, there we are watching your great-grandmother in awe and amazement like we'd never seen a woman before or something, and right when Mark goes to hop off the boat, one of the little kids runs into the water to chase after the ducks. Sophie starts to panic. I mean, she could swim like a fish but she had twelve other kids to watch after, and now one was almost drowning! So, I hop off and after a swift twenty yard dash, jump into the water—nearly twisting my ankle in the process—and grab the kid before his head goes completely under."

"Was he okay?"

"*He* was fine, but man oh man, Layla, between my ankle on the dive and my back on the landing, I was a hurt pup. Plus I was drenched head to toe, but yes, the kid was okay. Your great-grandmother was standing over me when she took the little boy from my arms and then tried to help me to my feet. Mark rushed over to help as well."

"Naturally." Layla smiled.

"Yeah, trust me, he just wanted to get close to her. Finally I make it to my feet, the water's in my eyes, my hair is all a mess, my back is killing me—ugh, hardly the first impression I wanted to make. But the good thing was Sophie could not stop thanking me, and apologizing to me. 'Are you okay? Thank you so much, thank you,' and I said, 'I'm so embarrassed.' I admit, I milked it a bit."

"Zaide!"

"What else could I do? This was my *chance*. When I finally made it to my feet, I brushed my hair away from my face, wiped my eyes clear with a handkerchief she handed me, then—"

Albert paused.

"Zaide?"

"Hold on a second." He didn't want to get too choked up.

"It's okay, Zaide. You don't have to go on."

"No, no, I'm fine. You need to hear this." He took a deep breath. "Then I saw her eyes. And she just looked at me with those big bright eyes. I had never seen eyes like that before. She smiled and touched my cheek with her hand."

"*Awww*, Zaide," Layla cooed, cuddling up to his arm.

"I will never forget what she said. 'You fell for me.' That's what she said! And Layla, she was right."

"Gosh, she was a smooth talker too."

49

Albert burst out laughing. "I guess so. But in that moment, that split second when we looked at each other, I *knew*. I knew right then and there that I wanted to spend the rest of my life falling for *her* over and over and over again."

"Then did you whisk her off her feet?"

"Well, kind of. I walked her and the kids back the school five blocks away, soaked and covered in sand and dirt but holding her hand the entire way. It took all my strength not to limp. I wanted to look tough."

"That's so romantic, Zaide."

"And *that's* how you have to feel before you take the next step with someone."

"So you think Jack feels that way about me?"

Albert turned to Layla and put his arm around her. "I can't say for sure, sweetheart. I can only hope he does. Layla, nothing is set in stone with love and sadly, nothing is always as you want it to be in life. There's no map. There's no guide. I know you try to make it that way, but not all love is like a job you can just up and leave when it gets too hard. Love, if real, is something you can't run from, because you don't want to. And you will only know that feeling when true love comes along. Not a day goes by when I didn't look into Sophie's face and thank God for her. Not one single day. And *that* Layla, that is how I knew then and I still know now." He noticed a tear trail along her chin. "Did I upset you?"

She wiped her face with the back of her hand. "No, Zaide, not at all. You said exactly what I wanted to hear. Exactly what I *needed* to hear."

Albert and Layla fell back into the sand, watching the sky move above them. The sun had left for the day, and the clouds collected into large bundles of gray. A storm was coming, and he turned his head to tell her they should go inside. When he looked over at her, she was gone. He hopped up and looked around. He called her name, but she was nowhere to be found. He could hear her voice in the distance, but the clouds were getting darker and lower. A fog picked up in front of him, and he could barely see his hands in front of his face as he waved in an attempt to brush away the mist.

"Layla?" Albert said, trying to push through the fog with his hands.

"Zaide, Zaide . . . I got you, Zaideeeeeee."

"Where are you?" Albert called out in a panic.

"I got you, Zaide."

He could still hear her voice, but it was getting darker, and fast. He called out again.

"Layla! Please, where are you?"

"Zaide, come here, Zaide."

His heart picked up speed, and then in the darkness of the clouds a bright light flashed at him, a blinding whiteness. His eyelids fluttered but the tugging in his hands was still real.

"Zaide, wake up!" Layla said, pulling at his hand.

He opened his eyes and saw Geoffrey standing at the door with his arms folded. "She's been here for twenty minutes, Gramps. What were you dreaming about?"

"It's not nice to sneak up on people," Albert retorted, ignoring his question.

"Tell that to your great-granddaughter." Geoffrey tilted his chin toward Layla.

"Oh, really? What great-granddaughter? Oh, you mean . . . *this* one!" Albert reached down and grabbed Layla's cheeks with his hand, tickling her neck. Layla flopped against the bed, half trying to escape, giggling with excitement. She climbed up and stood over him dressed in a blue Disney princess bathing suit, with her arms posted at her sides, like a toddler super hero.

"Zaide, get up, we're going to the club!" she announced.

"Is that so?" Albert snipped at her feet making her playfully kick back at his arms.

Geoffrey called out from the doorway. "Yeah, Gramps, I thought we'd go to the club for a bit and grab some breakfast while she swam. The café overlooks the indoor pool, and we can reserve a lifeguard to watch her."

Albert hated the club and its *holier-than-thou* attitude that most of Geoffrey's friends possessed. Geoffrey used to belong to a much more down to earth club, but Rose changed that too. Despite his dislike for the club, he knew Layla loved it there.

"Sure. Let me get ready."

"Yay!" Layla shouted, throwing her hands in the air.

"You want to use the driving range too, Layla bear?" Geoffrey asked her.

"I love going to the driving range, Zaide!"

"You play golf now?"

"Yup. Daddy says I can be the next Arnold Palmer."

"You'd be surprised Pop, she's got a pretty good swing. Well, for a six-year-old that is."

"It's better than yours, Daddy!"

"That-a-girl, Layla." Albert grinned, high-fiving her.

"Thanks for your support," Geoffrey joked. "Okay, go grab a snack real quick and I'll call to see if we can reserve some time at the range."

Layla bolted off the bed and settled onto the sofa in the living room with a small pack of pretzels, and Geoffrey pulled out his cell phone and stepped into the hallway. Albert wiped his face and gently smacked his cheeks to life. He didn't want Layla to hear the call to Cedarmere, so he reached for the phone next to Sophie's picture. It tore at his insides every time. He held the phone between his cheek and the pillows, pulling the blankets up to his head, hoping to muffle any possible reaction he may have to news he might not want to hear.

"Good morning, Cedarmere Hospital." It was Jennifer this time, another young woman in her twenties. Unlike Hollie's strong Long Island voice, hers was a southern sweetness, like a beauty pageant contestant. She was from Tennessee, and always wore something orange in honor of her alma mater, the University of Tennessee.

"Hi, this is Albert Abraham, I'm calling to check on—"

"Hi, Albert! How are you today?"

"I'm fine, thank you. How is Sophie?"

Like the rest of the nurses, Jennifer was very familiar with Albert. She knew his questions and gave him the time to ask.

"Doin' great."

"How was she through the night?"

"Slept like an angel."

"And her feeding tube? Dr. Menning said they were getting a new one in."

"Yes, they did the other day. I believe Hollie checked on it as well."

"Her blood pressure?"

"Perfect."

"Fevers?"

"Nope. A perfect 98.7 degrees."

Albert paused.

"Mr. Abraham, are you there?"

Albert didn't respond. He was lost in thought, concerned for Sophie as always. Every day he called the hospital, and every day she was fine. If she was fine, than what was there for him to do? In a way, this made him feel guilty. It was almost as if he wanted *something* to be wrong, so he could rush down there and save her like he did for so many years before she was hospitalized, and it was just the two of them.

"Mr. Abraham?"

"I'm here, sorry, my grandson was just calling me."

"Oh, Geoffrey? How is he? Tell him I said hi." Jennifer giggled.

"Thank you, Jennifer."

"My pleasure, Mr. Abraham. We'll see you soon."

"Goodbye."

Despite the nurses' friendly ways, Albert didn't share their demeanor. He wanted the calls as painless and as quick as possible.

If there is something wrong, tell me, if not, I'm hanging up. Short. To the point. Done.

Geoffrey reappeared in the doorway with his phone to his chest and whispered, still on the other end of his call. "Everything cool, Gramps?"

Albert nodded.

Geoffrey went back to his phone, appearing frustrated.

"What? What do you mean a *leak*?" He whipped his head around in exaggeration and banged his palm against his head. "No, Steve, I understand. Yeah, it's okay." He ended the call.

"What happened?" Albert asked, sitting up from his bed.

Geoffrey tapped his foot and massaged his temples. "There's a busted pipe in the kitchen at the club. There's water *everywhere*. The club will be closed for a week. Damn it! Layla will be so upset."

"What now?"

"You tell me." Geoffrey stared at the ceiling, and rubbed the back of his neck. "You know about fifty plumbers, or anyone with an indoor pool at their house?"

"So sorry, my boy. All I know is you." He smiled at the idea of Geoffrey's club being shut down. "Looks like you and your fancy little friends will have to go somewhere else for the week. Maybe Barbados, the Caribbean, Tahiti, or anywhere else you guys can spend a ridiculous amount of money just to go for a swim."

Geoffrey paced in the hallway. Then he looked up, and in what seemed to be a moment of divine realization, he turned on his heel.

"What?" Albert was trying to figure out why he was smiling at him without saying anything. "Son, what the hell are you grinning about?"

"Wait a second, you *do* know someone." He snapped his fingers.

"I do? *Who?*"

Geoffrey tilted his head and smiled.

"What is wrong with you?" Albert demanded.

Geoffrey casually walked over to the bed and sat down, placing one hand on his chest and crossing his legs at the knee.

"Oh, you know someone, Gramps. Oh yes, *you* do."

"Geoffrey, stop it. What the hell are you talking about?"

"Oh, Albey, you can come over to my house any time you like." Geoffrey spoke in a high-pitched voice and fluttered his eyelashes rapidly.

"Wait, no way!" Albert ripped off the covers and crawled out the other side of the bed, where Geoffrey met him. He grabbed Albert's arm and helped him to the living room, blankets fumbling at his feet.

Preparing for her swim, Layla had used nearly the entire bottle of lotion on her pale skin, making her look like a mummy wrapped in white bandages.

"Look at her, sitting there adding sun block to her little body," Geoffrey said. "A very pasty, oily, white, great-granddaughter who apparently thinks you need lotion for an indoor pool. You want to disappoint her?"

"Don't be ridiculous."

"Watch. Hey, Layla?"

Layla looked up at them, globs of lotion stuck to her face and in her hair. "I'm sorry sweetie, but there was an accident at the club. We can't go swimming today."

"What do you mean? Why? I was waiting for this all week." Then, as if on command, she started crying.

Geoffrey leaned over to Albert and whispered in his ear. "You see that, Gramps? Way to go."

"You are a cruel and evil man."

Geoffrey agreed with a wink.

Albert started to turn back to his room and Geoffrey took hold of him.

"Come on, Gramps, just call Ella. It will be great to see her and you need to get out of this house!"

Albert was growing impatient with Geoffrey's badgering. He looked down at Layla, who was squeezing his hand and pouting.

"Geoffrey, it doesn't matter anyway, I don't even have her number." He was glad he'd thrown it away.

"Really? Because I do." Geoffrey displayed a picture of the note on his iPhone. "Yeah, I took a picture of it just in case."

Albert ground his teeth. "That's low, son."

"I also saved the one you ripped up. You can throw it away again if you like, but it's still stored in the ol' iPhone. Don't you just love technology?"

Albert was on the verge of shredding Geoffrey with a barrage of curse words, but he couldn't lose his temper in front of Layla. She was watching him, waiting for his reaction. He bent down and wiped a glob of lotion from her forehead.

"You really want to go swimming today, don't you?"

"More than anything I've ever wanted in my whole entire life."

"You hear that, Gramps? More than anything in her whole entire life."

Albert rolled his eyes. *Oh, if only wanting to go swimming was the most important thing to me.*

He knew he was caught, and there was no way out.

Albert stared at Geoffrey, still mad at him for cornering him like that. *He has no idea what he's asking me to do.*

"Gramps?"

Albert didn't respond. He was still caught in a myriad of emotions, all of which did not sit well with him.

"You okay?" His grandson reached out for his arm, seeming troubled by his lack of response.

Albert swiped his hand away and shot him an intense look. "You owe me."

Geoffrey clapped his hands together, then rubbed Albert's shoulders. "This will be good for you, Gramps. Oh, I mean, Albey."

Albert went to his bedroom to make the call in private.

"You be nice now, Albey," Geoffrey shouted from the living room, mimicking Ella's southern tone and laughing at Albert's awkwardness.

He sat on the edge of his bed, staring at the phone. The phone only added stress to his life. He only called the hospital, Geoffrey, David, or takeout. The same few numbers on the phone were even worn down from his fingerprints over the years. Now he was calling another number, one he never imagined he would ever have to dial.

His eyes began to dry out from not blinking as he watched the phone mocking him, almost hoping it would dial itself. He was immobile, and the feeling did not sit well with him. He noticed his reflection in the glass frame that held Sophie's image as he did every day. He felt as though she was watching him, but he wasn't sure what she was thinking.

"You are the only woman in my life, Sophie. You always have been and you always will be. This is for Layla."

Albert couldn't possibly expect Geoffrey to understand how hard this was. He was only thirty-eight, which was a little more than half of the time it had been since Albert and Ella last saw one another. On top of that, he had not left her the way he'd planned. This was never supposed to happen.

He drummed the base of the phone with his fingertips. He wiped his wet palms on his ratty sweatpants. From behind he heard a knock at the wall and saw Layla waiting in the doorway. She turned away just as he looked back. His heart was beating and his breathing was exhausting him.

Just pick up the phone and call, you jack ass!

Each number had a loud echoing beep, as if he were dialing in a deep cave. It rang once, then twice. Each pause between rings seemed like an eternity, and he wished it would go to voicemail. Then a familiar voice answered.

"Well, well, well, this is a pleasant way to begin the morning, Albey." Ella's voice sounded hoarse.

"How'd you know it was me?"

"Caller ID, hon. Man, we really need to get you up to date with these things. I bet you don't even have a cordless phone."

She was right.

"Um, well, kind of."

Ella roared with laughter. "Albey, just because we are in our eighties does not mean we can't live young."

"I uh, I guess."

"So, Albey? You called?"

"Yes, I was thinking, well, I was wondering . . ." Albert's voice skipped an octave.

"Spit it out, Albey."

57

Albert cleared his throat. "Sorry. If the offer from the other day still stands, um . . . well, Layla would like to go swimming today. But I know this is short notice."

"Oh my Lord, of course!" Ella shouted. "You comin' over now, hon? You can if you want to. I'm ready."

"Are you sure, Ella? I mean, I don't want to barge in."

"Albey, now you stop that right now. I told you, you can call me today, tonight, tomorrow, or next year, and it will never, *ever* be barging in," Ella assured him in between coughs. "Heck, you can just show up without calling!"

"Ella, please, I will understand. It sounds like you have a cold."

"Albert, I could have the damn plague and I'd say yes. You are always welcome."

Albert managed a smile, thinking of how happy Layla would be. He had saved the day.

"Thank you, Ella. She will be very happy to hear that."

"Okay now, I'm going to order us some breakfast and lunch and y'all will stay for dinner too, right?" She didn't give him a chance to say no. "Oh, of course you will. It will be fun."

"You really don't have to do that, Ella. It's just swimming. She's only six. She'll probably get bored after an hour or so anyway," Albert insisted, worried Ella would feel obligated to entertain them.

"Bored? Here?" Ella burst into laughter. "Albey, trust me, no has ever used the word boring when referring to my home. But just to make sure, I will have to up the excitement factor for good measure."

Albert didn't respond right away. He still couldn't believe he was talking to Ella after all those years. She sounded so casual.

She has to remember what it was like when I left.

"Albey? Albey, you still there, hon?"

"Yes, thank you, Ella. Layla will be happy to hear this."

Ella's voice was calm and gentle. "Albey, I am so glad you called me today. You have no idea how happy I am to see you again."

When she gave him her address, he realized she lived closer than he ever imagined, and even more surprising, she lived along the same country roads Geoffrey drove him on almost weekly. Chills rolled up the back of his neck.

I pass by her house every week! All this time?

"Do you know where it is, Albey?"

"Yes. Yes, I do."

He tried to forget the coincidence and quickly thanked her again. As he hung up, he noticed his hands were covered in sweat, and his shirt was moist against his chest and the back of his neck. He calmed down with a tepid glass of water on his nightstand.

Anything for Layla, he told himself. *Anything for Layla.*

Layla and Geoffrey were waiting for Albert when he left the room.

"Well, Zaide?" Layla asked, tense with anxiety about the possibility of not going swimming.

Albert winked. "Grab your towel, baby girl."

Layla jumped in the air with uncontrollable energy. She hurried over and hugged Albert's legs, leaving large blotches of lotion on his pants. Geoffrey nodded to Albert, thanking him for making the call.

Albert handed Geoffrey the paper with the address and directions on the back. His eyes widened.

"Hey, I think we know where this is, Gramps."

"I'll go get dressed," Albert said before walking into his room.

"Gramps, don't wear your Speedo. You're not that young buff teenager she once knew."

Geoffrey and Layla both laughed uproariously.

Albert glanced over his shoulder at Geoffrey. "There was no leak at the club pool, was there?"

59

"Why, whatever do you mean, Albey? Would I ever lie to you?" Geoffrey crooned in a southern accent.

"Listen to me. If I want to leave, we leave, do you hear me?" Albert snapped, his back turned.

"Yeah. Sure thing, Gramps."

Albert was visibly shaking, his eyes watering. He didn't like being lied to.

7

Behind The Gate

Now arriving at your destination.

An automated voice from Geoffrey's navigation system guided them into Ella's long driveway of flattened pebbles, lined with flowers of every color. Fifty yards down, they were stopped by a security guard standing in front of a twenty-five foot high gate, with a gold *P* in the middle, connecting the doors with massive ivory columns that look they belonged in the Coliseum.

"What's this, Fort Knox?" Geoffrey said, astounded.

Albert said nothing. The well-built, middle-aged guard, wearing a tight red polo and khaki shorts with large sunglasses and a white sport's visor, motioned for Geoffrey to roll down his window.

"Hello, we are here to see Mrs. Perlman."

"Yes, of course, Mr. Abraham." The guard nodded, speaking in a deep, raspy, cigar voice and breathing heavily through this nose. "Mrs. Perlman said you would be arriving. My name is Walter, and I'm Mrs. Perlman's personal driver and go-to-guy. You need anything, you ask me." He stuck out his hand and shook Geoffrey's, then peered over at Albert and back toward Layla. "Good day, Albert," he said, tilting his hat. "And you must be Layla! Mrs. Perlman said you were cute, but she didn't say *how* cute!"

Layla waved back to Walter.

Walter invited them to proceed forward. The gates parted with deep growls from the heavy iron bars, as the large *P* swung back, hanging onto the left side of one gate, leading onto Ella's property.

"Not too shabby, old man. Your girl's got taste."

"I'm surprised Rose hasn't asked for a gate like this," Albert retorted sarcastically, hoping to shut Geoffrey up.

Geoffrey acknowledged the dig by biting his bottom lip and nodding slowly.

They moved down the seemingly endless driveway, with large oak trees and deep chocolate brown wooden benches in between. Albert figured he'd need a place to sit if he were to walk the driveway. There were flowers around the base of every tree, alternating in colors, producing a pattern of purple then yellow the entire way.

On the right was an old barn with several horses milling around, a trainer feeding them. To the left was a large pond about the size of a baseball field, filled with ducks that quacked as the car went by, causing them to scatter and take flight. Layla's mouth hung open at the spectacle that was Ella's life. The palms of her hands and her face were pressed against the window. She rocked back and forth with excitement.

"Daddy, do you see the horses, the ducks, and geese!" she shouted, practically out of breath.

"I do. Maybe Ella will let you see them later." Geoffrey was caught up in her excitement, nearly speechless at the site of the massive estate.

Albert nudged Geoffrey with his elbow. "We'll see, Layla."

They pulled up to the house that could easily double as a small hotel. What Ella called home was a white brick mansion, a spitting image of the White House. Four large columns stood in front of the huge wooden door, with a large United States and Maryland state flag fluttering in the wind.

Bright green shrubs surrounded the stairway, flanked by dozens of rose bushes, kept in pristine order. Geoffrey stopped the car at the top of the driveway by Ella's door. They climbed out slowly, still taking in the sight. Albert held his bag as Geoffrey unbuckled Layla. He picked her up in his arms and walked around the back of the car to Albert on the other side.

"Gramps, does this place remind you of something?"

"Tacky," Albert grumbled.

"More like *amazing!* I saw this house profiled last year in Baltimore Magazine. I had no idea it was so close to us."

"If you like this kind of thing," Albert said, acting unimpressed.

"It's the frickin' White House, Gramps." Geoffrey gasped, admiring Ella's unique style and incredible eye to pull off the exact look.

"Let's get this over with."

"Stop being a grump, we just got here."

A voice from the second floor balcony echoed across the large front yard.

"Good day, Abrahams! I'll be down in a second," Ella sang, clad in a slightly see-through white robe over a leopard one-piece bathing suit, large gold sunglasses perched over her eyes.

"Looking good, Gramps." Geoffrey raised his eyebrows, and nudged Albert.

"Shut up." He leaned over so Layla couldn't hear him. "Please, let's not make this an all day thing."

"Like you have something *better* to do?"

The main doors to the house opened simultaneously, as if Ella was taking the stage, and she walked out with her hands extended to embrace her visitors.

"I'm so happy y'all are here!" She gave each of them a kiss on the cheek. Geoffrey hugged her as if they'd known each other for years, Layla in between them. Albert stayed put. She stepped back to eye up her company, and placed her hands on her hips.

"Well, good morning, Albey. I see you are just as excited as always."

"Hello, Ella." He was hardly able to speak.

"You know, Albey, if we are going to be spending all day together, you might want to offer up more of a conversation. After all, it has been some time now."

"You hear that, Albey?" Layla added, wagging her finger at him.

Ella reached out toward Layla as Geoffrey gently let her down. Layla only wore her bathing suit and flip-flops; the day couldn't begin fast enough for her. Ella crouched down at eye level with her, clearly trying to hide the pain in her knees by squinting her eyes tight.

"Are you ready to have fun today, Layla?"

"You bet!" she exclaimed, pumping her fists in the air.

"Good, because I brought a very special friend to swim with you today, if that's okay."

"A friend? Who?"

As if on queue, from behind Ella a tall young college-aged kid appeared in the doorway, wearing baggy red swimming trunks and a backwards Baltimore Orioles baseball cap. He walked over to Ella, towering over all of them—even slightly taller than Geoffrey—then placed his lanky hands over her shoulders.

"You must be Layla," the man said, smiling at her.

"Wait a second, I know you!" Geoffrey said, pointing in disbelief.

Ella and the young man exchanged a familiar smile. "Well, I would hope so, Geoffrey," Ella said musically. "The entire world knows who Kenny Harmon is by now."

Geoffrey clapped his hands together. "That's it! You're Kenny Harmon, the . . . the *swimmer!*" Geoffrey fumbled to find the right words, nearly out of breath at the shock of meeting a famous athlete of Kenny's caliber. "You won three gold medals last Olympics."

"And one silver," Kenny added.

Geoffrey lunged forward and shook Kenny's hand vigorously. "Dad, do you see this?" He looked back at Kenny, and back at Albert, then back at Kenny. "I bought your Wheaties box! We watched you all the time. *Man!*"

"Now, now," Ella said. "Kenny is here for Layla today. He's going to watch over her in the pool while Albey and I catch up. Geoffrey, I thought you wouldn't mind starting out with a massage?"

He gushed like a little kid. "Are you kidding me?" He slapped his knee again, still in shock. "He was on the cover of *Time Magazine*!"

"Twice actually," Kenny said with a smile.

Albert remained unimpressed, his hands in his pockets, his bag at his feet. "I don't think that's necessary, Ella. We probably won't be staying that long anyway."

Both Layla and Geoffrey looked back at him in shock. As far as they were concerned, they had no intentions of leaving any time soon.

Ella folds her arms. "Albey, y'all aren't going anywhere. I have a very nice day planned for us."

"Let's go, Layla," Kenny said, taking her hand. "The pool is waiting."

She waved goodbye, skipping along with Kenny.

"Ella, can I ask how you know him?" Geoffrey said.

"Oh, I've known Kenny since he was a small boy. His mom worked for Perlmans for over twenty-five years, and he worked at one of my stores for a couple years, bagging groceries, catering, you name it. Before he turned pro, that is. A real great kid. I thought Layla would enjoy hanging out with him, and this way you two can relax, knowing she's in good hands."

"So you just called him up? This morning? Just like that." Geoffrey shook his head in amazement, still not sure if he was imagining one of the world's most famous athletes babysitting his daughter.

"Yup. Just like that. You'd be surprised what a little phone call can do when it's from me. Now let's go have some fun, boys." Ella laced her arms around Albert and Geoffrey's, walking in between them. She guided them around the back of her house, where a stone pathway led through gardens of wild flowers, tended by various workers she greeted along the way. Ella began to talk about the house and the additions she had put on over the years.

"The design is very *interesting*," Geoffrey noted.

Ella playfully rested the side of her head on his arm. "I know, I know, a little much, right? But my husband Norman, God rest his soul, grew up in DC after his family moved here from Scotland. They used to take him to the Mall in DC to see the monuments and museums. He was a real history buff. One of our first dates was to DC, in fact. We still have a house in Georgetown. Over time we became good friends, from parties and events with some of the politicians, and after we met JFK for the first time at *the* White House, Norman could not stop talking about how beautiful it was. I do miss that man. Such a sweet family man." She paused to press a handkerchief to her lips.

"As I was saying, we have several homes, each decorated in our own way, we never really went over the top with them. You know, we wanted something totally different. So, when we decided to spend more time in Maryland, not in Florida and North Carolina, I figured, what the heck, let's have some fun and get people talkin'. After all, the house was already white, already had two nice columns, so you add in some more, bring in some stone, tweak the garden. *Et voila!* I mean, why not, right? Have fun. Live a little!"

Geoffrey beamed, still amazed.

Albert stared off into the distance, already dreading the entire day.

She led them around the estate gardens, heading toward the backyard where the pool was located.

"I have to admit, I think it's kind of cool." Ella looked toward the house, her silver-white hair gleaming in the sunlight. "Would have liked it a bit bigger but the county wouldn't allow. So we'll settle for a nice replica."

"*Bigger?*" Albert muttered under his breath.

"Well, look who decided to wake up." Ella slapped him playfully on the arm.

"I'm just saying, it's pretty big now. That's all."

Ella turned and tugged her large sunglasses down to the tip of her nose, meeting Albert's jaded expression with her bright eyes.

"I bet you tell that to all the ladies, Albey." She threw her head back, laughing boisterously at her own joke.

Geoffrey joined in, laughing so hard he almost cried.

Albert grumbled and waited for them to collect themselves.

When they arrived at the pool entrance around back, Ella turned to face them, gesturing with her delicate hand and manicured nails.

"Abrahams, we are now at the lovely Perlman indoor swimming facility."

Lovely was an understatement. Ella's Olympic size pool was split in half by a glass structure that on hotter days could be removed by remote, connecting the indoor pool to the swimming area outside. The glistening water of the infinity pool on the outer section seemed to run off the edge like the cliffs of a waterfall, overlooking the deep forest at the back of the property. Even from indoors, the full effect could be felt.

A bridge made of rock stretched over a narrow canal of water between two sides of the pool's paved decks. Overhead, two sliding boards went down from four different angles, leading into different locations. Ella said that on a normal weekend day, there could be anywhere from twenty to thirty of her family members and friends swimming well into the night.

Albert tried to take in the enormity of Ella's house while remaining as stoic as possible. He was still trying to act is if nothing surprised him. Geoffrey, on the other hand, didn't bother hiding the fact he was impressed.

"Ella, this could be the largest pool I've seen in my entire life." He spun around on his feet, trying to take in every bit of detail—the impressive indoor gardens raised by artistically placed rocks, the intricate yet tasteful statues of angels that seemed to watch over the surroundings, and the way the sun streamed in, feeding the tropical plants that reached toward the top of the glass enclosure.

"It's the fifth largest residential indoor pool in the Mid-Atlantic area, to be exact," Ella said. "And if it wasn't for that wide receiver for the Ravens and his over-the-top mess of a pool, I would have been number four. Damn shame."

A loud screech came from the far slide as Layla and Kenny slid down together into the pool. Kenny landed with Layla on his lap before going under water.

"Zaide! Come on in!"

Albert waved back, but shook his head.

"Gramps, do you want to go in now?" Geoffrey asked, sounding hesitant.

It was clear to Albert that his grandson felt his discomfort, and so did Ella. Instead of answering, he folded his wrinkled hands before him, and watched Layla splashing in the pool. Seeing a smile on her face was the only thing that made this day worth it.

"I'm just going to watch Layla." He made his way down the long stone deck that led to the poolside, then sat down on a small stool and watched Layla as she swam with Kenny. Nothing contented him more than seeing her happy.

***

Ella took a deep breath and bit the inside of her cheek, knowing Albert was avoiding her. When he slumped on the stool, he looked so diminutive. She remembered a different Albert, and wondered where he had gone.

I told myself I would never allow him to walk away from me again, and there he goes.

Ella shook her head, recalling the last time she'd seen Albert. She could tell Geoffrey was uncomfortable as he shuffled his feet where he stood, perhaps feeling badly for her, when she had shown nothing but intense excitement at seeing Albert again.

Despite her generosity, she was being ignored.

Geoffrey put his arm around Ella and patted her back. "You just have to give him time. He's a pretty quiet guy these days. Please don't take it personally."

She kept her gaze on Albert, who sat with his back to them.

"You know, Geoffrey, last month I ran into a girl at the mall who worked for me when she was fifteen. She's twenty now, and she was home for the weekend from college. She came up to me, gave me a big hug, and we ended up talking for an hour over coffee—right out of the blue. Right there at the mall, like old friends." Ella turned and looked up at him. "But I haven't seen your father in over sixty years and he hasn't so much as smiled at me."

Ella sat on the edge of a lounge chair overlooking the poolside. Cabanas were scattered across the pool's exterior, exotic plants and small palm trees decorated the inside, antique light fixtures lined the walls. Pictures of family and friends were everywhere—all sizes, professionally framed. In every photo of Ella, she was laughing and smiling, hugging those she loved. She wished Albert were as happy to see her as they were.

"Sit with me, Geoffrey. Let's get to know one another a little better."

Ella stretched out on the lounge chair. Her large dark sunglasses covered her eyebrows and the tops of her cheeks. Geoffrey took the chair beside her, sitting up with his elbows on his knees and his fingers tented.

"Tell me about yourself," Ella said.

"Me? Well, I'm thirty-eight. I used to be in real estate. Still am, I guess, but now I own a few bakeries around town. I have a lovely wife named Rose, and of course my angel, Layla."

"And she certainly is an angel." Ella smiled at Geoffrey's obvious adoration of his beautiful daughter.

"Aside from that, I like movies, a good glass of whiskey, and some fine dining now and then. Pretty much your average guy, I guess."

"And your wife?"

"My wife? She's very sweet and a great mother."

"She couldn't make it today?"

"Um, no, she's busy at the moment."

"You told her what you were doing and she *still* didn't want to come? Who wouldn't want to come to my house?" Ella could sense his nervousness, and she wondered what his wife was *really* like.

"Actually, she didn't know we were coming today. I was over at Albert's house last night and we were playing phone tag this morning."

"Why are you staying with Albey?" Ella prodded, tipping her glasses down at Geoffrey.

He shifted where he sat, clearly uncomfortable, as sweat began to bead on his forehead. "We're getting the house redone, so I thought I would hang with Albert for a while. Plus, Rose has a big case coming up, so she's staying at a hotel downtown off and on, closer to her office. There's dust, and people coming in and out, you know. One less person there is best."

"Uh-huh." Ella placed a gentle hand on his knee and patted softly. "I know, Geoffrey, I *know*."

"What about you, Ella? You seem to have the life here." He looked around at the vast estate through the foggy windows surrounding the indoor pool.

"I like to think I do."

"I didn't realize the connection at the store, but I actually met your husband once at a culinary conference a couple years ago in Miami. He was giving a speech on the success of your franchise. You must be very proud of what he's accomplished."

Ella chuckled knowingly. "Geoffrey, my dear, allow me to let you in on a little family secret. Millions of people believe all the Perlmans' success rested solely on the broad shoulders of my husband. We *planned* it that way."

"Excuse me?"

"Geoffrey, you're one of the very few people outside of the Perlman circle that know this information. But to me, you're family, so welcome aboard."

"I'm honored."

"Growing up, my father was a very successful man. He had land, and many different businesses. He would often lecture me on things like investments, making deals, negotiations—things most little girls my age wouldn't want to hear about. I always admired his hard work, and made it a goal to pursue something on my own. I could have easily gone into banking or even the shipping industry but I had to find my own path. You know, something I could say I created." She took a sip to clear her throat.

"Same thing goes for Norman. His family had even *more* money than mine. In fact, we met because our families were friends. Turns out Daddy didn't mind

70

playing matchmaker for me. Norman followed at his family business, while I tried to figure out what I wanted to do. So Perlmans Grocery technically started when I was a door-to-door saleswoman back in the fifties. Doing business that way was catching on, and if you were a pretty girl like myself, you'd be surprised how many doors opened for you. Gosh, I sold everything I could get my hands on. Then I sold out of my house. I even did stuff like those Tupperware parties, but for different kinds of food and household products, explaining them to women around the neighborhood. I was doing this on the side as Norman managed the family bank. But then the crowds got so big I had to expand, which led to a small convenience store—" She stopped short and coughed hard into a napkin, a familiar shudder overtaking her.

"Ella, are you okay?" Geoffrey placed a hand on her shoulder to steady her.

She took a deep sip of lemonade and let out a relaxing hum.

"Oh yes, just allergies. Okay, where was I? Yes, the convenience store. So, I saved every penny I made to open the first Perlmans Grocery in Owings Mills, only twenty minutes from where we sit. From there, we got one more in Pikesville, then farther out in Columbia, Towson, Western Maryland. Even started some gas stations next to them too. Then Norman quit his family bank operation and joined me at the top. We moved very fast after that. Another popping up on the eastern shore, and so forth. At one point, we were opening two stores a month, up and down the east coast." She paused, then winked. "You know the rest."

She took another sip of her lemonade.

"Wait a second, *you* are the Perlman behind Perlmans? Not your husband?" He was speaking to the wizard behind the curtain herself. "He sure left *that* out of the PowerPoint presentation."

"He was supposed to, Geoffrey. In the fifties and sixties, not many women were in the workforce like I was, let alone owning the largest grocery store in the area. And Norman was smart, charming, attractive, patient, and people were drawn to him instantly. You see, people at that time didn't like dealing with a woman as the owner, or having to negotiate with a woman. So we told people Perlmans was his, even though everyone knew I started the whole show."

Ella paused to take another sip and cough. "Excuse me. As I was saying, Norman took credit for the expansion, which was the plan, when really *I* was the one writing *his* checks. And Geoffrey, at the end of the day, when we looked at what we'd done, I didn't mind lettin' people call *him* Mr. President." She took another long sip and smacked her lips with a satisfied, "Ahh."

"That is amazing! I had no idea. Ella, I must admit, you are one impressive woman. I wish Albert would have introduced us earlier."

Ella's mouth opened slightly as she searched for the right words. She paused and then spoke carefully. "I do as well."

"But look at it this way, we're here now and you guys can start hanging out again."

Ella raised her eyebrows and looked out at Albert and Layla. She took off her glasses and rolled them playfully in her hand.

"Did your grandfather ever tell you about me, Geoffrey?"

"No, he hasn't."

"Not even about who I was . . . to him?"

"Albert doesn't talk much these days."

"Even about me? After we saw each other at the store? He didn't say nothin'?" She didn't bother to hide her annoyance.

"No, I'm sorry. Should he have?"

Ella placed her glasses to the side and turned in her seat. "Listen, we're adults here, Geoffrey, so I hope you don't mind if I'm straight and honest with you."

"Please."

"Your grandfather—he was my first. You catch my drift on that?"

"*Oh.* I didn't know that."

"And after your grandfather, there was only one other, and I had to bury him years ago."

"I didn't realize you went back . . . *that* way." Geoffrey blushed.

72

Ella took another deep breath and glanced up at the clouds overhead, through the large glass opening in the ceiling, as if the distant memory of her life with Albert was peeking through the sky like photographs in a dusty album.

"I met your grandfather the first day of high school when I was only fifteen." She smiled fondly at the memory. Talking about it was difficult, but something pushed her on. "He was a friend of my cousin and I had seen him around, here and there, but never spoke to him prior to that day. Oh, Geoffrey, you should have seen him. He was so confident, so strong, and funny too!" She chuckled, shaking her head. "And you should have seen him on the baseball field. Nothing got by him. When he was up to bat, everyone got quiet. *Every* girl wanted Albert." Ella relaxed her body against the lounge chair. "And he chose *me*."

"I didn't know this, Ella." He reached out for her hand. "He doesn't talk too much about the past, but I wish he did."

"Me too." Ella gripped his hand in return.

"So what happened?"

"I wish I knew." She shook her head. "The military I guess? Many boys went off to the military even after the war, mainly for the work. I thought maybe he had. I even thought he died." Ella lifted a hand to her mouth, trying to hold back her tears.

"It's okay, Ella." Geoffrey rubbed her arm.

"One day we were making love under the stars by Cunningham Falls, planning our future, and the next day . . . he was gone like the wind blowing through my hair." Ella snapped her fingers. "Just like that! The last time I saw your grandfather, he was seventeen."

"I don't know what to say, Ella."

"And all this time, he was practically living in my own God-damn backyard." She glided her finger around the edge of her glass, watching Albert as he waved to Layla. "How did we never see one another?"

Ella hoped she wasn't upsetting Geoffrey, but she could tell from the look in his eye that he was troubled. Was it anger she spotted in his blank expression as he turned and watched his grandfather sitting by the pool?

"He's changed so much over the last several years," Geoffrey said. "Seeing Layla is pretty much the only thing that really drives him to do anything at all. My grandmother had a stroke years ago, and Gramps can't seem to understand it or deal with it at all."

"Oh honey, I'm so sorry to hear that." Ella sat up to face him, patting his knee again.

"Thanks. It's been tough, but we still see her. Gram's been at Cedarmere the entire time."

"Cedarmere, you say?" Ella put her arms behind her head and leaned back. "I know some people there, Geoffrey."

"I don't doubt that, Ella." He smiled knowingly and leaned back as well.

A man tapped Geoffrey on his shoulder, almost startling him. "Sushi, Mr. Abraham?"

"Sushi? Sure! Thank you." Geoffrey accepted a small sushi roll as the young man offered some to Ella as well.

"Oh my Lord. This is damn good sushi, Ella!"

"It better be, for what I pay."

The two of them lounged back and lapsed into silence as they sipped cold beverages, while Layla swam with her Olympic hero, and Albert watched on.

8

Don't Be A Stranger

The morning faded away and the humidity from the artificial indoor summer heated up the afternoon. Layla had yet to leave the water, and Geoffrey barely left his chair, using the day to relax and catch up on email with his phone, while Ella tended to some business in the house.

Geoffrey noticed Albert didn't budge from his chair the entire time, keeping his focus on Layla. Whenever Ella walked over to check on them—even standing right beside Albert—he moved his body away and focused his energy even more intently on his great-granddaughter.

Kenny stood in the shallow end of the pool with Layla, tossing her in the air and letting her splash into the water as her arms and legs flailed in various directions. She laughed louder with every splash, yelling out, "Again, again!"

"You should come in the water, Mr. Abraham. It feels great," Kenny said.

"No thanks. I'm okay watching you guys."

Geoffrey's phone rang and he briefly considered not answering it. After all, the massage was putting him a Zen-like frame of mind. Being a workaholic, he grudgingly picked it up, fearing an emergency from the shop or a deal with his real-estate company. Instead, it was Rose barking orders about having Layla back in time for her friend's birthday party. Geoffrey excused himself to the side of the deck, away from Ella.

"Rose, she is having fun here. She doesn't even *like* that girl." He gritted his teeth, trying to keep his voice down. "We'll be back in an hour. One hour. I said *one hour!*" He paused and listened. "Why not? You know what? *Fine!*"

He hung up and crossed his arms over his chest. His wide shoulders rose and fell as he tried to calm himself. He slowly walked over to Ella and sat down beside her, wiping his face with his hands.

"Ella, listen, I'm so very sorry but I think we have to go now."

"Oh sweetie, so soon?"

"I'm very sorry." He could tell by the look in her eye that she'd overheard the conversation, and she was on to him. "Trust me, this has been a fantastic day. *Beyond* fantastic!" He looked out at Layla as she swam and splashed, never tiring. "The food, the massages, the Olympic babysitter—definitely not a normal day for us. But I should get her home."

"Well, if you are going to leave prematurely, then you must promise to come back soon," she insisted.

"You have a deal, Ella. I promise." He bent down and kissed her cheek. She held him in a tight hug and rubbed his back with her hands.

"Thank you, Geoffrey. Don't be a stranger, hon."

"Never. You can count on that. I'll go get them." He walked over to Albert and tapped him on the shoulder. "Gramps, we have to go. Apparently, my little girl has a party to go to." He shouted over to Layla.

"Good. I've been ready," Albert said, standing and stretching.

Layla was climbing on Kenny like a monkey. "But I don't want to leave. I don't want to go to the party!"

Geoffrey stood poolside next to Albert. "I'm sorry, kiddo, but your mom promised. Don't worry, we'll come back soon."

"We will?" Albert sounded shocked.

"Thank you, Kenny, she had a great day today and it was wonderful to meet you." Geoffrey unfolded a towel for Layla to dry off.

"My pleasure." Kenny nodded his head in their direction. "Layla, you work on the strokes I showed you, okay?"

"You got it, Kenny!" Layla exclaimed.

As she swam toward the ladder, Geoffrey leaned down to whisper in Albert's ear. "Gramps, Ella has opened her house to us and you haven't said one word. Now please go thank her."

"I'm not a child, Geoffrey. I'll say goodbye when we leave."

Layla ran to Geoffrey and fell into the towel. Once she was dried off, they gathered their things and followed Ella around the side of the house. She walked in front of them, quietly strolling along.

Geoffrey gave Albert another pointed look, indicating he should say something before they departed.

Albert wiped his brow again and unbuttoned his top button, revealing a matted down chest of hair. "I wanted to—"

"You want to what? Come over here again?" She grinned. "Good, because you are, tomorrow night."

"That's not what I was going to say."

"Well, you haven't opened your mouth all damn day, and who knows what you were going to say. So I said it for you. Have him here tomorrow at six, Geoffrey." Ella leaned in to kiss his cheek, and Albert blushed.

"On the dot, and no later," Geoffrey agreed, placing his hand on his grandfather's back." Albert clearly wanted to snap at them, but there was no way he would do it in front of Layla.

Ella bent down to the little girl, who had taken to wearing the towel around her neck like a cape.

"Layla my dear, I want you to know that no matter what I am doing, where I am, or what time of day it is, you can come over any time. You have your daddy call me and I am here for you."

Layla reached out and hugged Ella close. Both Albert and Geoffrey were surprised and impressed; they had never seen her hug someone so easily. Sophie had never met Layla, and Geoffrey knew how much Albert wished that wasn't so.

"And I didn't forget about that necklace either," Ella added. "I never forget. I just wanted to make it a little more special, so tomorrow night when Albey comes over, I will have it ready."

"Wow! Thank you, Ella!" Layla squeezed her tighter.

Geoffrey's car arrived, driven by Walter, looking brand new. Apparently Ella had Walter wash and detail it while they were swimming. Geoffrey chuckled at yet another thing she did best—making sure her guests were fully taken care of.

They said their goodbyes and climbed in the car. Layla placed her hand on the window and Ella placed hers on top. From the front, Albert was watching Ella interact affectionately with his great-granddaughter. Then she walked to the front window and motioned for Albert to lower it. Geoffrey did it for him.

"Do you remember that necklace you gave me when I was sixteen, Albey? For my birthday?" Ella's voice was soft.

Albert swallowed hard.

"I'll take that as a yes. I still have it, Albey, I've kept it all this time." She stopped herself and glanced out to the pond. "I held it for all these years, just in case, Albey. Just in case." She reached in the window and tapped his shoulder. "I'll see you tomorrow." She backed away from the car, waving. "Now y'all have a good day, and Geoffrey, you make sure this young man is here tomorrow."

"You got it, boss." He leaned over Albert so Ella could see him. "You know I will."

Albert stared ahead, once again avoiding eye contact with Ella.

Geoffrey pulled out of the driveway, waving to Walter as they left. Layla was already fading in the back seat, exhausted from all the fun she'd had. They turned onto the winding country road they'd traveled so many times before, and headed home.

9

In A Busy Street

Albert didn't sleep well. His stomach was hurting. He was nauseous and cold, trying to keep warm by rubbing his feet together. He pulled the blanket over his head, but it didn't help. Nothing ever seemed to help.

He refused to get up for another two hours, trying to catch up on sleep. Despite how big the bed was he stayed on *his side*. Sophie's side remained untouched for her return.

She will come back.

He found solace in watching her empty side of the bed and imagining Sophie with him—her hair always kept behind her ears, her lips moving slightly as she dreamt. She used to move her lips when she read too, something he eventually took on as one of his own traits.

He always marveled at how Sophie managed to sleep only on her right side—never her back, stomach, or even flipping between. Albert used to fall asleep in dozens of positions without thinking twice.

He stretched out his hand and ran it across the flat side of her bed. He imagined it was her arm he was rubbing, and she'd take his hands and kiss them—

just like she used to. The simple motion calmed him, and Albert soon shut his eyes. Finally.

Geoffrey knocked on his bedroom door and opened it enough to peek inside, causing Albert to grumble and moan.

"Hey grouch, I'm heading out with Layla, be back in a few."

Grumble.

"Oh, don't forget, be ready by quarter of six. Layla is going to an afternoon riding class, then a friend's house afterward, and I'm in meetings all afternoon, but I'll be back here to get you."

Albert pulled the covers down tighter over his head.

Grumble. Moan.

"Come on, I'm serious. Five forty-five."

"Geoffrey, I don't need a babysitter. I can get there on my own."

"Gramps?"

"Your grandfather is a big boy. I've been driving myself to and from places longer than you've been alive." Albert's muffled voice rose and fell under the sheets.

"Please take your head out of the covers."

"Damn it, Geoffrey, I almost fell back to sleep!"

"You *will* be there, right?" '

Albert stuck his hand out from under the sheets and gave Geoffrey a thumbs up.

"Okay, fine. But I'll leave a directions on the table, just in case."

Albert purposely snored louder to annoy Geoffrey and drown him out. He heard him sigh heavily.

"Later, Gramps."

Layla yelled goodbye from the other room, and Albert pulled the sheet away only to reply, "Bye-bye, sweetie!"

Then he ducked his head back under like a turtle retreating into his shell.

Albert waited to hear Geoffrey pull out of the driveway before he threw the covers off. He ached, moaning as he straightened and rubbed his eyes. He sunk his shoulders and did his best impression of Geoffrey, mocking his authority:

"Be ready, Gramps, be ready . . . quarter of, Gramps, quarter of."

Then he remembered there was nothing to get too upset about. This was Geoffrey's personality—always the fixer, always the good guy. That was what Albert loved about his grandson.

Albert was old enough to make his own decisions. And the decision *he* made about dinner tonight was made the second Ella told him about it.

The newspapers were waiting for Albert, like they were the first morning Geoffrey was there. Knowing him, he'd probably highlighted the best parts already.

Before reading the paper, Albert decided to make his usual phone call while it was still early. He dialed slowly as he had done twice a day for the past six years. Time only moved forward, and Albert feared Sophie's time was running out.

"Cedarmere, this is Jill." Albert could envision her bright Midwestern smile bursting through the phone. Jill, like Hollie and Jennifer, were always extra nice to Albert.

"Hi Jill, this is Albert Abraham."

"Well good morning, good morning, good morning to you, Mr. Abraham. How are you?"

"I'm fine, thank you. How is—"

"I just came back from your lovely wife's room, and Mrs. Abraham is doing great. She just got done with a check-up from Doctor Bryson and breakfast is on its way."

Jill's country-girl manner of drawing out her vowels entertained him.

How could you not like Middle American girls?

Albert sighed in relief, knowing nothing was wrong. Even though he wished for more answers, more results, he knew that as long as red flags weren't being waved, it bought him at least one more day.

"Mr. Abraham?"

Albert was still in deep thought, staring out at his kitchen window, thinking about Sophie.

"Mr. Abraham, are you there?"

"I'm here, Jill. Sorry. Okay, thank you. Goodbye."

He hung up and rested his elbows on the kitchen counter, rubbing his scalp in an attempt to diminish the stress headache he developed every time he made that call. He rolled his neck, feeling the muscles pop and pull with every move.

"I hate being old."

Albert plopped into his recliner and flipped on the *Today Show*. A random interview with some average citizen and their bizarre looking dog followed news about the arrest of a teen celebrity—nothing that interested Albert. He clicked around to different channels, and apparently death and tragedy were very popular that day. He turned the TV off and stretched out his legs before falling asleep.

While he napped, Albert's mind was clouded with worry. He once told Geoffrey that inside his head it was as if he was standing on a thin yellow line in a busy street, as hundreds of cars whipped by at top speeds, just moments from hitting him. If he twitched, moved, or tried to walk away, he would be crushed. The cars were his thoughts, and the line was his stability.

The idea had frightened his grandson, and Albert almost wished he hadn't told him. He thought about Sophie again and the evening shift at Cedarmere last night, thinking they were more concerned with checking the internet than checking on his wife. He hated the evening nurses, and always thought the lazy ones chose that shift since almost nothing happened in the evening.

Geoffrey always reminded Albert that it was crazy to theorize that way, but in Albert's mind, anything was possible when it came to Sophie's stay there. He woke up in a mild sweat, and practiced his breathing to calm his heart. Then he slid his hand in the opening of his shirt and rubbed his chest. When he noticed the time on his watch, he realized how long he'd slept.

"Seven hours!" Albert exclaimed.

The sheer thought of sleeping that long ever, let alone in the middle of the day, was about as shocking as Layla sitting still for seven minutes. He kicked his feet forward and stood up, nearly tipping. His back was still sore, but after digging a tight fist into his side to ease the kinks, he was able to walk more comfortably. The clock read eight minutes after five. Just then, Geoffrey called.

"Gramps, you almost ready?"

"Huh?" Albert grumbled, still waking up.

"Gramps, your plans with Ella. You have to leave in like a half hour."

"Oh, that. Yeah, I know."

"Are you okay?"

"Yeah, I'm fine. Just dozed off for a bit."

"Do you need me to come get you?"

"No, I'm fine."

"Wait there, I'll be there in fifteen minutes. I can wrap up my meeting."

"No, don't do that. I'm fine. Get back to your meeting," Albert assured him.

"Gramps?"

"Go! I'm fine. I'll see you later."

"Okay. Have fun. Be a gentleman, please. You know, talk to her, ask her questions like a *normal* person," Geoffrey teased.

"Son, I'm fine." Albert gritted his teeth to keep from telling him off. "I'm going to grab something to eat real quick."

"Dad, you're going to dinner!"

"Goodbye, Geoffrey." He could hear him shouting at him as he lowered the phone, but he didn't care. He didn't need someone to tell him what to do.

Albert hurriedly brushed away leftover crumbs from breakfast that were still stuck to his shirt, then flattened his hair down before getting his hat and jacket. He picked up his keys and headed out the door.

***

Ella waited in her bedroom at first. After all, it was suitable for man to enter the house and then have the woman walk down to greet him. Like in the old days when women took their time to get ready and the men waited patiently by the door, like Albert used to do when he picked her up in high school.

She checked her lipstick in the mirror and adjusted her dress. Butterflies swirled in her stomach. She felt like she was fifteen again. Ever since she first saw Albert at the grocery store, a burst of energy had grown within her. With her health the way it was, that feeling was welcomed with open arms.

It'd been a long time since she thought about Albert as she did now. He was part of her daily activities, even if only in thought. After Albert left her, she was crushed. But over time, she had to move on, and slowly he stopped being the main focus of her day. She never forgot about him, not even after marrying Norman, but she forced herself to push Albert to the back of her mind, rather than the front of her thoughts.

Since their meeting at the store, she thought about him constantly. She wondered what he was doing at all hours of the day. When she was taking her daily walks, she wondered, *Is Albey taking a walk now?*

When she ate breakfast, she thought, *What is Albey eating for breakfast?*

Even when Walter drove her to the office or to a meeting, she wondered if Albert might be taking the same route. She would even look out the window, wondering if she'd see him in the car next to hers.

She couldn't erase the smile from her face as she thought about seeing Albert again.

"It will be just like old times," she told Walter on a drive earlier that day. "Me and Albey used to talk for hours on end when we were kids. We have a lot to catch up on, and I can't wait to talk for hours once again."

After not seeing Albert for so many years, and him being so silent before, she figured a nice dinner out would be a great opportunity to catch up. After all, there was a lot to talk about. Getting out would be good for them both.

Aside from her usual cough, she felt great. The cough had worsened these past few years, but it was nothing Ella couldn't manage. Even though her handkerchief was sprinkled with blood, she still had hope. She would throw it away and fetch another white silk cloth—one of the hundreds she owned. If she was going to cough uncontrollably every day, to the point that her throat was shredded to pieces, she was determined to do it with elegance.

After twenty minutes of sitting on the chaise lounge by her window overlooking the stables, she began to grow restless. She walked down the long staircase to the main entrance and hoped to see Albert waiting for her, his arms filled with roses, or, if no roses, at least on his way up the driveway. She didn't see either. She prayed nothing had happened to him on the way there. After all, it was dark, and most people their age didn't drive after the sun set.

Ella picked up her cell phone. She fiddled with it, debating whether or not to call Albert or Geoffrey to make sure everything was okay.

She waited.

She paced.

She checked her watch.

She paced some more.

Thirty minutes went by, and she continued to pace, her high heels tapping on the marble floor.

Forty minutes.

She sat, but got up quickly. Now she was furious, and knew exactly what had happened.

Fifty-five minutes passed. No longer angry, she felt naïve and hurt. Ella peeked out the side windows one last time, but saw nothing. She wanted to be optimistic, thinking traffic might have slowed him down, or a flat tire. But she knew that wasn't the case.

After an hour, Ella coughed hard into her handkerchief and wiped her tears away with the fresh side. Her makeup smeared, but she didn't care. She wouldn't be going out tonight anyway.

She was embarrassed, crushed, and sickened.

She thought about sending Walter out to go look for Albert, but she knew it was a waste of time. She bit her bottom lip and shook her head in frustration.

Why is Albey being so distant? What did I do? What did I ever do?

She was mad that Albert stood her up, and upset with herself for being a fool. She tapped the window, getting Walter's attention from outside, where he was wiping the car with a rag one final time for an extra shine. He walked swiftly to the door.

"Yes, Mrs. Perlman?"

"Walter dear, call the Oregon Grille and tell them I will not be needing the private room tonight." She turned her back to Walter so he could help her out of her jacket.

"Is everything all right, Mrs. Perlman?" He hung her coat up, his expression betraying his curiosity. It was rare Ella ever showed any sign of annoyance.

She kept her back to Walter, not wanting him to see her face as she made her way up the stairs to the bedroom.

"I'm just tired, Walter. Please tell Sydney I appreciate her keeping the room for me, and that I will still pay." She stopped a few steps shy of the top of the staircase. "In fact, take the night off, Walter. Take the reservation and treat your family to a nice dinner. On me."

"Really? Thank you, Mrs. Perlman! Thank you so much. I will call them right away."

When Ella slammed her door, the chandelier in the foyer rattled from the vibration.

A few miles away from his house, Albert sat at a counter seat of the Ashland Diner, sipping a strong cup of coffee and picking at a blueberry muffin. When the waitress came over for a second refill, he checked his watch, then kindly declined and asked for his bill. It was 8:45 when Albert passed the street leading to Ella's house. He didn't slow down, or stop. He knew she was probably mad at him, but it didn't matter . . . he knew he'd never see her again anyway.

10

You Have No Idea

Geoffrey had given the spare bedroom to Layla and settled for sleeping in the living room on the old couch, which could barely hold his long frame. Albert knew it was his way of trying to make the visit seem as casual and short as possible, even though he wasn't fooling anyone.

When Albert woke up to use the bathroom in the middle of the night, he'd go check on Geoffrey. If he wasn't on his laptop hammering away emails, or walking around using his phone on the deck, he was sleeping with his legs bent nearly to his waist in a fetal position. Albert would pick up his legs and place them gently across the armrests and drape his lanky arms over his belly.

Geoffrey awoke later than usual, around eight, and his body rose slowly like a vampire creeping out of a coffin. His head and body lifted up in a perfect line and then his arms stretched so high it looked as if he was trying to touch the ceiling. He was tall, but when surrounded by Albert and his small living quarters, he looked like a giant in Santa's workshop. When he dug into the refrigerator for something to eat, he had to duck his head in the doorway and lower his neck like a crane searching the ocean for food along the shoreline.

He let out an elongated yawn, followed by a very poignant "Shit!" after he glanced at his watch. He popped up and swatted at his pants for his keys, still dressed from the night before. He searched frantically for them, shuffling things around in the kitchen.

Albert didn't know why he was in such a rush, since he usually headed to the bakery at noon, then hopped from shop to shop until the bakeries were all visited and everything was accounted for. Then, if he had time, he would catch up on his real estate deals.

Albert was very proud of his grandson, and had every right to be. Geoffrey had become quite popular for his "drop-ins" and his employees were grateful; they liked him and enjoyed the endless energy he always brought with him. Plus, he was known to slip the staff a few twenties each to thank them for their dedicated work.

Albert marveled at Geoffrey's ability to master so many things in his life yet remain a calm and collected person. The hours and attention to detail he spent on the bakeries alone seemed like a task for ten people. Not to mention managing his real estate empire. He moved so fast and with hardly any sleep. To top everything off, Geoffrey's devotion to Layla and Rose was too remarkable for words.

Despite the millions of dollars each year his businesses brought in, the work to make that happen would have made most other men quit, yet Geoffrey never skipped a beat. Whereas most people in his financial position would rather cash it all in for an early retirement, Geoffrey was working even harder.

Albert watched from the dining room as he paced and searched for his belongings, then crouched down and shot his hand under the couch where he found his shoes and keys. He sat on the edge of the sofa, checked his phone, sighed, and then started to tug his shoes on. When he reached into the left shoe, he pulled out a small pillbox filled with different shapes and colors. He grabbed two and swallowed them without any water.

"What are those?" Albert asked.

Geoffrey jolted as if he'd been shocked with electricity.

"Damn, Gramps, you scared the shit out me!" he exclaimed, his hand on his chest.

"What did you just take?"

"Vitamins, and some Tylenol. I woke up with a massive headache. You should be taking vitamins too, by the way." Geoffrey wiggled his feet into his shoes.

"Those don't look like vitamins I would take."

"What's this, health tips from a guy who still eats bacon and mayonnaise sandwiches?"

Albert rolled his eyes.

"Gramps, what do you expect, Flintstone vitamins like Layla eats?" He picked up one pill at a time, holding them up so Albert could see them. "This one is for cholesterol. I should probably stop tasting my own cakes. This one here is for iron, can't ever be too safe. And this one is for my *chi*, it keeps me balanced." He held it out. "You want to try one? You could use some chi for sure."

"Oh, stop it." Albert turned and headed into the kitchen. "Those things will kill you."

"You have no idea," Geoffrey mumbled under his breath before swallowing two more.

He followed Albert into the kitchen where he'd already started browsing the paper, deep into the sports section. Geoffrey leaned against the refrigerator, crossing his arms over his chest.

"What're your plans for the day, Gramps?"

"Well, I'm going to read these papers for a bit. Then call the hospital. Go back to the papers and watch some TV. Same as I've been doing for years, my boy." Albert didn't look away from the paper. "Oh, and your brother is coming over later so please make sure you're back to see him."

"I'll try to, but I'm already running late and still need to stop back at the house."

Albert kept his gaze down, and raised his eyebrows. Geoffrey didn't sound too thrilled about seeing his brother.

"Oh, and Gramps, I'll be back here by five to get you ready for your date."

Albert set the paper down and looked up. "What are you talking about?"

"Don't play dumb, Gramps." Geoffrey searched through his phone, probably reading another email. "I know you didn't go last night."

Albert ignored him and went back to his paper.

"Ella called me last night." Geoffrey held his cell phone, showing the call log. "She didn't hear from you and thought maybe something had happened. You didn't call her, so she got worried. Odd, right? I could have sworn you *promised* me you'd be there."

Albert continued to ignore him by turning the pages of the newspaper slowly.

"Well, it doesn't matter, because you have plans with her again tonight."

"What?"

"I know you heard me, Gramps."

"You don't tell me what to do, son! And you *don't* plan my days," Albert snapped.

"This is not an argument. You lied to her and to me!" Geoffrey fixed his belt one loop tighter. "We had a deal."

"A deal? That's a stretch." He watched Geoffrey finish fixing his pants, and noticed his grandson was looking a little skinnier than usual.

Geoffrey went into the living room and stiffly rearranged the cushions.

"Gramps, you *are* having dinner with Ella tonight. You agreed to come over at six o'clock before and I gave her my word to make sure you were there. If I have to carry you to her house myself, I *will* do it."

Albert stood, waiting for Geoffrey to say something more, but he'd become too obsessed with cleaning up his space.

"I didn't agree to anything," Albert retorted firmly. "*You* may have, but *I* did not." He went over the sink and put his mug away, then headed back to the living room.

"Gramps, stop it now. You promised." He'd changed his tone, pleading in a soft voice as if he were talking to Layla.

Albert slid into his recliner and firmly pressed the buttons on the remote, surfing through random channels, hoping his body language would give Geoffrey a hint. Instead, he sat down on the couch next to him.

"Gramps, I love you, but you have no choice but to go."

He poked angrily at Geoffrey with his remote. "I don't have a choice? I'm eighty-two years old and I don't have a *choice*? Look here, Geoffrey, my days on this planet are numbered, and excuse me if I want to be a little choosey with how I spend them. And I'll tell you one damn thing, it's not going to be with Ella!" Frustrated, he turned his focus back to the television.

Geoffrey stood up and looked down at Albert, his large frame filling the air around the tight little room which Albert spent the majority of his days sulking in. He walked over to the door, then turned and pointed a firm finger in his grandfather's direction.

"I don't get it, Gramps. Ella is sweet, fun, and cooler than half the people I know. All she wants to do is have dinner. Why can't you do that? She said you used to be . . . friends.

"You have no idea what you're getting into, son."

"Well, until you tell me why I can't possibly understand what's going on, you will be going." Geoffrey put his hand on the doorknob, his back to Albert. "I'll be back at four-thirty. You'll be ready and I will drive you. If you fight, I'll throw you in my trunk. These fancy luxury cars you tease me about have very roomy trunks."

Albert's gaze sharpened on the television, but out of the corner of his eye, he watched Geoffrey's car pull away. When it was out of sight, he threw the remote hard against the wall, cracking it in half as the batteries flew in different directions.

11

What Do I Have?

Geoffrey pulled up to his house to find Rose carrying an overnight bag to her girlfriend Michelle's car. Michelle was the only one of his wife's friends that Geoffrey could tolerate, along with her husband, Brandon. The four of them usually went out on the weekends. This time, it appeared Geoffrey wouldn't be joining them. When he parked behind Michelle and climbed out, Rose was already walking in his direction.

"Michelle and I are going to Montauk for a few days, maybe the week. I'll need you watch Layla when she's not at her friend's house. I've made arrangements and wrote down their numbers on the table. I emailed you the information as well."

She'd skipped the greetings. Geoffrey remembered a time in the not-so-distant past when she would have kissed him hello, but that rarely happened these days.

"Um, okay then. I didn't know you had plans."

"Oh, Geoffrey, I told you two weeks ago about Michelle's shore house, and this week being the only one I could do." She had one hand on her hip, the other holding her BlackBerry as she scanned her text messages. "Stop acting like you don't know!"

"When will you be back?" Geoffrey asked, half wondering if she would return at all.

"Geoffrey, God, I don't know! Stop hassling me. I'll call you later." She shoved her phone into her tight jeans and pulled her glasses down over her eyes before looking back at him.

"Rose, wait." He spoke softly, reaching out for her hand. But before he could make contact, she was in the passenger seat of Michelle's car. "Rose, wait! Please!"

She was already fastening her seatbelt and reiterating instructions through the cracked window. "Layla is at Noah's house now for a play date, she'll be home at three. Her weekend plans are listed on the counter, as I told you before. Did you hear me when I said that? The rest is up to you." She pressed the automatic window shut. Rose waved her hands at Michelle to leave quickly. Geoffrey stood and watched as Rose disappeared again.

"Great start to the day, Geoffrey," he mumbled.

He walked slowly to the door and crumpled on the front steps, exhausted. His routine was blown. With the amount of medication he needed to consume in a day in order to keep his *chi* in check, he had to be up at five in the morning, no later. Anything less would cause a tremendous inner meltdown, which apparently had already begun.

Time was going to drag more than usual, and he knew he needed help if he was going to watch Layla by himself for the next few days. He called Nick Scott, the man who'd been his best friend since second grade, now his right hand man and business partner in the bakeries. Nick had been by his side since the first store opened, making sure all aspects of the business ran smoothly.

When he got him on the phone, he asked Nick to do the drop-ins for the next few days. As usual, Nick agreed, but this time with a great deal of hesitation. The drop-ins had been Geoffrey's idea, and since the first shop had opened years ago, he'd never missed a day if he could help it. Even when Geoffrey went on vacation, he'd call each store twice, sometimes three times to check in and ask how everyone was doing. He didn't do it to micromanage, but simply because he cared about his employees. If anything happened they were concerned with, he wanted to know right away so he could fix it.

"Everything okay, buddy?" Nick sounded uncertain.

"Yeah, Nick, I'm fine. It's my allergies again giving me another killer migraine. You know how the change of seasons does that to me." Geoffrey hoped Nick was buying it.

"Totally understand, Geoff. I'll make the stops, and afterward why don't we go hit some balls at the range? I just got a new club and I'm itching to test her out."

"Nah, I'm gonna kick back today and take it easy. I'm going to see Sophie and swing by Albert's place again."

"Okay, well, call me later. I'll come over and we'll shoot some pool. I'll pick up pizza."

Geoffrey ran his hands through his hair, massaging his scalp, trying to ease the tension. "I'll let you know. I have something with Albert tonight. But yeah, I'll call you, I'll call. Listen, I gotta run. These allergies, man."

"Call me later. We'll talk then," Nick said before Geoffrey hung up.

Geoffrey wiped away his tears, and shook his head in disbelief about what his life had become. Even to this day, over a decade after he'd become a multimillionaire, he still couldn't wrap his mind around what he owned. He couldn't get over the fact that just the custom pavement on his driveway cost more than the house Albert lived in. He looked at his car, knowing it cost more than most college tuitions. And the watch he wore was more expensive than the Volkswagen Albert bought him in high school. He didn't like who he was now.

He thought about all the things he wished for himself as a young man. Children? Yes, Layla was the best. Money? He had plenty. A thriving career? He had that as well.

Albert always stressed that working hard would get you whatever you wanted in life. Geoffrey had worked harder than anyone he knew. Now he wished for a simpler life. He laughed at the irony of his situation.

Life should have been simple for him. His land was worth millions, he had so much money he could easily retire if he wanted to, he had local celebrity status, he was the father to a great little girl—yet he was still miserable.

Geoffrey wasn't sure when that started, but he knew things were getting worse when Nick noticed a change last year. He'd encouraged him to see a doctor about his migraines, and Geoffrey dismissed the idea. Nick had insisted. Since then he'd had an array of medications prescribed to cure his pain. But the doctor never prescribed the amount and the frequency of medication Geoffrey took now. No doctor would.

He flipped up his jacket collar and pulled the top in close to keep his neck warm. He didn't want to go inside because he didn't want to know what the inside had become. One thing was for sure, it wasn't the house he had envisioned when he bought it. He reached into his pocket and pulled out his pillbox.

Only three tablets left. Shit.

He needed a refill. Fast. He'd make that call next.

He leaned back against the door and squinted his eyes tightly as he swallowed the remaining pills. In twenty minutes the migraine would be gone, and he would melt away.

***

Albert couldn't forget that morning's dispute with Geoffrey. He hated that things were left the way they were. He knew he was responsible, but Geoffrey didn't understand. He never would. His situation with Ella was far beyond anything he could comprehend, and it was nothing he cared to discuss. He never thought he'd see her again, and he'd made peace with that. He looked at his watch—noon. Time to call the hospital again.

"Good afternoon, Cedarmere Care Center, this is Hollie."

Call it like it is. It's a hospital, not a care center, Albert thought.

"Hi, this is Albert Abraham, I'm calling for my wife, Sophie Abraham."

"Mr. Abraham, come on now, how many times have we talked over the years? I know your voice, you don't have to say your whole name."

"I'm sorry."

"And you don't need to apologize either, silly. We're friends."

"Yes. I guess."

"Good. But so you know, I have your gorgeous wife's chart right in front of me, and she is all good. Perfectly happy."

Happy?

"Are you sure? You sure I don't need to come down today? I'm planning on coming tomorrow with my grandson."

"Mr. Abraham, you are more than welcome to come as much as you like. But I promise you she is okay. And I can't wait to see you tomorrow, and Geoffrey too." She'd always been smitten with his grandson.

"Okay. I will see you then. Thank you." Albert hung up before she could say goodbye.

He sat back in his chair and watched his chest rise up and down as he breathed slowly. His day was complete.

I'll call back in a few hours.

He turned the television on, and watched ESPN.

***

Albert had been asleep for about an hour, when he heard people talking nearby. But he wasn't sure where they were or where he was.

"What should we do?" a voice asked.

"I dunno."

He couldn't open his eyes. He was trapped in his dream.

Wake up, Albert, Wake up!

"You want to pinch his nose?" A deep voice asked.

"Yeah, that would be funny," the second voice said, laughing.

"Go ahead, do it."

Albert felt a slight squeeze on his nose. The pinch was followed by the smaller voice whispering.

"*Zaideeeeee, Zaideeeeee.*"

Albert flicked open his eyes to find Layla sitting on his lap with her elbows folded on his chest, her tiny fingers playfully poking at his face. Albert wiggled his nose.

"Does this nose say Property of Layla Abraham?" Albert asked playfully. "Well, now you'll have to pay the price!"

"Pay? I'm only six, I don't have any money."

"Oh well. I guess you'll have to pay in . . . tickles!"

Albert poked at her sides as she squirmed and struggled for help, laughing until tears came. Then he wrapped his arms around her and kissed her cheek.

"What brings you here?"

"What, a grandson can't bring his daughter to see her Zaide?" Geoffrey butted in, grinning, his hands on his hips. Albert shot him a glare.

Layla hopped off Albert and ran to her backpack, where she had a stack of books and toys she'd brought with her. Geoffrey sat next to Albert, as Albert adjusted his seat and pulled out the remote that had fallen behind him during his nap.

"Gramps, about today—"

"*Ehh*, it's nothing, son." Albert raised his hand and swatted the air.

"Thanks. So, you're going?"

"Goddamn it, Geoffrey!"

"Gramps, hey!" Geoffrey pointed his chin toward Layla.

"You said this was dropped."

"Wait a second, no I didn't. I apologized, but never dropped it."

"Geoffrey, you're fighting a losing battle, son."

"Really? Is that so?" He turned to Layla. "Layla? Tell Zaide what you asked me on the way here."

Layla looked up from her book. "I wanted to know when we were going back to Ella's house, Zaide. She said she'd give me a charm necklace like she wears, remember? When are we gonna go back?"

Albert and Geoffrey locked eyes.

"So, you feelin' lucky, punk?" Geoffrey asked.

"This . . . this isn't a game, Geoffrey." Albert pulled him closer by his sleeve. "Son, you have no idea what you're doing. You have no idea."

He locked eyes with him, angling forward in what he hoped was a threatening manner. Suddenly the phone rang, and Albert startled.

Sophie! My God!

"I'll get it!" Layla shouted from the floor, then lunged for the phone before Albert could reach for it. "This is Zaide's house, how may I help you?"

Albert and Geoffrey watched her, both hoping Layla would not be the first person to hear anything had happened to Sophie. Then her voice rose in pitch.

"Uncle David! Where are you? Here? Where? *At Zaide's?*"

Layla dropped the phone and ran to the door where David was already halfway in, slipping his cell phone back into the pocket of his double-breasted suit.

"Uncle D! Uncle D!"

"There's my Layla!" David reached down and kissed her cheeks.

Geoffrey walked over to shake his little brother's hand—no hug. "Hey, Dave, how's things?"

"Me? Great as always. *Like a boss!*" He spoke in a conceited manner, as if everyone should know this already.

This was classic David; a young, smart, rich, arrogant man-child who thought the world should be grateful for his presence. He ran through women and colleagues faster than the expensive bottles of wine he regularly purchased. Despite being incredibly pompous, he didn't care to alter his ways. He knew exactly who he was and for good or bad, he had no desire to change. Change was a hard issue for any of the Abraham men, and David was no different.

As always, he wore a suit. He never left the house without one, and always traveled with a spare. To him, status was everything, and wearing anything but the best clothing or jewelry was unacceptable. Even at the mall or the movies, he'd wear a suit. The most casual he got was in the spring and summer when he wore a lightweight suit, unbuttoned to expose his chest, and thousand-dollar loafers. It sickened Albert.

At five-foot-nine and a hundred and seventy-five pounds, David was a solid block of muscle, which made him look like a 1920s wise guy, hustling some sort of bootlegged liquor deal, especially when he wore his pinstripes. His hair was a slicked back mop of chocolate brown. His photograph had been on every legal website in the world, he interviewed constantly, and occasionally he appeared as a guest on CNN round tables. The only time David dropped his guard was when Layla was around. Something about that little girl made all the Abraham men turn into mush.

"Uncle D, you smell funny." Layla tipped her head back.

"'It's called *Depth*, a rare cologne only sold in South Africa. It costs your Uncle D seven hundred and fifty dollars a bottle." He spoke as if Layla should be impressed.

"You spent *seven hundred and fifty dollars* on a bottle of cologne?" Albert was aghast.

"Gramps, there are only like sixty bottles made a month," David replied, as if that made it okay. "Old Spice doesn't cut it nowadays." He turned to Geoffrey. "Well, for *some* of us it does." He chuckled, clearly expecting Geoffrey to pick up on his humor.

Geoffrey remained stone-faced. "So, David, what brings you around today?"

"Same as you, I suppose. Thought I'd see Gramps on my way out of town and check in on Sophie."

"Where you going, Uncle D?" Layla asked, swinging his hand in hers.

David knelt down. "Well, Layla, Uncle D is going to France. Do you know where France is?"

Layla's face scrunched up as she considered this. "Do they make fries there?"

"Sharp kid, bro," he said to Geoffrey sarcastically. "Hey, Layla, I'll bring you back something really cool. Sound good?"

"Cool!"

"France?" Albert wondered why David would be going there.

"Yeah. I rep this big time Hollywood agent. Last month one of his clients started directing some big action movie that's taking place outside Paris. He invited me out any time so I figured I'd go now, right? Should be fun. But the plane leaves in a few of hours, so I gotta run."

Albert was well aware David only visited when it was convenient for him. He'd accepted this for better or for worse. He smiled, acting impressed, because he knew David would want him to. "That should be fun."

"Yeah, it should!" David turned to Geoffrey. "If by fun, you mean a private jet, hot stewardesses, a yacht waiting, and three grand per night for a villa."

"That's uh, pretty impressive, David," Geoffrey said.

"You know it, bro." He punched him on the arm.

The conversation stalled as it often did when they were around one another. David bragged, Geoffrey listened, flattered his little brother a bit, and then they refocused on something else.

"I had a chance to see Sophie," David said. He stopped when he noticed Layla sitting on the floor, flipping through one of Albert's newspapers.

Sophie was a non-issue with Layla. She was aware she had a great-grandmother and that she lived in a hospital, but they left it at that. The Abrahams were in agreement they would not bring it up around Layla.

"Sorry. I saw our *friend* today. She's doing well. Looks good."

Albert's eyes widened. "Is the feeding tube working correctly now? I asked about that last week. I should go tonight." He began to panic at the mere mention of her name.

"No!" Geoffrey exclaimed. "I mean, you can't go tonight." He shot him a glance, and Albert replied with a similar gesture even though he had no idea what he was talking about. "He can't, not tonight. We're having a game night. The three of us."

"What?" Albert said.

David raised his eyebrows. "Wow, gosh. Sounds absolutely riveting, you guys. So sorry I won't be here for that. *Really!* And to think I thought the private jet

100

and luxury service would be a blast. Then you throw in game night? Way to make me jealous."

Geoffrey crossed Albert's path and bent down to pick up Layla. "Isn't that right, Layla? Game night tonight."

Layla clapped her hands together. "Uncle D, you like Jenga? I rule!"

"I'm sorry, sweetie. How about next time? Rain check?" Layla smiled and agreed. David bent to kiss her cheek. "Okay, baby girl, I gotta run, but take care of these two goofballs while I'm gone."

Layla liked the goofball comment.

"You just got here, David. Sit down for a bit, and have some coffee," Albert pleaded.

"Yeah, well, it's game night and I know you're eager to get that going. Plus I have a bottle of 1985 Pinot and a filet awaiting my arrival." He slipped on his sunglasses.

"Have fun, David," Albert said, settling for a hug.

"Always do, Gramps. I'll call you tomorrow when I get settled. Layla, you're my girl! Don't forget it. When I get back, we're playing Jenga, so you better practice."

Layla ran over to give him a hug.

Just like that, the magical celebrity known as David Abraham, Esquire, completed his disappearing act.

As soon as the door shut, Albert grabbed Geoffrey's sleeve and pulled him toward the kitchen. "We need to talk."

Geoffrey followed him and blocked the entrance so Layla couldn't hear as she flipped loudly through various newspapers on the floor.

"Listen here, son. I've told you this before and I'm starting to lose my patience. Ella is *not* my friend and I don't want to see her. I don't want to visit her. I don't want anything to do with her! Do you understand me?" His voice was rapid and stern.

"Gramps—"

"I said, do you understand me!"

"Okay, okay, not so loud."

Albert pushed him aside to leave the room, but Geoffrey grabbed him from behind to stop him.

"Gramps, you have to explain this to me."

Albert slapped Geoffrey's hand away and jabbed a finger at his chest. "I said this is beyond you."

Before Geoffrey could argue, the doorbell rang. They exchanged a glance, both wondering who it might be. David wouldn't ring the doorbell, and Albert's entire social circle was already in the house.

Geoffrey shrugged. "It's *your* house."

Albert walked to the door and saw Ella's driver, Walter, waving and smiling. He opened the door slowly.

"Walter?"

"Mr. Abraham, good evening. I'm here to take you to Mrs. Perlman's house for dinner."

"What are you talking about?" Albert turned to Geoffrey, who appeared just as surprised.

"I didn't do this," Geoffrey insisted, raising his hands.

"Mrs. Perlman thought you would like a ride to her house tonight for dinner. I will bring you back as well. No need for you to drive tonight."

"It's only four-thirty," Albert said, his frustration increasing.

"Mrs. Perlman just wants you to know you can come earlier if you'd like. I can wait. Whenever you are ready. Now, ten minutes, thirty, or as scheduled. Your call." Walter looked back at the shiny black Lincoln Town car. "But no later than five forty-five, please." He tapped his watch with his finger.

Yeah, you'll be waiting for a while, all right. Albert had no intentions of going to Ella's house tonight or any other night.

"Well hello, Mr. Abraham." Walter peeked over at Geoffrey.

"Great to see you, Walter." Geoffrey extended his hand over Albert's shoulder. "And what a nice ride, my man."

"Mrs. Perlman does have good taste in cars," Walter said as they exchanged a quick laugh. "She has a rather nice collection. I can go back and bring over another sedan, or convertible, or SUV, if you like?"

"No, no this is fine," Geoffrey said, startled by the invitation.

"Anyway," Albert interrupted, "this won't be necessary, Walter, but thank you. Tell Ella I'm not really feeling well today."

Geoffrey firmly gripped Albert's neck, and Albert winced.

"How about you give us a moment to get ready and we'll be out soon," Geoffrey said.

"Not a problem, Mr. Abraham, I'll be in the car. Please, take your time."

When Walter walked away, Albert threw Geoffrey's hands off with a quick shrug.

"Gramps, you are being ridiculous!" Geoffrey argued, watching him head toward his room. "Just go for one night, for one hour even. What is the harm?"

Albert waved him into his room. Layla watched with interest, then ignored them, and continued flipping through newspapers, ripping out photos she liked, and neatly stacking them.

He sat down on his bed, his elbows aggressively planted on his thin withering legs. He rocked slowly back and forth, trying to calm down, shaking his head in aggravation from side to side. His breathing picked up, which annoyed him the most. He was not supposed to be getting this worked up. He had been trying to save all his energy to mourn Sophie's eventual passing, since that alone would wipe out every ounce of his strength. The last thing he needed was someone antagonizing him.

Geoffrey sat down next to Albert and put an arm around him, slowly rubbing his side. Albert allowed it. His grandson reached around him like a toddler clutching a teddy bear. He hated arguing with anyone, let alone Geoffrey. They had a close bond despite any hiccups here and there, and he knew that, but their disagreements still made him uncomfortable.

"I think you need this," Geoffrey said softly. "I don't understand why you are being so tough with her."

He tried to answer, but the words wouldn't come.

"Gramps? You can tell me what's wrong. Is it about Grandma? I don't think she'd mind."

Albert looked over at the picture of Sophie. "There is more about Ella than you know. It's nothing worth rehashing. My focus is on your grandmother."

"Gramps, she's a friend. It's dinner. What's the harm?"

"Son, you don't—"

"How about this, you go Ella's house and I will call the hospital every hour to make sure Grandma is okay. Does that work? If there's a problem, I'll call Ella and pick you up immediately."

He continued rubbing his back. For once, they were speaking in soft tones, not arguing. From the other room, Albert heard paper ripping as Layla played with the old newspapers.

"That's not it, Geoffrey."

"Then what?"

"Nothing."

"Look, if anything, at least go for Layla's gift."

"Fine, for Layla," Albert said, finally giving in.

"Great. You go have a good evening."

Geoffrey went over to the closet and started pushing through Albert's shirts.

"I thought your fridge was bad, but your closet is an embarrassment. You've got nothing nice to wear. We're going to the mall tomorrow." He retrieved the cleanest shirt he could find, a white button-up, and found an old pair of dress shoes to match a pair of black slacks. "Well, Gramps, not exactly what I would call fine fashion, but this will do." He held the shirt up to his chest.

"Geoffrey, please."

"I know, I know. But look at it this way. Layla is expecting you to bring home a present, so at least do this for her. I will call the hospital, I promise. All grounds are covered."

Albert went over to his closet and nudged Geoffrey aside. "There is *nothing* wrong with my clothes."

12

More Questions

Albert was quiet during the fifteen minutes it took to get to Ella's house, even though Walter tried to make casual conversation with him. He figured Ella probably instructed him to be extra nice to him, but he didn't care. He was too concerned with the itchiness in his dress shirt. He tugged at it the entire way.

Why do I have to get dressed up to go to her house?

Albert longed for his sweats and slippers. It took him some time to settle, and when he did he found comfort resting against the cool window, staring at the fields and trees he'd seen so many times before.

His place of peace and relief was now clouded with confusing emotions. The houses he'd admired for so long no longer seemed so distant, since he would be inside the biggest one of all in a matter of minutes. He saw horses lined up along fences, people feeding them just as he and Layla did. He wished he was in one of their cars instead.

Albert considered playing sick again, maybe asking Walter to pull over so he could vomit, and then turn around. But he didn't. He had to do this for Geoffrey and Layla. And despite Geoffrey's campaign for convincing Albert, he still felt he didn't have to do this for himself.

He wasn't sure what Ella had planned for the evening, but undoubtedly it would end up with him having to explain why he left and why he never spoke to her again. He knew she wouldn't like his answer, and he didn't like having to give her one. Geoffrey and David could think of ways to get out of talking about something so awful, but Albert lacked the street skills his grandsons had acquired in business.

It's been over sixty years. Maybe she already knows why I left.

The leaves scattered in a deep rusty rainbow. The thick autumn colors pressed through the window, reflecting off Albert's white shirt. He looked down and felt as if he could actually touch the leaves right there. It seemed so surreal for such beauty to be held on such a small stretch of road that wasn't even a dimple on any map.

Albert clung to images like this as if they were precious gold. There were few things he loved outside of his family, and this road was one of them. He thought about all the rides he'd taken with Geoffrey, good or bad. He hadn't made a final call on which category this ride fell in.

Albert heard Walter call Ella from the car to let her know they would be there shortly. When he heard her voice on the other end, his mind went back to when he last saw Ella, all those years ago.

They were young, vibrant, and in love. There was no reason beyond blind ambition that would make either of them believe they wouldn't be together forever. Back then, *forever* was something they spoke about often. They had big plans for their future. They often escaped to the fields on Ella's parents' farm and lay in the grass for hours, out of sight. They'd bring food and some wine and let the freedom youth allowed them to wash over their bodies like the smooth comfort of the Chesapeake Bay waters, which they would retreat to nearly every weekend.

On the weeknights they would take long walks in the woods behind her parents' house, maybe set a fire and listen to the rushing waters of Strongwood Creek. When they had long afternoons, they would drive over to Cunningham Falls, an hour and a half away, where they would swim, rest, and hold one another.

He'd kiss Ella's neck, as he laced his fingers with hers until the last second when they had to leave for home.

Whenever they would hold hands, Ella would look into Albert's eyes and utter the same words she always did when she felt his touch.

"Laced fingers means we're going to kiss, Albey."

And they would.

For hours.

The last day they spent together at the falls was no different. He kissed her deeper and with more passion than ever before, never knowing it would be the last time. She caressed his face with her hands.

"I love you so much, Albey. Never let me go."

"Never," Albert promised.

"Never." Their gazes locked before she pulled Albert in for another kiss.

As Albert sat in the car, he could still see Ella. He watched her come out of the water, pushing her long hair away from her face and holding her hands out to him. It was as if she was standing right there in front of him again. Her bright green eyes and auburn hair shone with a youthful glow. He could even hear her voice.

"Albert, so great to see you."

Her voice, still as sweet as he remembered it.

"Albert?"

"Ella?" Albert tried to adjust his eyes.

"I'm right here, Albert. Albert? Can you hear me, Albert?"

I can Ella. I'm looking right at you. You're as beautiful as ever. He couldn't stop smiling.

"Walter? Walter, help me please!"

Walter? What is he doing at the falls?

"Mr. Abraham, are you all right? Do you hear me, Mr. Abraham?"

As Walter lifted him to his feet, Albert realized he was real, but the image of Ella continued to toy with his mind.

"I'm okay, I'm okay," Albert insisted, suddenly realizing where he was. He'd been so deep in his imagination he was unaware the car was parked at Ella's house.

She's here! I see her.

The woman spoke, the one he could have sworn was her.

"Mr. Abraham, are you okay?"

"Are you?" Albert mumbled.

"I'm Madilyn, Mr. Abraham. I'm Ella's granddaughter. I'm so happy to meet you."

Albert took off his hat and wiped his eyes with the back of his hand.

"You look . . . You look just like her." He could hardly believe it wasn't Ella.

"You know, Mr. Abraham, I've heard that same exact thing every day for thirty years." Madilyn laughed softly.

She held Albert by his arm, helping him to the front door. He couldn't take his eyes off her face, as if he was seeing a ghost from his past.

"I know, it's pretty uncanny, right?" Madilyn winked. Albert's mouth hung open; he was still shocked at the incredible similarity.

She brushed her thick wavy hair behind her ears, keeping hold of him with her other arm. "Albert, you're going to catch some flies if you keep your mouth open like that," she warned.

He was drawn in by her smile, that *same* smile. It was the exact same smile he'd kissed more than half a lifetime earlier. It was wide and bright, with a line of perfectly straight white teeth. And at just about his height, he was eye to eye with her.

"Good evening to all!" Ella exclaimed, swinging the door open.

She was clad in a glamorous outfit, too beautiful for a dinner at home. Her turquoise dress, held snug on her small frame, ended just shy of her knees. The outfit was something Albert had never saw any senior citizen wear before. A gold headband pushed her hair back, and jewelry decorated her fingers and wrists. She approaches with open arms.

"Well, Albey, I see you have already met my lovely granddaughter, Madilyn. I had her fetch you since I was still getting ready. Madilyn, will you be staying with us for a bit? We have plenty of food."

"I'm sorry, Grandma, but I have to skip out." She turned to Albert. "I know you guys have a lot of catching up to do, but I hope to see you again soon. When are you coming back over, Albert?"

Before he could reply, Ella blurted out, "Don't count your blessings, Maddy, it took me over sixty years to get him here tonight, and Walter had to practically kidnap him."

"That's not true," Albert mumbled, not wanting to appear rude, even though Ella was right.

"Plus, he stood me up last night. *Me!*"

"About that, Ella—"

"Water under the bridge, Albey, water under the bridge. But if you do it again, I'll have Walter take you to the backroom and rough you up like he used to do to the cheaters at the casinos."

Walter nodded, his arms folded across his wide chest.

"Really?" Albert said, feeling somewhat frightened.

Walter and Ella both laughed. "It works every time, Walter."

"Well, when you do decide to come back, I'd love to see you, Albert." Madilyn leaned in to kiss Albert's cheek.

"You knock it off, Maddy, this is my date."

"This is *not* a date," Albert said firmly.

"Oh, for Christ sakes, Albey, stop being such a big old baby. I was just playing around." Ella stepped out to hug Madilyn goodbye. Madilyn waved as she walked toward her car, which was parked alongside Walter's. Ella reached for Albert's hand, and he moved it away fast and shoved both hands in his pockets.

"Okay, okay, I understand," Ella said. "Here, I'll just loop my arm in yours, how about that?" He didn't answer, but allowed the gesture. "Walk this way, Albey."

He didn't know what to make of her house. If what he'd seen last time was impressive, the part he saw now was beyond words. There was gold, marble, hardwood, and crystal everywhere. A gigantic chandelier hung in the foyer with large silver and gold charms swimming in crystals. The walls were papered with angels and religious ornaments. The floors were wooden, shiny, and thick. The ceiling was so high it made him queasy just looking up. Elaborately framed pictures of all sizes hung floor to ceiling, as they had in the pool area. There were family photos, pictures of Ella with celebrities, parties, magazine articles featuring Norman, and awards of all kinds.

Their footsteps sounded like they were walking in a cathedral. He took in as much as he could, but it was very overwhelming.

Tacky, but overwhelming.

He looked away from the glamour, reminding himself to get this over with as quickly as possible.

They walked slowly to the back patio that overlooked her estate, where Ella had a small table for two prepared. It was elegant and beautiful. Albert hadn't even been to restaurants as nice as this. Large heat lamps warmed the outside patio, allowing them to enjoy a comfortable evening under the stars.

"You can have a seat right there, Albey. You can take your hat off if you'd like." She sat down across from him. He tried to look settled, but he knew he wasn't hiding his discomfort very well.

He took off his hat and admired the view Ella woke up to every day. He couldn't help but think how breathtaking it was. Pristinely kept hills toppled over one another for what seemed like miles. Each heap was greener than the last and more manicured than the most prestigious golf course he'd ever seen. Orange and yellow trees dotted her backyard. He could hear the ducks in the background, from the farm. Her house was like a photograph.

This can't be real.

For years he'd driven past these houses as an onlooker, never knowing what was hidden behind the fences. He imagined what it might look like, but his imagination didn't compare to reality. Everything a person could wish for—she had it all.

Ella leaned in. "You like the view, Albey? We can take a walk around if you like."

He didn't answer. It was hard for him to fathom the teenage girl he used to be in love with lived this way. When he knew her back then, her family was very wealthy, but it was nothing like this. She lived in a way they'd once longed for. He'd promised her a life like this once. But she didn't need him for that after all.

"Or, better yet, I have some golf carts. Walter could drive us around."

He didn't budge. He just stared out into the sky.

"Okay, we'll eat and then go for a ride later maybe?"

Albert turned to his plate slowly, not looking at Ella.

"Are you okay, Albey?"

"It's very nice, Ella," he said, barely lifting his head up.

"All right, words! We have words, ladies and gentlemen," she joked.

He said nothing.

A young man approached with two glasses of wine. Albert sipped it slowly, raising his eyebrows at the delicate taste. He loved wine, and Ella had chosen one of the best. She peered over the tip of her glass, watching him.

The young man who brought the wine returned with shrimp cocktail. He handed Albert a chilled glass of five large shrimp hanging over the edges, and gave one to Ella.

"I remembered how you loved shrimp, Albey. I had the chef from Tio Pepe make his shrimp cocktail here earlier."

He nodded, robotically placing the shrimp in his mouth one by one. Ella waited, but she seemed irritated.

Finally she hit her limit.

She slammed her fork down on the table, crashing it hard against the fine China. She stood up and threw down her silk napkin, speckled with spots of blood. Albert saw this, but didn't have much time to consider it.

"That's it!" she snapped. "If you don't want to be here, go the hell home, Albey! I'm too old to put up someone being so damned rude!" She turned her back to him with her arms crossed, walked to the edge of the patio, and rested her arms on the brass railing above the steps.

Albert nearly choked on his shrimp, and quickly wiped his mouth.

"I'm sorry, I'm sorry, Ella."

She shrugged, staring off into the distance.

"Everything is nice, very nice. Please sit back down," he said, hoping Walter hadn't overheard.

She smiled wanly and turned back. "Good. Now we've gotten that out of the way. So, where shall we begin?"

He feared she wanted him to explain why he'd left. "Begin?"

"Albey, we haven't seen each other in so many years, we have so much to catch up on."

"Yes, it's been a while."

She raised her glass in a toast as she sat back down. "Think of tonight as a new start, or the *restart* of our lives together."

Albert raised his glass. They touched glasses, and took a sip. Both poked at their salads, waiting for the other to speak. He sensed she was watching him and waiting for him to begin. He took a deep breath, trying to think of something to say.

"Madilyn seems very nice."

"Thank you. I'm very proud of her," Ella said, beaming. "She's quite the looker ain't she, Albey?"

"Yes, she is. You're very lucky."

"Maddy is very special, you know. She takes good care of me. I need that. Although I wish sometimes she would focus on helping herself more than me."

"Why's that?"

"You know kids these days. Their minds. Their priorities. I want her to be happy. She seems so, so . . . *alone*. I hope Maddy can find someone soon. She seems troubled or something. Distant at times."

"She seems fine to me."

"Oh, she's fine, yes, but her and that asshole of an ex—it's just a disaster. I want her to find someone who will treat her the way she deserves to be treated."

"I know what you mean."

"Really?" Ella tilted her head to the side. "Geoffrey, right?"

Albert wobbled his head back and forth, catching himself before answering.

They exchanged a knowing glance, and despite all of Albert's efforts to keep her at arm's length, it was obvious they'd found common ground.

***

The waiter brought another dish, even more dazzling than the last, but Albert could tell Ella couldn't concentrate on eating. She had more questions about Geoffrey.

"It must have been fun having two young boys around to play ball with, Albey. Bet you could have shown them a thing or two."

Albert rolled his eyes. "Geoffrey was never one for sports. He had the build but didn't get into it. David, on the other hand, now he had a good arm. Played second base in college too. I used to go watch him play whenever I could."

"I remember watching you play ball in school. I thought you would have turned pro one day."

He sighed. "I didn't stand a chance with those guys. I played minor league ball for a year after the military, but it wasn't the way to make a living at the time. I had to move on."

"Well, I think they should have bumped you up, Albey." Ella winked.

He shrugged at the thought, and continued to eat his meal.

"You know, my husband, Norman, was an athlete too. Soccer, or futball as they called it in Ireland. He played in college, and taught the girls. He even started a league for the employees to play on."

Albert glanced up from his plate. "He sounds like a very nice man, Ella. And it's amazing he was able to give you all this." With his fork still in his hand, he gestured to the landscape and then returned to his dish.

She chuckled. "Oh, Albey, all of this was a joint effort. In fact, I was talking to Geoffrey the other day about this same thing. Did you ever take me for a woman who would sit back and never do her own thing?"

"What do you mean?" For the first time he was genuinely interested.

"Albey, you know my father's work?"

Albert nodded.

"I could have gone to his company and found a comfy corner office, or joined Norman's family business and done the same, but I wanted more out life. Something to show my kids their momma was a self-made woman. Perlmans is just a name. The creation is all yours truly." She spread her arms wide.

"You did all of this?"

"*Ta-da!*"

"I didn't know."

"Had you reached out to me earlier, you could have known. And I would have loved for you to meet Norman as well. He reminded me a lot of you."

Albert wiped his mouth, and took another sip. "In what way?"

"Oh Albey, he was so adventurous and funny, like you! And just like we did as kids, we'd go on drives for hours. In fact, for our honeymoon, we took off work for two months and went around the world."

"That doesn't sound like me, Ella."

"Okay, well not like that, but we used to talk about traveling all the time, back in the day. Do you remember those talks?"

Albert nodded again slowly.

"I miss those talks, Albey. But now look at us! Two old friends. We'll have plenty of time to talk about the old times and what's happened since. I mean, it's been so long! So much has happened." She coughed into her napkin again, and waved Albert off before he could ask about it.

He tried to keep up as she talked about her trips with Norman, and her family, but she spoke too rapidly as she tried to fill him in on everything he'd missed—which was a lot.

"Albey, here I am blabbing away. It's your turn now."

"I'm sorry, Ella, my life is not nearly as exciting as yours."

"Granted, yes. But it's been so long. What have you been doing all these years? Work, family, *life*?"

He took another sip of wine, and leaned back into his chair. "Okay. Well, after the military—"

"Which branch, Albey?"

"The Navy."

"You always loved the water. We used to spend so much time together on the water."

"Yes, well, it wasn't quite that interesting. I spent more time cleaning boats and taking orders. After I left the Navy, I took some odd jobs while I worked on getting my degree in architecture."

"An architect! Albey, that's amazing. You were always so good with math and had an eye for design."

"I wasn't exactly doing homes like this, Ella. It was basic commercial structures."

"I'd love to see what you built though. We can have Walter drive us around one day, and you can show me. Can we do that?"

"Um. . ."

Ella leaned closer. "Sophie is a lucky woman, Albey."

Albert's body language shifted and his back straightened. "I'm the lucky one."

"I would love to meet her one day."

"Ella, I don't think that's possible."

"I'm sorry if I overstepped. Please don't be upset."

He paused before changing the subject. "My son Clark played soccer too. Like your Norman."

"A son, Albey?"

"Clark. . . he's passed but you would have liked him."

Ella reached forward and put her hand on his. "Oh my Lord, Albey." Her eyes watered. "Can you tell me what he was like?"

Talking about him was always hard, and speaking to Ella only made it worse. He took a deep breath.

"Clark was handsome, strong, brilliant, everything a father could want. Some drunk asshole took it all away."

"Oh." Ella was overtaken with emotion. She covered her mouth with her napkin.

"There are some things in life that don't make sense, and losing a child is at the top of that list, I believe." He was staring down at his plate, slowly pushing a piece of lettuce around his plate with his fork.

"Albey, I hope I didn't ruin the night by asking about your family." Her bottom lip quivered as she spoke, her eyes moist with tears.

"You didn't. It's fine."

She cleared her throat. "Do you remember my cousin Chase?"

"Of course. He introduced us." Albert was relieved she'd decided to change the subject.

"Do you remember the homecoming dance when he borrowed my uncle's car?"

He rolled his eyes. "Borrowed? No, Ella, he stole it."

"So you do remember."

"You kidding me?" He managed a weak smile.

"He still says it was your fault." Ella let out a peal of laughter, fighting off the sadness of the last topic of conversation.

"My fault?" Albert burst out laughing. "I told him that road was too muddy but he ignored me."

"I still don't know how we got out of that ditch."

"Because I pushed with my bare hands while he shot mud in my face, spinning the tires like a maniac!"

Ella began to cry from giggling.

"You and your girlfriend, Samantha, sat in the car laughing your heads off as I dug my shoulder into that bumper and got a face full of sludge. That was the only suit I had. In fact, it wasn't even mine, it was Matthew's that I borrowed! I can't believe they let us in the dance after that."

She held her stomach from the pain of laughing so hard. "Two hours late as well. . . Albey, I swore, I never laughed so hard in my life!"

"You all heard me shouting, I know. Man, Chase was a riot."

Ella dotted her eyes dry. "Well, he's still around. I can invite him over one day."

"Gosh! Chase MacArthur." Albert's eyes widened. "I'd love to see him again."

She raised her glass. "To old times, Albey."

"To old times."

***

My God, I missed him.

Despite his initial reluctance, they had gone from being strangers to talking about their family, and even connecting on the past. Ella was able to make Albert warm up, and she didn't want the feeling to go away. She cared so much for him that she couldn't help but feel as if she was a part of his family. She wanted to be there for him. And most of all, she wanted to make sure he never left her again.

Waiters came in and out with hand signals from Ella as if she were conducting an orchestra, offering them refills on their drinks or more food. She had more wine, and he settled for a soda. She excused herself throughout the meal to dab her eyes, and paused between stories as her throat grew dry and she had to cough into her napkin. When she calmed down, she pretended it never happened, hoping Albert didn't notice.

The young man cleared the table of all the dishes, leaving their glasses behind.

Ella sat back and tapped her nails on her wine glass.

"Albey, you have to admit you are having a good time."

He grinned out the side of his mouth.

"Go on, admit it."

"Yes, Ella, this is a nice change of pace for me."

She turned and admired the dark magenta of the sky. The evening was coming to an end quicker than she'd planned.

"Albey, can I ask you something?"

"Sure."

"Why did you leave me?"

"Ella, please."

"I need to know."

"It's been so long. Why does it matter? We were kids . . ."

"It matters to me."

"I don't want to hurt you."

"You won't. I swear it. Anything you tell me is fine. Please tell me."

"I can't."

Ella's patience waned thin. Beneath her calm exterior, she had years of boardroom debates and negotiation skills she could turn on if she needed to. If she has to bully him, so be it.

"Albey, I've waited more than sixty years to see you again and I have you here now. You ran off in the middle of the night! You didn't call. You didn't write. I asked your friends, your family, and no one responded. For all I knew, you were dead. *Dead!* And now you're here, I need this. We aren't young kids anymore. I'm a grown woman who has handled more bad news and hard times than any ten men behind me, and don't think for a damn second I can't take what you have to say."

Ella looked away to cough into her handkerchief, then took a deep drink of wine before continuing. "I won't be mad. I'm done being mad. I spent the majority of my late teens and early twenties being mad. Now, I just have to hear it from you." She leaned in closer, and touched his hand. "Who knows what will happen tomorrow. I may never see you again after tonight. I can't die not knowing the truth."

"It's not that simple." He slid his hand from under hers.

"Was is it something I did?"

"Oh no, not at all."

"Something I *didn't* do?"

"No."

"Then what the God damn was it!" Ella snapped, throwing her hands up, then crossing them over her chest.

He pushed back his chair and took a few steps to the edge of the stone patio. He bent his head back and looked up at the stars.

Ella, don't lose him again!

She went to meet him, and slowly reached for his hand. He pulled it away, and Ella settled for placing her arm around his.

"Okay, okay. This is fine, Albey. I'm sorry I raised my voice again."

He looked forward, avoiding eye contact.

"Tell me, please tell me," she whispered.

"Does it really matter after all these years?"

"I know it may sound silly, but to me it does."

"Ella, look at what you have." He spread his arms. "And think about your kids and grandkids. You would have had none of this with me in your life."

"But *you* were my life."

She dropped her arms to her sides. For a moment she saw him as the teenage boy she fell in love with, standing in front of her asking if he could kiss her for the first time. As she watched him squirm, his body stiffening with anxiety, she knew he wasn't the same. The Albert she saw now was someone else—as was she. His

120

body had changed, but so had her own. She wanted to find him, and she wanted to find her old self as well. She needed him to do that. She begged him in her mind to hold her hand again, or for him to need her the way she needed him.

"Ella, I had fun tonight."

"Really?" It wasn't what she wanted to hear, but it was something.

"I knew I was going to, and I did. I'm sorry I was rude before."

"It's fine."

"I may need some time."

"Oh, gosh, Albey, I don't want to rush anything, I just want to see you again! When will I see you again?"

"Maybe we can get coffee some time."

"Tomorrow?"

He rolled his eyes.

"I was just kidding." Ella grinned sheepishly at her own eagerness. "That is, unless you want to? Albey, you're saying you want to see me again, and I look forward to that. How can a girl say no?"

"I do have a small confession."

"Oh my, what?" She held her handkerchief to her mouth.

"I've seen you over the years."

"What? You saw me . . . You should have come over and said something!"

Albert wrung his hands nervously. "Only once in person, Ella. But I saw your picture in the papers."

"Oh, Albey. How long ago?" she asked, saddened their paths were so close but never crossed.

"Three years ago at Miss Shirley's Cafe."

"The one in Roland Park, on Cold Spring Lane?"

Albert nodded. "Geoffrey and I go there at least twice a month."

"Oh, I love it there too! In fact, I know the owners very well, the Dopkin family. I can make a call right now if you like and we can have a table all to ourselves tomorrow morning."

He seemed to ignore her comment. "On warm days, we sit outside at one of the tables along the sidewalk. The day I saw you, it was brunch time on a weekend in May. A car pulled up right by the entrance, only a few feet from where we were sitting. When people got out of the car, I happened to look up from my plate. I don't know why, really. People come in and out all the time, and I never notice. But *something* told me to look. I didn't know it was you. Then I heard your voice, when the hostess said your name." Albert managed a smile amidst his guilt. "You had passed by before I could see your face for me to make sure, but I knew it was you."

"Only a few feet away? And you didn't say anything . . ."

"I'm sorry about that."

Ella paused before responding, partly because she was out of breath from coughing, and because she didn't want to yell at him for having not stopped by. "Well, you've hid long enough. Now I've found you."

"I guess you did, Ella. But I think I should go now. It's getting late."

She nodded. It was getting late. They walked back through the house. Walter was waiting for them. He opened the car door for Albert, placing a hand on the small of his back for support.

"Wait! I almost forgot." Ella hurried back into the house. She returned moments later, carrying a tiny purple box wrapped in a gold ribbon. "I promised Layla I'd get her a charm just like mine, and I would never want to disappoint her."

"You don't have to do this, Ella."

"I know, but I want to. I had it inscribed as well to make it even more special."

He took the box and placed it on his lap. He rolled down the window, placing his hand on the edge.

"Ella, thank you for inviting me over."

She reached for his hand but he moved it away. "Oh that's right, we don't do the hand touching thing," she said, realizing there were some things she'd just have to get used to. Not holding his hand was one of them.

"Can I see you tomorrow, Albey?"

"I don't know."

"Good, so tomorrow it is."

"What? I said—"

"I got you now, turkey," she said, leaning in close. "I'll have Walter pick you up at three."

"No. I am not free then." Albert's brow furrowed. "I go . . . I go to see . . . I have to be at Cedarmere at that time."

"Oh, dear, I'm so sorry. I understand, Albey. I'm so sorry, that's fine. Forgive me."

"No, I mean, if you want, I can see you afterward. I mean, I owe you for buying this for Layla."

"You don't owe me a thing. It was my pleasure. When should I schedule Walter to pick you up?"

"I'm usually free, except for my time at Cedarmere. I'll have to check with Geoffrey."

Ella couldn't believe Albert had willingly agreed to see her, despite using Layla as an excuse.

"That would be fantastic. I have a great idea too!" She held her hands out and spun around like a child dancing in the rain. "Albey, you are going to *love* what I have planned!"

"Ella, please don't go out of your way or anything. I'd like to stay in, like we did tonight. This is fine."

"Then maybe the day after. You know what? Give me a day then. I will make it even better! Either way, don't worry, I hear ya. Keep it small, nothing too big, *blah, blah, blah.* Ain't you caught on yet?" She pointed over to Walter and blew Albert a kiss goodbye through the window. "Walter, you make sure he gets home safe and sound. I'll see you soon, Albey."

***

As the car drove away and he left her behind, he thought about the truth behind his leaving, and how badly Ella wanted to know. He knew it would hit her harder than

123

she could imagine, and he couldn't bear to deal with that now or ever. When he left so many decades ago, he told himself he would bury the past, and he'd kept that promise.

Even if I did tell her, where would I begin?

During the ride home, Albert clutched the box for Layla in his lap. He didn't know what Ella wrote as an inscription, and the temptation to find out pulled at him. But this was a gift for his great-granddaughter, and she should be the first to open it.

He looked down at his watch and thought about the inscription on the bottom of it: *Today I married my best friend.*

He couldn't help but feel guilty making plans with Ella, and again the thought of telling her the truth gnawed at his insides. There he was dining on more expensive food than he'd ever eaten before, served to him by a private waiter on the patio deck of a mansion on a lavish estate, with a woman he'd once planned to marry. All the while, Sophie was in a hospital bed clinging to life.

What am I doing?

The guilt settled like an anchor. He rested his head against the cool window and allowed the car's vibration to ease his mind as he closed his eyes.

***

Geoffrey watched for Albert after he put Layla to bed in the guestroom. He sat for an hour, fingers pressed down on the blinds, eyeing the driveway like an overprotective parent waiting for their teenager to come home from a first date.

Finally the lights of Walter's car flooded the front of the house and Geoffrey quickly sat back, reaching for the nearest magazine. He could hear Walter wish him a good night, and something about returning in a day to pick him up again.

Again? He's going to see her again? Geoffrey fought back his smile and tried to look as nonchalant as possible.

When Albert entered, he hung his jacket on the coat rack by the door, and placed a pretty box on the coffee table. Geoffrey assumed it was Ella's gift for

Layla. Without saying a word, Albert headed through the living room toward his bedroom.

"Gramps?" Geoffrey peeked over the magazine.

"Sorry, son, I didn't see you there."

"So?"

"So, what?"

"Gramps, come on, how was your night?"

"How's Sophie?"

"She's fine. How was your night?"

"That's good. I want to go see her tomorrow . . . early."

"Not a problem. How was your night?"

Albert glanced at the magazine, then back at Geoffrey. "You weren't waiting for me all night, were you?"

"Please, Gramps, don't be silly."

"Been reading the whole night?"

"Yup, the whole night." He tipped the magazine toward Albert.

"Really? I find it hard to believe you like reading the AARP Magazine . . . let alone *upside down*." He shook his head and walked off.

"What? Damn it!"

"Good night, son," Albert said before shutting his bedroom door.

13

The Day It All Changed

Albert's hands were sweating and his breathing skipped with a mixture of excitement and nervousness. He flexed his hands to keep the blood flowing through his body before he knocked on Ella's door. He knew she'd be gone for a while with her mother, shopping in town, and her father would be home alone.

As he waited for the housekeeper to answer, he rehearsed his lines. He practiced controlling his excitement to appear calm and collected. When she came to the door, he asked for Mr. MacArthur. He always called him Mr. MacArthur and never by his first name, Collin. Everyone in town knew about Ella's father.

The housekeeper nodded and went to get him from the study. Albert took a seat on the large front porch looking out at the sprawling estate, picturing the ceremony and reception he and Ella talked about every day. If the weather was nice, they'd hold it outside. If not, they'd use a large tent her family often prepared for early spring functions. Everyone would laugh and dance until they collapsed from pure exhaustion, just as he and Ella had imagined.

Albert and his brother Matthew had built a traditional Jewish *chuppah* for the wedding ceremony out of pine and oak earlier that month. When Albert told his father his plans, he gave Albert his *tallis* brought over from Russia at the turn of the century, which Albert's father wore at his own wedding. Everything was coming together.

Albert had met Ella's father many times, but he was a stern man who spoke short and firm. He had little time or desire to associate with anyone outside from his inner circle of business associates and immediate family. For nearly three decades, he'd ruled the Mid-Atlantic as the leading legal figure for politicians and wealthy European investors that wanted to business in the States. Being from England, but having lived his adult life in Maryland, he had every connection from England and used it to make deals throughout the country. Yet his accent was barely discernable. When Collin spoke, he was a southerner. Along with being highly connected in various business circles, he was part owner of the largest bank in Maryland, and one of the largest landowners in the state.

Collin had intimidated Albert ever since the first day he'd arrived at Ella's door, which made him cower in his presence and avoid him at all costs. However, Collin always quietly welcomed Albert and Ella's friends to the house. But as a boy in front of his girlfriend's father, he couldn't help but be nervous.

The door swung open and Collin MacArthur stood in the doorway.

"Albert?" His deep southern voice was scratchy from years of smoke and booze. "Ella's not home now."

Albert jumped to his feet and fumbled to remove his hat. "Mr. MacArthur, h-h-how are you today?"

"I'm fine, Albert, and you?"

"Oh, I'm great sir, I'm doing fine, thank you." Albert heard the uncertainty in his words, inducing more sweat. "Did you hear about the game last week, Mr. MacArthur? I had two homeruns, and a triple."

"Albert, what do you need? I have about another hundred pages of contracts to read before dinner."

"Okay, sir, I don't want to hold you up," Albert said apologetically.

"Then don't."

"Um, let me get right to it, then." Albert stepped closer, clutching his hat. "Well, sir, I'm here to ask—" He took a deep breath, his heart pounding. "Sorry sir, I'm a little nervous. I'm here to ask you if, well, if I can—"

"Albert let's walk, shall we?" Collin said, stepping past Albert and out to the front lawn.

***

Again, Albert didn't sleep well. This time, his bladder and dreams weren't the issue. His heart felt heavy. Guilt ran through his body like a virus, painfully pulling at his insides. He had to see Sophie.

When he walked out of his room, Geoffrey and Layla were sitting at the table, reading through the papers and eating breakfast. Layla had a mouthful of cereal, and Geoffrey was sipping a large cup of coffee.

"There's my man!" Geoffrey said, winking.

"Zaide! Can I open my present?"

"Layla, I said to wait for Zaide to sit down, please."

"It's okay." He slumped into his chair and looked for the Sports section. "Sure, Layla, go ahead."

Geoffrey handed Albert the paper and watched him, as if waiting for him to say something. Layla leapt out of her chair and ran to the coffee table, then ripped the ribbon off her gift and tore into the box.

"Careful," Geoffrey warned.

Her face glowed as she pulled out the small violet box that filled her tiny hand. She opened it as Geoffrey and Albert looked on.

"*Wowwwww!* Look, Daddy, look!"

Albert lifted his chin from the paper, craning his neck.

Geoffrey opened the box and jumped to his feet.

"Oh my God! Gramps, did you know what Ella got her?"

"No, I didn't ask. Why?"

"Layla, listen, this . . . this is a special occasion necklace, honey." Geoffrey handed the box to Albert.

"What's wrong, Daddy? I want to wear it. It's mine." She tugged on her father's shirttail.

Geoffrey knelt down. He looked up at Albert, who shrugged his shoulders.

"Layla, this is a very, very nice necklace." He held her hand, locking his gaze with hers. "How about we call Ella and thank her first. Okay?"

"All right." She lowered her head, frowning. "But why can't I wear it now?"

Neither of them knew how to explain to a six-year-old that other kids her age didn't wear the equivalent of an entire year's private school tuition around their necks.

"How about I hold onto it, since you have to go riding soon, and then tonight we'll all go out for dinner somewhere nice and you can wear it then?"

Layla appeared thoughtful for a moment, then nodded.

"I can't tonight," Albert interrupted.

"Why?" Geoffrey asked.

"I have . . . plans."

"Really!" Geoffrey chuckled. "That's great, Gramps."

"But I can cancel—"

"The hell you will. You're going."

"Can I go call Ella now, Daddy?" She bounced up and down, too excited to stay still.

"Sure, sweetie. I'll dial for you."

Albert grabbed the necklace for a closer look, not sure why Geoffrey was making such a big deal out of it. He knew it would be gold, since Ella said she would get Layla the same one she'd worn, so he expected it to be pricier than Layla's normal jewelry. It was a little big for such a small girl, and heavier when he held it in his palm. He could hear Layla enthusiastically thanking Ella on the phone. Geoffrey stood over her and glanced back at Albert, grinning. Layla spoke fast as usual. Geoffrey and Albert both listened raptly.

129

"I can't wait to wear it! Well, tonight I will. I'm going riding soon and then Daddy is taking me somewhere really nice for dinner . . . I don't know where though. Hey, Ella, do you want to come to dinner with us tonight?"

Albert leaned over and reached for the phone as quickly as he could, stubbing his toe on the corner of the end table in the process. He winced in pain, grabbing his foot and biting his teeth down hard.

"Oh, okay, well maybe tomorrow? Really? You will, that's awesome! Okay . . . here's my daddy." She handed the phone to Geoffrey and wrapped her arms around Albert.

"Ella is getting us a limousine, Zaide. A real limousine!"

"Oh, God," Albert mumbled. He listened to Geoffrey thanking Ella over and over, and telling her the limo—like the necklace—wasn't necessary.

"I know, Ella . . . Yes, yes, she'll look beautiful in it . . . Um, no, sorry, my wife won't be able to make it. Oh for sure! Next time she will, of course."

Albert rolled his eyes, knowing that a *next time* with Rose meant *never*. Geoffrey hung up and scooped up Layla, swinging her from side to side.

"What? What was I supposed to say, Gramps?" He lowered her, who scampered into the living room. "She's very convincing."

Albert may have been warming up to Ella—mainly out of guilt—but they had a past, one he was not ready to bring to the forefront of his life. Albert was annoyed he hadn't put his foot down when it came to people making plans for him.

"You could have lied to her, son."

"Gramps, it's *one* day. Dad, you were seeing her again anyway. I thought you are okay with all of this now?"

He threw his hands up. "Who cares what I think anyway, right? It's just *my* life. It was supposed to be just one day yesterday and the day before, and now we're planning our lives around her."

"Settle down." Geoffrey put his finger over his mouth, then pointed in Layla's direction.

"This is for her, Geoffrey, not you."

"That's fine with me. I mean, look how happy she is."

"That big grin over some silly necklace." Albert shook his head, watching her dance about, her eyes bright and shining. "If I'd have known she'd get this way, I would have bought it myself."

"No you wouldn't have, Gramps," Geoffrey retorted with an expression of smug confidence.

"Why not?" He tilted his head back. "They sell stuff like that at every store on Reisterstown Road."

"Oh, no they don't."

"Sorry, I forgot. I know, I know, Ella Perlman bought it, so it must be nicer than anything anyone else could buy," he retorted, his voice laced with sarcasm.

Geoffrey leaned in and paused for a second, choosing his words carefully.

"That necklace cost *more than your car*, Gramps." He slapped Albert on the back, and sat down to read the paper. "I have to admit, the lady has style."

14

The Need To Be Closer

"Damn." Geoffrey searched through his duffel bag. "I could have sworn I brought it."

"Brought what?"

His body jolted, and then he relaxed just as fast, not wanting Albert to ask more questions. "My hair products, Gramps. If I wasn't such a calm guy, you could have given me a heart attack." He slammed his bag down after digging through and coming up with nothing.

Albert shrugged and made his way to the door.

"Where are you off to this early?" Geoffrey asked.

"To see Aunt Abigail and your parents." Albert fumbled with his cap, then placed it on his head.

Geoffrey walked over to him and placed his hand on his arm. "You want me to drive you?"

"No, Geoff, I've been doing this for a while now. But you should try to visit. How long has it been?"

Geoffrey smiled wanly, but ignored the topic. He didn't visit the cemetery very often, and he didn't like to talk about the death of his parents.

"Plus," Albert continued, "you need to go buy more hair products. I wouldn't want to inconvenience you with having to drive me around."

"Jealous much?"

"*Jealous?* You spend forty-five dollars on something that looks like *drywall*."

"Jealousy's not very becoming of you, Gramps."

Albert rolled his eyes and picked up the brown canvas bag he kept under the coat rack that held the cleaning supplies for the gravestones.

"I'll see you later, handsome." Albert stepped outside.

Geoffrey leaned out the door for one last joke in his favor. "Don't be mad because the last time you used hair products was at your bar mitzvah!"

Albert's shoulders rose and fell in tiny beats of laughter.

When he drove off, Geoffrey looked in the large wall mirror next to the door. He patted his short hair in place, trying to make the best of it, and quickly gave up.

"Oh well, I needed to go to the store anyway."

***

"I'll be there soon, sweethearts." Albert patted the outside of the bag tenderly. The contents were more than just tools, they were a connection to his children.

The bottle of cleaner shined their tombstones, and soft towels wiped away the debris and dirt. Albert thanked the objects every time. When he was done cleaning, he always felt better. He never had a chance to bathe Abigail as a child, and keeping her gravestone clean and polished after all those years helped him keep his promise to his daughter. Losing his son and daughter-in-law was one thing, but the life Abigail never had continued to rip him apart inside.

"I will never forget you, my loves. You will never be without your father."

Albert parked in his normal spot, closest to the grass. When he pulled in, his body went into an awkward mode that teetered between nervousness and rejoice. He turned off the engine and waited. The car settled down, and Albert watched as other mourners crouched over their loved ones' graves. He leaned against the window, the keys still in the ignition.

He waited.

When he was ready, Albert took his bag and followed the path to the gravestones, which he knew so well he could walk it blind. He knew where the stone walkway sloped twenty yards into the cemetery, and he'd memorized the crack they had yet to fix which so many people tripped over. He knew where the flowers bloomed the brightest, alongside the old oaks in the left corner on hot days. He knew where the shade was heaviest, on the south perimeter. Over the years, this had become Albert's second home, and he could recite its patterns like his favorite song.

Albert looked down at the gravestones, all sitting in a row. "Good morning, my loves. It's a beautiful day, isn't it? I love this time of year. The trees look amazing. I spoke to the grounds keeper, and he's going to make sure there aren't too many leaves covering you. If he screws it up, I'll be sure to take care of it. Don't worry. Geoffrey said he'd hire a private landscaper to come by each week if they don't do what they promised, but I'm not sure it's allowed. He didn't care though. He said he'd make it happen. Gotta love him." Albert chuckled.

"All right, my loves, let's get you all cleaned up now, shall we?"

Albert took out a rag and cleaner, then began scrubbing the gravestones. From top to bottom and in between the engravings, Albert cleaned thoroughly and recited the Mourner's *Kaddish* in Hebrew.

Albert took out a large bristled brush to scrub the more difficult areas. He continued with the remaining lines of the prayer.

When he was finished, he sat with his legs crossed and rested the bag on his lap.

To his right, an elderly woman cried over her husband's grave. Behind him, two teenagers sobbed, comforted by their parents.

Albert had been to the cemetery so many times that seeing someone cry was commonplace. He felt badly, though—especially when it was someone he'd never seen before.

At one time, crying was all Albert could do. He'd arrive at Abigail's grave and cry endlessly for hours, never saying a word. When Clark was buried, the crying nearly destroyed him. But gradually he built up a tolerance, as all mourners do. Healing was not easy, but Albert trained himself over the years. The cemetery was a challenge, a fight he took on with great fortitude. Death had come too soon for his daughter, then his son, and it would catch up to him one day as well. But he wasn't ready yet.

Despite other mourners seeing the visit as a time of sadness, for Albert it was a time to remember joy. In Abigail, he saw a child who never had a chance to live in the world. In his son, he saw the pride he had from watching him grow up, and the promise he made to take care of Geoffrey and David.

Albert always spoke to Abigail as if she were a full grown adult. Over the years, Abigail was always there for him. Talking to her came naturally, but changed over the years without Sophie around.

"Mom's doing well. I know you probably know that, and thank you so much, sweethearts, for watching her." He smiled slightly, proud of his children for being her guardians.

"The days when I'm not there, it's always good to know you are there with her too. I will visit her soon with Geoffrey. David already visited."

The wind picked up and small, fallen leaves brushed over Abigail's stone. Albert was quick to remove them.

"I wanted to talk to you about Geoffrey. I'm worried about him." He paused for a moment. "He . . . he just seems *bothered* or burdened. And not by me! I swear. I promised I wouldn't do that to him. I don't think I have. But for the life of me I don't know how a young, rich man like him can be worried about *anything* at all. Something just doesn't seem right. He's staying with me now too. I told you that last week, but I didn't think he was going to be there as long as he has. Odd, right? Yeah, I think so too, sweethearts." He rubbed the grass between Abigail and Clark's stones with his hands.

"I think it's his marriage. It has to be. It's Rose. I know it's not nice to speak badly about her, but she's not right for him, kids. I told you that when they got married, and how many times have I repeated it since? A million, right? I can't put it any nicer."

He placed his left hand on Abigail's side and right hand on Clark's. He leaned his weight onto his arms, forcing his body farther into the ground.

He needed to be closer.

He needed to feel the ground as if it were them, to hold them again.

"I don't want this to affect Layla. God help me if Rose takes her away from us! I couldn't stand to see anything bad happen to Layla."

Albert stopped to wipe his tears away. "I know, I know, kids. I shouldn't be crying. I know I promised you I wouldn't." He pulled his sleeve across his face. "I know you don't mind, and thank you, but I don't like you to see me like this. I'm just so worried for him. What should I do?"

He gripped the grass in his fists tighter than before, with as much strength as he could manage. "What should I do? Please help me. I wish you were here to help me."

He squeezed the clumps of grass between his fingers.

"I wish you were here . . ."

He calmed himself with some of his breathing exercises.

"Your birthday is coming up soon, sweetheart," he said to Abigail. "I'll bring you a nice batch of roses. I know, yellows and oranges. *Seasonal*. This is my favorite season, too. You're just like your daddy." Albert waved his hands at her headstone. "No, no, you stop, I'm your dad and you're my daughter. It's what dads do."

He smiled back at her, then leaned back on his hands and watched the stone staring back at him. "I should be going now, my loves, but I'll be back soon, I promise. Before your birthday too, Abigail."

He kissed the top of Abigail's headstone after he stood. He traced his fingers in the engravings of her name, then leaned over to Clark and Valerie's stones and did the same.

One last time, he recited a verse from the *Kaddish*, lowering his head in prayer.

As always, after he said the *Kaddish* in Hebrew, he repeated it in English. "During your lifetime and during your days and during the lifetimes of all the House of Israel, speedily and very soon. And say, Amen."

Albert reached into his pocket and pulled out a few tiny stones. In honor of the Jewish tradition, he placed one each on the top of their stones, right where he'd kissed.

"I'll be back soon. Please watch over your mother for me. I love you all, always and forever."

He blew them a kiss before leaving, and walked slowly back to his car.

***

As Albert's car pulled away, a black Escalade parked by the entrance and the back window rolled up.

"Are you ready, Mrs. Perlman?" Walter asked, after Albert's car was clearly out of view.

"Yes, Walter. We can go now." Guilt rose in her chest. She'd been spying on Albert all afternoon, trailing him from his house, to the gas station, and finally to the cemetery.

"Would you like me to continue to following Mr. Abraham, Mrs. Perlman?"

"No, Walter, that's enough for today."

Walter began to back the car up, and Ella suddenly raised a delicate hand.

"Wait, Walter. Pull over to that gentleman with the rake."

"Yes, Mrs. Perlman."

Walter lowered Ella's window for her.

"Excuse me, sir, I was just wondering who runs this cemetery," Ella called out.

The maintenance worker looked up from his task. "EWA Incorporated, Ma'am."

"Thank you, young man." She closed the window. "Now, Walter."

As they drove, Ella reached for her cell phone and called her assistant.

"JoAnn, look up a company called EWA Incorporated and get someone on the phone as soon as possible. I'd like every Abraham family member's lot to be manicured to perfection, every single week. Also, call Betty at the flower shop. I want three dozen roses, delivered immediately."

15

A Chance Encounter

Geoffrey ordered a latte and scone from the coffee shop at Perlmans before starting down the aisles to find his hair gel and other items he may need for his time at Albert's house. He casually strolled down the organics aisle again, taking his time to see if anything new had come in. He turned the corner into the specialty breads section, then stopped abruptly. In front of him was a young woman, possibly in her late twenties. She was holding a loaf of bread in one hand, her cell phone in the other.

Geoffrey couldn't help but notice that his feet seemed to be stuck to the floor.

The young woman smiled curiously. "Hi there, mind if I just move around you?"

His eyes widened, but Geoffrey didn't answer. He wasn't easily stunned by a gorgeous woman. After all, Rose was about as pretty as they came. But there was something about *this* stranger that had him transfixed.

"Listen, how about I just scoot on over here," she said uncomfortably, inching around his crooked cart, which blocked the aisle. "And um, you have a nice day now," she added, tapping the side of his arm as she walked by.

Geoffrey, what're you staring at, you fool? Get it together!

"Madilyn, how are you?" A voice called out to the woman.

138

Geoffrey turned and saw her hugging an older woman who wore a Perlmans Grocery shirt.

"I just saw your grandma in here this morning," the older woman said. "I just love when she comes into the store."

"You know her, she's always running around here." Madilyn laughed.

Geoffrey faced the rack of food, trying not to be noticed as he listened intently.

I can't take my eyes off her. He took two small steps sideways in her direction.

"It is so great to see you. Please tell Ella it's always better when she comes around."

"She will love to hear that. I'll make sure to pass it along," Madilyn said, thanking her.

"*Ella? Madilyn?*" Geoffrey gasped, suddenly realizing who she was.

Madilyn and the store clerk parted, and a moment later she was out of sight.

Where'd she go?

The shopping cart wheels screeched off balance as Geoffrey raced around the aisle to find her. His shoulder bumped the rack of potato chips, causing a few bags to fall as he made the sharp turn. When he straightened out, Madilyn was standing in front of him.

"Okay," she began guardedly, "I don't know *who* you are but I don't like you following me." She leaned on her back foot, starting to walk away.

Geoffrey stammered for an explanation. "No, no, please I . . . I know you."

Madilyn looked puzzled and stepped back faster.

Geoffrey reached out his hand to stop her. "I know your grandmother!"

"A lot of people know her, but that doesn't explain why are you following me."

"I'm, uh—"

"Look, if you're some food company rep, you'll have to talk the sales manager about placing your product in here. I don't deal with that, so talking to me won't get you anywhere. Excuse me, please."

"No wait, I'm Albert Abraham's son," Geoffrey blurted out.

Madilyn's mouth opened in shock and then she smiled.

Those eyes!

"You're Albert's son Geoffrey? Oh, I didn't know. I'm sorry about before. I know that may have seemed awkward, but people will do the wackiest things to get a meeting with my grandmother."

"It's fine."

"I've heard a lot about you," she said, stepping closer.

"And *you're* the wonderful Madilyn I hear so much about."

"I don't even want to know what my grandmother told you about me."

"Not enough. Sorry if I scared you."

"No, please. I was just caught a little off guard."

"I'm sure you have freaky guys staring at you all the time," he said, hoping to make her laugh.

It didn't work.

"So, you're saying only freaky-looking guys would stare at me?" she asked, raising an eyebrow.

"Oh no, not at all. What I meant is that—"

"I'm kidding, Geoffrey."

That laugh! That smile. Part of him worried she might hear his thoughts, and he found it difficult to talk.

Madilyn seemed to be waiting for him to say something, and when he didn't, she said, "Well, it's nice to meet you, Geoffrey. I hope to see you again."

He could only offer an awkward smile. *Snap out of it, you asshole! Man up!*

"Okay then, I'll tell Ella you said hello." Madilyn turned her cart and began to walk away.

Geoffrey realized he was losing her, and for some reason, he knew he couldn't let her go. Hurriedly, he spat out the first words that came to mind.

"Madilyn, do you like Mediterranean food?"

***

Geoffrey gave her directions to one of his favorite Mediterranean restaurants, The Wild Pea, which sat in the heart of Mt. Washington Square just inside the city lines of Baltimore. It offered the hip atmosphere of a city but the coziness of a small town hideaway. After they left the store together, Geoffrey raced south down route 83 to make sure he arrived before Madilyn. He didn't want her to have to wait for him. He spent ten minutes on the phone chatting up the owner, Blake, to make sure a table would be ready for him, since he had an "important guest" meeting him there.

Geoffrey sped into an open spot, ignoring the meter, and ran two blocks to the restaurant. He found a chair outside, sat down, and fanned his shirt from under his jacket, trying to catch his breath and act casual. He couldn't stop his right knee from bobbing.

Settle, Geoff . . . settle.

He reached into his jacket pocket, pulled out his pillbox, and emptied two tablets into his mouth. Shutting his eyes, he tilted his head back as the gentle ease of overmedication rushed through his body.

A musical voice sounded out, with a teasing lilt to it. "Is it okay if I wake you?"

He opened his eyes and saw Madilyn standing next to him.

"I was just fixing my contacts," he mumbled.

Her light brown hair was pulled back, a few loose strands of hair hanging over the left side of her face, gently covering one of her angelic emerald eyes.

She took off a pair of tortoise reading glasses, and placed them in her jacket pocket. Her crimson red lips stretched wide across her face as she spoke. He had never seen a smile so wide and welcoming.

When she brushed a thread of hair behind her ear, she revealed a small mole on her jaw line that Geoffrey couldn't help but find incredibly sexy. He couldn't take his eyes off her. He tried to play off his nervousness, but he knew she could see right through him.

He quickly stood and offered her his arm. "Shall we?"

She looked away and blushed as she laced her arm around his. They sat down at a small table by the window, Geoffrey's favorite spot. The waitress came over with his usual appetizer of fresh hummus and warm pita bread.

"You come here often?" Madilyn asked, referring to the quick service.

"Is that a pick up line?" He offered her the plate of pita slices.

"Good one, Geoffrey. I walked into that, didn't I?"

"But to answer your question, yes I do. I actually sold the owner this property. And these tables, I even helped build with a friend of mine in his wood shop. We used restored wood from an old barn out in Carroll County." He knocked against the table with his knuckles.

She placed her elbows on the surface and leaned in. "Very impressive. Do you always take *random* girls to your favorite restaurant?"

"I'd hardly call you random."

"Meaning?"

Geoffrey relaxed his shoulders, enjoying their friendly banter. "From what Ella has told me, I feel like I already know you."

She leaned back against her chair. "I don't know if I want to hear what she told you. She'll talk about me to anyone. It can be a little embarrassing sometimes."

She pulled out her hair clip as if she were undoing a soft ribbon tied around a present, and her hair fell against her back.

Geoffrey's feet fumbled over one another under the table as he tried to control himself. *I said, settle Geoffrey . . . Settle!*

"She told me you're her favorite grandchild, and that if I ever met you, I should treat you to dinner. I hope this is okay?"

"Oddly, even though I know you're kidding, that *is* something she would say."

Geoffrey took a sip of water and drummed his fingers against the glass after setting it down. "Actually, it is something like that. She told me you live in Baltimore, while everyone else in your family seemed to leave town."

"She's right. I never really think about it that way since the family is always in and out of town visiting. Especially as of late."

"As of late?"

"It's nothing. I shouldn't have said anything. Just . . . *nothing.*"

"Is everything okay?" he asked, coming in closer.

"It's Ella." Her eyes began to water.

"Is there something wrong with her?"

"Geoffrey, I hope I don't ruin the meal by crying."

"No way! You kidding me? It's totally fine. Not ruined at all. You leave *that* part up to me. I've been known to ruin many of meals in my day."

Madilyn chuckled but not enough to stop her tears. "God, this is so embarrassing!"

"Not at all, trust me."

"She's been sick for a long time, really since she was a child. I'm sure Albert would know. Over the years it got worse, but lately we think she's not telling us exactly what's going on. She moved back up here mainly for the care she needed, and to be by family. I don't know for sure how bad it is. She goes through handkerchiefs like candy, coughing into them with more and more pain."

Geoffrey figured as much, from when he'd seen Ella coughing into her napkin, only to come up with specks of blood. He didn't want to reveal this to Madilyn.

"Look, it's Ella! She's unstoppable. Anything wrong with her, I'm sure she can fix it."

"You're right. She'll be fine." Madilyn stared down at her glass.

"Are you okay? Do you want to leave? We can leave if you like? I'll understand."

"No, please no. I'm fine." She padded her eyes dry with a napkin. "Okay, now that I've ruined my makeup. So, you were saying you sold this place to the owner? But I thought Ella told me you own bakeries?"

He laughed, knowing how often he was asked about his odd choice of careers. When he first launched his bakeries, it was a big hit with the press. The media loved it: *Real Estate Mogul Cooks Up More Than Custom Homes.* The public ate it up faster than they could his cakes.

"What, real estate and cupcakes don't mix?" Geoffrey joked. "So, the summer of my sophomore year in college I decided I'd work like a madman to make enough money to buy my own car, a black Mustang convertible." He grinned as he pictured his dream car. "I got a job with a promotion company in D.C., doing some parties at clubs, events, big concerts, stuff like that, and it ended up doing very well. All cash under the table. It was a dream job."

"Trying to impress the ladies with some VIP passes to a bar crawl, I see?" Madilyn teased.

"I was nineteen. Of course I was!" Geoffrey chortled. "It was a great gig, fast money too. After a couple of months, I had this wad of cash, around six thousand. I mean, that's a lot for an office job, let alone a summer job, right? But the day I was going car shopping with Albert, my fraternity got a letter saying the house was being sold and we'd all have to move out. No one had *any* money. If we lost the house, we would all have to find apartments and end up paying at least triple what we paid at the frat house. So, here I am with more money than I've ever seen, and I started to think the car might have to wait. I convinced Albert and Sophie to cosign for me, toss in a few extra dollars to help, and then I bought it."

"Wow, I don't know many college kids that are homeowners."

"Trust me, it was a gamble, but it just felt right. Plus, I got it real cheap too. It was a dump. No person in their right mind would live there unless they were college kids. We didn't care what it looked like. As long as there was heat and air conditioning, the place was a palace to us. Plus, I charged a fair rent to all my frat brothers, and Albert even called their parents to vouch for me. The place paid for itself."

He took another sip of his drink to calm his throat. He was trying to impress Madilyn and was talking much faster and more animated than usual.

"I took the money I made off the rent, and when another one down the road went up for sale the next year, I grabbed that one too. Rented it to a couple sorority girls I knew. They took care of it much better than we did. Six months later, I did it again. I didn't need Albert for that. In fact, I paid him back his initial loan to me, and went on my own. I was buying these dumps, hiring a local guy to fix them up for me, and do maintenance when needed. The next thing I knew, I had three homes by the time I was twenty-one. I took off the next semester to give real estate a try."

"Looks like you did the right thing."

"Albert didn't like me dropping out of college so close to finishing, but at the time, it was too good of an opportunity to pass up. I got my own place, hired a small staff, and really hit the ground running. The market was at a great point."

"Okay, I see how *that* worked, but the bakeries?"

"Now *that* is my real love. Again, something that just came out of nowhere. When I launched my firm, I was reading all these books about how to bring in buyers for open houses, like tips on how to make them feel at home. I wanted them to walk in and say, *'This is my future home!'* One book talked about how people love the smell of fresh pastries from the oven. Sounded easy enough. I figured I would bake a cake or two for the open house to keep the homes smelling cozy, and a little something extra for the guests to enjoy.

"Doing like four or five open houses a month, people started to expect them. Then the other agents asked if I could make them for their open houses. After a while, I found baking to be incredibly therapeutic. Next thing you know, I get a call from a local store about selling them for parties. I hired another chef, handed him my recipe, and a year later I decided to open a small shop of my own. Shortly after that, I had a food truck to hit up the city. You'd be surprised how many college kids are ready for fresh cupcakes outside a bar at two in the morning. Then, I just kept expanding."

"Wow! No wonder my grandmother likes you. You have the same drive she does."

"She's a smart woman."

"She's my hero. But with all the success in real estate, you don't exactly sound too jazzed about it."

Geoffrey rolled his eyes and bit his lip. "Don't get me wrong, I loved selling homes."

145

"You said *loved*, not love."

"*Ha*, yeah, you're right. And it's the truth." He shrugged. "After a while the people just became dollars. I'll admit the greed factor got to me. I was riding high in this new lifestyle that wasn't exactly the best for a young kid. And I was still a *kid*. But I couldn't stop. The money came in faster than I could count it. Along with building and selling, I started doing home loans too, which was great for me, but I was just going through the motions of getting better numbers each day. I didn't care who they were, what their income was. If you wanted the home of your dreams, I'd make it work. Maybe that's not the best thing for a businessman to say, but there's a very thin line between what makes good sense for your wallet and what makes good sense for your soul."

"What do you mean?"

Geoffrey leaned forward, clasping his hands on the table. "I'll never forget this guy from my college who came to my office about a loan for a house. This kid was twenty-four, making fifty thousand a year at Goldman Sachs, which is not bad for a college grad. He came to me with a list of expensive homes that I knew were way out of his comfort zone. But he pushed and begged me. So after some tweaks here and there, I ended up securing a home loan for a house that cost six hundred and fifty thousand. Based off just his salary, not having a spouse, or someone helping him out. There was no way on earth that should have ever gone through." He shook his head at what a huge mistake it was, and how much he regretted it. "I *knew* it was shady, but my partners . . . and even *me*, Madilyn, we saw nothing but dollar signs. He lost the house within eight months. I felt sick as a dog over it. I even gave him ten grand in cash out of my own wallet just to make up for it. I realized that business wasn't for me. I was tired of *just* looking at the money and *not* how I got it. I still have the business but I'm not as active as I used to be."

"That poor kid."

"But that, as they say, is in the past." Despite this, he was still hurt by the memory of it.

The chef and owner Blake made his way over, just in time to change the mood of the conversation, placing a hand on Geoffrey's back and extending the other to shake Madilyn's hand. Blake was tall, dark, and fit, like a yoga instructor. His olive skin, clean shaved head, and black tattoos with his children's names on his forearms gave him an exotic look that always helped in running a business catering to the hip diners of Baltimore City.

"Geoffrey, Geoffrey, *now* I know why you called me in such a rush." Blake grinned. "He's a good guy, you know."

"I'm finding that out," Madilyn said.

Geoffrey blushed.

Blake ran down the specials for the evening and Geoffrey ordered for the both of them.

"So, you called in a rush? Why's that?" Madilyn asked coyly as she took a sip of water.

"No, it's—"

"I want to hear more. Keep going." She placed her napkin over her lap and put one hand under her chin, resting her body on the edge of the table as she playfully skated a slice of pita around her plate, filling it with hummus.

Geoffrey let out a deep sigh, calming himself down. "Okay, more? Well, you heard most of it already. I'm just a normal type of guy really. I like sports, beaches, I have a place in Bethany, and of course I love to eat good food. And a little secret, despite being a bakery owner, I can't cook anything that doesn't have flour, sugar, and water as the main ingredients. That's why I come here so much. But when I'm not running around in my shops, I'm running around with my daughter."

Madilyn stopped mid-chew. "Your daughter!" She gushed. "Tell me about her."

"How much time do you have?" Geoffrey asked proudly.

That made her smile wider.

"Her name is Layla. She's my life. I love her more than anything. She's just so . . . I don't know. I don't know what I'd do without her."

"That's very sweet, Geoffrey," she said, reaching out for his hand, while her gaze remained focused on his.

"It's weird, but when I first found out I was going to be a dad, I was so nervous. I mean, since I was a sophomore in college, I did nothing but work, work, work, and of course party, you know? Then all of a sudden, it's like *BAM* you're a father! Albert was young when he had my dad, and my dad was young when he had me, but I was young in age and maturity. I still keep the sonogram picture in my car from the first time I saw her, and the ID band from the hospital around my gearshift. Then when she was born, I just became an entirely new person. Work, life, *money*. . . All of that means *nothing* without her. She made me want to rethink my life and where I was." Geoffrey stopped and shook his head, embarrassed. "Oh man, look at me. I'm *babbling*. I'll stop now."

"No, don't. I like it."

"I just wish my parents—my *birth* parents—had a chance to meet her."

Geoffrey felt a lump in his throat and quickly took a drink. He looked down, and realized Madilyn's fingers were gently touching his. He was taken aback that she was holding his hand, and more surprised by how wonderful it felt. He extended his fingers to her palms. All of a sudden, she seemed to notice what she was doing, and pulled her hand back, her cheeks flushed.

"Oh, sorry about that," she muttered.

"No, please, it's fine. It's . . . *very* fine." He reached back for her hand, and this time she didn't pull away.

"Have you ever taken Layla to their gravesite?" Madilyn asked, sounding hesitant.

"Nah. I don't know if she'd understand. In fact, *I* haven't been there in a long time, come to think of it. Albert practically lives there. But I go once a year, on the day they passed. It's a . . . You know, I'm . . ." Geoffrey fumbled for the right words.

"It's okay, I'm sorry. I shouldn't be prying."

"Never. Please don't think that." He reassured her with a smile.

A waiter arrived, setting plates in front of each of them, and they separated their hands and dug in. The aroma seemed to warm the conversation. He watched Madilyn bring her fork to her mouth, his gaze drawn to her face.

Those lips! He tried to keep his legs from shaking.

"This is delicious!" Madilyn exclaimed, enjoying the entrée Geoffrey had recommended, mango curry chicken salad.

"Best in town!"

She took another sip of wine. "So, apparently our grandparents have quite the past. Did you know that?"

"Ella told me, but Gramps hasn't said much about it." Geoffrey was eager to hear what Ella may have told Madilyn.

"Really? I wonder why."

"From the beginning, he's been standoffish about her. I think it's because he feels like he's betraying my grandmother for having a female friend or something. But that's so outrageous. Ella just wants to talk to him. He can be difficult sometimes."

"To be honest, I'm not sure either. She is vague too."

"You would think that after all these years, they'd love to talk to one another. At least just to have a friend, if nothing else. I mean, sixty years! I can't imagine seeing someone after that much time. I'm on Facebook and can see people I went to nursery school with, but sixty years and not ever having seen a photo . . . or not even talking to them? I can't wrap my brain around it."

"Let's make a plan. We'll each do some investigative work and see what happens. Bottom line is that these two need to connect again. There is too much of a history there, regardless of whatever happened. Deal?" She raised her glass to Geoffrey.

"Cheers to that for sure. You have a deal."

The waiter returned to relight the candle on their table that had burned between them. The soft light illuminated Madilyn's face, creating gentle shadows around her chin and cheeks, framing her lips and making her eyes glow almost iridescently when she looked up at Geoffrey.

I have never seen anything so beautiful in my life.

Just as the thought comforted his heart, he reminded himself there was another woman in his life, even though Rose had never looked at him the way Madilyn was looking at him now.

"Okay, my turn. Tell me about yourself," Geoffrey said.

She took a deep breath. "Where to start? I just turned thirty, from here in Baltimore as well. I *was* married, but quickly divorced. That's another story for a much longer meal." Madilyn smirked. "No kids, but . . . *hopefully* one day. I've always wanted a big family of my own. I've been a preschool teacher ever since graduation, which I absolutely love. And when I'm not teaching, I like to bike ride and jog. I'm a pretty simple gal, Geoffrey. No chain of restaurants or real estate empire on this side of the table."

"Ha-ha! Well, you can help me out at my shop any time." He hoped she would take him up on his offer.

"Trust me, you're better off if I keep my day job. But if you have an opening as a taste tester, *then* we're talking."

"Where do you teach?"

"I'm in between right now. I just got back from a year in Durham, North Carolina. After the divorce, I had to get away for a bit, so took a job at the school I used to substitute teach during my senior year at Duke."

Geoffrey almost choked on his water. "Wait a second, wait a second. You're a . . . a *Blue Devil*?"

"Is that a problem?" Madilyn asked, grinning.

"By *problem*, you mean for *you*! Were you kidnapped and taken there for ransom or something? Did your parents lose a bet? Was it a dare? Tell me it was a dare. I mean, tell me it's *something* other than you voluntarily applied, and attended Duke?"

"Oh great, here we go again."

"Again? Meaning someone else has pointed out how evil your college is?"

"Once or twice," she said, rolling her eyes.

"Well, let me tell you again."

"Let me guess, you're a *Terp*."

"That's right, I'm a Terp! University of Maryland, all the way. You want me to do the cheer? Because I will! I don't even know if we should be dining together?" Geoffrey teased.

"Great. Another Baltimore boy turn Terp, who hates Duke because we won more championships than they ever will," she shot back, her nose in the air.

"We're arch rivals!" Geoffrey exclaimed.

"Hey, news flash, buster, the University of Maryland is *not* a rival for us!"

He threw down his napkin. "Okay, that's it! Blake, we'll need to cut her off now, she's had way too much to drink."

"If you like, I can send you a picture of all of our NCAA championship trophies. That's right, I said *trophies*, as in plural. And then you can show me the *one* that you have?"

"Wow, low blow! Looks like we have a trash talker here!" Geoffrey rolled his neck and cracked his knuckles. "Let's go, what'd ya got?"

Madilyn laughed hard, then crumbled up her napkin and threw it at Geoffrey's face. It bounced off his chin.

"Nice hands, Terp boy!"

They laughed like old friends, neither believing it'd only been a couple hours since they first met.

"When I first met Ella, she told me how much I looked like Albert but it's incredible how much you look like your grandmother," Geoffrey said.

"I think Albert was rather shocked too."

"Really?"

"When he arrived at the house, I think he must have dozed off in the car, and when he saw me he had a hard time looking at me. I think because I look so much like Ella when he last saw her. It may have spooked him a bit. It's funny, but part of me thinks it also helped them both."

151

Geoffrey stopped before taking another bit of hummus. "What do you mean?"

"There's something there, Geoffrey, and I think it's more than just two kids who used to hook up behind the bleachers at school."

"I agree. Ella mentioned they were rather *a*-hem, *romantic* back in the day, if you catch my drift."

"I know, Geoffrey," Madilyn said with a wink.

"Oh. . . Well then."

"My grandmother is not one to hide things. She told me she loved him very much. And I'm pretty sure he felt the same way too."

"Maybe that's why he's so scared."

"Love will do that to you, Geoffrey."

"Indeed it will, Madilyn."

Their eyes met in a different way for the first time. They didn't have to say it but they both seemed to have a mutual understanding about what kind of love they wanted out of life.

Other diners came and went, but they stayed. Blake refilled their wine and they shared a slice of homemade cheesecake.

The check was placed on the table and Geoffrey swiped it without asking, adding his credit card in an equally fast motion. She thanked him, and he shrugged, insisting it was no big deal.

"Let's go walk off that cake," he suggested, reaching for her hand.

They strolled along the crowded Sulgrave Avenue, past the other shops in the Square. The temperature had dropped several degrees, and Madilyn put on her coat. Geoffrey watched her as she placed one arm in each sleeve, then buttoned it up to her collar. She tucked her hair behind her ears again.

They walked two blocks until coming to a city bench alongside the quiet stream that ran the south end of Mt. Washington Square. Geoffrey asked if Madilyn wanted to grab a seat. He always found the sound and motion of the tiny stream to be soothing to his soul, and hoped she would see the romance in it as well.

Geoffrey cleared off a few leaves from the bench and held her hand as she sat down. She leaned beside him, her shoulder touching his. They rested their feet on the steel rail that separated them and the stream, and listened to the night.

"I love this weather, Geoffrey. Don't you?" she said, leaning her head back and breathing in slowly.

He couldn't take his eyes off her.

The smell of nearby restaurants filled the air with a mix of cultures from American to Mediterranean, to French, and Chinese. At every slight turn Geoffrey could taste a different flavor on his tongue. Surrounded by the varying cuisines he thought about where to take Madilyn on their next date. Then realized a large part of him wished it were a real date and more than just two people building a friendship.

A teenage couple walked by, hand in hand, and took the bench a few yards down. The boy leaned into the girl, holding her close around the waist as she placed her hands over his shoulders. They began kissing.

"First kisses. Gotta love 'em." Geoffrey playfully nudged Madilyn.

"Do you remember yours?"

"How could I forget? Candice Franklin. Middle school. I don't think it was my best work, though. With my mouth full braces, I'm pretty sure it was like kissing a robot." He laughed. "And you?"

"Mine? Mike Keane. A strikingly handsome goalie on my seventh grade soccer team."

"I get it. You're into the jocks, huh?"

"I was twelve, *of course* I was."

"I never would have had a chance," Geoffrey joked.

"I don't know about that." Madilyn tilted her head to the side and winked. "I may have given you a shot."

"You have just given nerds of the world a reason for hope, Madilyn."

Geoffrey's phone beeped. It was a text message from Nick, not Rose as he was hoping. He squinted in frustration, and bit his bottom lip.

"Everything all right?"

"It's my wife . . ." Geoffrey stared down at his phone. "I haven't heard from her in a while."

Madilyn's body language changed abruptly. She straightened up and leaned back. "You're married?"

Geoffrey glanced up at her. "I didn't mention that?"

"No, you didn't." Madilyn rose to her feet to adjust her jacket.

Geoffrey followed her. "Really? It must have slipped my mind."

"Do you think your wife would mind you having dinner with me?"

Madilyn sounded somewhat distraught. Even though he knew Rose was not wondering who he was having dinner or where, the heaviness of guilt returned, weighing on his mind. Despite her betrayals, Geoffrey had always been a loyal husband. The guilt dissipated when he recalled how he and Rose had parted the last time he'd seen her.

"Honestly?" Geoffrey crossed his arms over his chest. "I don't think my wife would mind if I went into outer space with the entire roster of the *Sports Illustrated Swimsuit Edition*."

Madilyn tucked her hands into her side pockets and stepped closer to Geoffrey. Her upper body pressed against him, right below his chest, and she tilted her head up, meeting his gaze.

"Then we'll have to go to the moon next time." She spoke softly, and he could see her breath in the air.

Geoffrey gulped, and the hairs on his neck stood up.

"You're flushed, Geoffrey Abraham." She leaned her head to the side and brushed a strand of hair behind her ear.

"I, uh—"

She seemed to be waiting for something. He wanted to kiss her, but he knew it wasn't right. He was married.

Despite this, they locked eyes with one another, caught in the moment. Madilyn seemed to be letting her guard down; she placed her palms on his chest, cocking her head to the side as if anticipating something. Probably the same thing he was hoping for.

"I had a lot of fun tonight, Geoffrey."

He took her hands in his. "I did too."

Take her, kiss her. Now! Forget everything else, and just kiss her! Still, he knew it was the wrong thing to do—for him and for Madilyn.

"I should be going." She spoke softly, squeezing his hands.

Geoffrey didn't want her to leave. He didn't want the night to end. But he couldn't tell her that. They remained close together.

"When can we meet up again?" he asked.

"We have some homework to do on Albert and Ella. See what you can uncover, and when you're ready, you know where to find me." She winked.

"Okay. . . I'm ready now," he retorted, trying for flattery.

Madilyn was captured by his charm, giggling as she pressed her head against his chest, and then looked up to smile at him. She stood on the tips of her toes, and kissed his cheek.

He leaned into her, holding her back but unable to move any other part of his body. He was frozen.

"Don't be a stranger now, Geoffrey." She stepped back to leave.

"I won't."

"And you should visit your parents, too. I think they'd like that."

He nodded. "I think you're right."

Madilyn waved goodbye, then turned to walk to her car.

Geoffrey let out a large gasp of air, as if he hadn't taken a breath in the last two hours. He bent over, hands on his knees, breathing heavily. He placed his hands on his hips and stumbled in her direction.

He knew he shouldn't pursue her, but there was a greater force pulling at him. Right or wrong, he was falling for Madilyn. She was everything he ever fantasized about and never thought he'd find. She was everything Rose wasn't, and everything he wished she was. She made him feel good about himself—confident—which was something he hadn't felt in a long time.

After only having known her for a couple of hours, Geoffrey felt a divine connection, and a force pulling them close together. He juggled his keys around in his palm and called out to Madilyn, who was quickly disappearing in the crisp, city night.

"Madilyn, wait!"

She turned, clutching her jacket close to her face. "Yes?"

"You know the funny thing about first kisses?" He had to shout over the wide distance between them.

"What's that, Geoffrey?"

"You always remember your first kiss, but it's the *last* kiss that tells you when you've found that special someone."

Madilyn beamed. "I'll let you know when I find my last kiss then, Geoffrey."

He looked down at the ground and shook his head at his attempt at being poetic.

That's your line, Geoffrey?

"Goodnight!" She called out over the wind before finally disappearing into the darkness.

"Goodnight, Madilyn," he mumbled. He tilted his head up to the sky. "You are one dumb shmuck, Geoffrey Abraham. You know that?"

16

The Empty Room

Albert and Geoffrey both looked forward to seeing Sophie, but they knew she was getting worse every day. It was a dark reality they had to embrace. Especially Albert, who tried to deny it, but knew it was only a matter of time.

Geoffrey missed his grandmother, and wished that Layla could meet her. He knew she never would. When he looked at his grandfather, it made him think of Ella and how Layla acted the first time they'd met. The thought wore heavy on him.

They didn't talk much during their ride to the hospital, but that didn't stop Geoffrey from watching Albert out of the corner of his eye. As usual, Albert was lost in the drive like a dog with his head out the window—minus the delight. He seemed to be searching for distraction. Over the years, he had trained his mind. Geoffrey knew he was scared, but he didn't let it show.

The trip to Sophie's floor was slow, and both men over-analyzed the noises and creaks the old elevator made along the slow journey.

"What if I die from this piece of junk collapsing?" Albert wondered. "What if I die, on the way to see my wife who is dying? That would be my luck."

Geoffrey said nothing in response.

"Here we are, Gramps." He directed what he hoped was a smile toward his grandfather as the elevator doors opened.

The potent and overwhelming smell of urine filled their nostrils. Out of habit, they held their breath, but it would only kill the scent for so long. Geoffrey wondered how the nurses could live through this every day and not notice.

Sophie's room was down the hall, and they had to pass through the main lobby and a row of rooms to get to her. Patients meandered around the halls, talking to themselves, or standing stationary over walkers or slumped in chairs. It was the hospital's way of getting them out of their rooms to "socialize". Some patients would grab or pull at Albert and Geoffrey as they walked by, thinking they were their own family members. Some would scream or rant, but Geoffrey ignored them, ushering his grandfather along. They had been told not to interact. The nursing station was busy and the girls didn't notice as they walked by.

Before entering Sophie's room, they paused for a moment. Sophie wouldn't know how they were feeling, but they had to prepare themselves for what they were about to see. It was their routine. Geoffrey discreetly swallowed another pill by faking a cough and covering his mouth.

He touched Albert's arm. *It's okay, Gramps, I'm here for you.*

When they opened the door, Geoffrey gaped, watching as his grandfather appeared to take a sudden strike to the gut, all the air visibly racing out his lungs.

The room was empty.

Geoffrey's heart pounded quicker.

There could only be one reason for this.

Albert's knees buckled and his entire body dropped. Geoffrey caught him from behind and held him tight before he hit the floor. Albert was frantic, fighting his grasp.

"Where is she, Geoffrey, where is she! Where is she! Where! Where!" He was hysterical, shouting, his arms flailing and grabbing at anything for stability.

"Gramps, I have you! It's okay, Gramps." Geoffrey wrestled Albert close to him and tried to settled him down.

This was the day they'd dreaded. Geoffrey never knew how Albert would react the day of Sophie's death, but now he was seeing it firsthand, and was overwhelmed by his animalistic response. It took every bit of Geoffrey's strength to contain him. Possessed with fear and anger, he was no longer feeble or easily held back.

Sophie's bed was freshly made and all her belongings were gone. Albert's face was drenched with tears and sweat as he clambered to his feet, pulling at Geoffrey for help. Geoffrey half-carried Albert to a chair by the door.

"Sophie, Sophie! Where is my wife?"

Albert yelled louder, and the nurses were racing over. He screeched in higher octaves as he lost more control. Other patients gathered and watched as the nurses came in and grabbed hold of him, and Geoffrey tried to keep him down without hurting him.

"Where is she? Tell me where is she!"

Albert's screams were even more intense, his mouth foaming with saliva and tears pouring down his face.

"It's okay, Mr. Abraham, Sophie is okay!" Hollie shouted over him, putting her hands on his chest to get his attention.

Geoffrey gulped, suddenly unsure of what was going on and fearing Albert's reaction when the nurses would tell him Sophie had passed.

"My grandmother? Where is she?"

"She's fine, she's fine. We just moved her," Hollie said, struggling to keep Albert calm.

"Why did you move her?" Albert shouted, as two male nurses came in and placed their strong hands on his shoulders.

"Calm down, Mr. Abraham, you're going to hurt yourself."

"Calm down?" he roared, rocking his body up, trying to buck them off.

Geoffrey held him as best he could, surrounded on all sides by hospital staff.

"She's fine, Gramps, they just moved her, that's all. Hollie said she's fine." He didn't believe them, and through his confusion he realized his voice sounded different as he spoke—strained, worried, fearful.

"I need you to calm down, Mr. Abraham." Hollie's voice was firm yet soothing. "I need you to calm down now. She's fine. Trust me, she is more than fine."

"What do you mean?" Geoffrey asked.

Hollie's attention was still centered on Albert. "Can you remain calm now, Mr. Abraham?"

He was breathing heavily, his chest heaving. "Yes! Yes, I can. Get off me!"

The other nurses stepped back—though they looked ready for a fight—and Geoffrey helped Albert to his feet.

"Can you please give us a second, Hollie?" Geoffrey's voice was soft, more subdued.

Hollie agreed and the other nurses left the room as well. Albert's breathing was still rapid, as though he were in the throes of a panic attack. Geoffrey put his hands on his shoulders.

"Breathe, Gramps, she's okay. You're okay. Breathe with me." They breathed together in unison, until it resumed a normal pattern—reverting back to the practice Albert's physician told him to do in case he ever felt anxious. Geoffrey lifted his head and lowered it as he breathed in and out, slower and slower, urging his grandfather to do the same.

"Okay, we're cool, right?"

"Why would they move her and not tell us?" Albert stared blankly into Geoffrey's eyes. His breathing had finally settled to a more relaxed pattern.

"They said she's fine, Gramps. That's all that matters." Geoffrey had his doubts, but he decided to handle one thing at a time.

"They only move patients when it's their time to go. She can't go now, Geoffrey. She can't leave now!" Albert wiped his face and loosened the top of his shirt.

The door opened and Hollie peeked in.

"Are you ready, Mr. Abraham? We can go see Sophie whenever you like."

"I'm . . . I'm sorry Hollie."

"For what? Please, Mr. Abraham, it's *our* fault, I should have called you."

"Just tell me she's okay."

"Trust me, Mr. Abraham, she is in better hands now than ever."

They walked down the left wing of the sixth floor, through three sets of double doors, and past a nurses' station. Hollie and Geoffrey made small talk about the weather, anything to make the walk easier.

Sophie's room was at the end of a long narrow hallway of single bedrooms. Hollie led them down past four other rooms, two on each side. The last corner room by a large window was Sophie's new room. This hallway had no distasteful smell. It was fresh, clean, and decorated like a five star hotel, with framed paintings hanging on the walls and contemporary lighting overhead.

"Here we are," Hollie said. "This room is *gorgeous*. It's nicer than my one bedroom apartment! Twice the size of her other room, with a larger TV and double the staff. Much more modern, filled with all the latest technology. There's even a new tool that massages her legs to enhance blood flow, still in beta, but the hospital has it on trial, and Sophie gets that too. It's very cool stuff."

Albert appeared bemused. "What is she doing here?"

"I'm sorry, Mr. Abraham, I just follow my orders." Hollie peeked through the window of the shut door. "I see Dr. Glazer, Cedarmere's Vice President of Patient Relations, has already arrived. He can probably tell you more."

Geoffrey put his hand on Albert's back and turned to Hollie. "This all sounds very nice, Hollie, really it does, but why is she being treated like this? I pay a lot for her care, but no one mentioned this to me. How much does this cost?"

"I'm not the one to go over that, Geoffrey. I just take care of our patients." She peeked through the window again. "I'm sure Dr. Glazer can explain. He's the best, really. Just a super, super nice man. Everyone around here loves him."

Albert and Geoffrey had nothing to say, as they hadn't been told anything about what was going on. She knocked on the door and opened it slowly. She called out in a sweet, gentle voice.

"*Hellooooo*, Sophie and Dr. Glazer, we have some guests here for you."

The doctor was sitting on the edge of Sophie's bed with a stethoscope draped around his neck. He was a tall man of medium build, with thinning brown hair combed clean and firmly held to the side, and a light goatee, speckled grey. He hopped up when Hollie entered to greet both Albert and Geoffrey with steady handshakes.

"The Abrahams! It is so nice to meet you both." His smile was genuine, reaching his eyes. "My name is Dr. Glazer, but you can call me Brian if you like. I just checked Sophie's vitals and everything is perfect. She is doing great. I oversaw the move myself as well."

Albert stepped past Dr. Glazer as if he wasn't even standing there. He didn't acknowledge anyone else as he approached Sophie's bedside, and sat down on a small stool. They watched as he picked up her frail hand, cradling it like a wounded bird, and leaned in to kiss her fingers.

He brushed his hand through her hair and rested his cheek against her pillow. He caressed her neck and shoulders with such gentleness it almost seemed he was afraid she would fall apart. He wept quietly and stared into her face.

Hollie, Geoffrey, and Dr. Glazer decided to give Albert a few minutes to himself. They stepped outside, and Hollie excused herself. She wiggled her fingers flirtatiously as she waved goodbye to Geoffrey.

Dr. Glazer and Geoffrey stood side by side, watching through the door as Albert spoke softly to his wife.

"I can tell he loves her very much," Dr. Glazer said, breaking the silence.

"More than any man possibly can," Geoffrey affirmed.

"I heard about what happened in Sophie's old room, and I do apologize. I promise you we will call you as soon as anything happens, to the second. This is just faster than our usual turnaround."

"I'm totally confused here, Dr. Glazer. Why is my grandmother in this room?"

"What do you mean?"

"She's been in the same room for six years, and now she's in a much nicer place than most resorts I've stayed in."

"You don't know?"

"Doc, we don't know *anything*. We get here and see that her room is empty, and all her belongings gone. In this place, we all know that only means one thing. My grandfather almost killed two of your male nurses."

"Mr. Abraham, I had no idea—none! I assumed you knew."

Geoffrey shook his head. "Knew what?"

"Mr. Abraham, you have a friend who this hospital cares very much about. I got a call last night and we went to work making the proper adjustments immediately." When Geoffrey's brow furrowed in puzzlement, the doctor continued. "Ella Perlman, she called me last night on my cell phone and asked that Sophie be taken care of to the best of our ability." He nodded toward the room. "This is the very best of our ability, Mr. Abraham."

"Wait a second. You're telling me *Ella* called you and told you move my grandmother here? Just like that?"

"Yes, Mr. Abraham, just like that. When Mrs. Perlman asks for something, we make sure to follow through right away."

"Doc, I'll be honest with you, this must be costing a fortune. I mean, I pay a fortune just to have her in that other room! It's a nice gesture, but how much is this going to cost me?"

Dr. Glazer raised his eyebrows, then cleared his throat. "Yes, I'm aware of your commitment to Sophie. I looked at your grandmother's file before the move. You're a very generous grandson, Mr. Abraham. But you need not worry about that anymore. You will no longer have to send us any payments. Everything has been covered."

"Excuse me?" Geoffrey gasped in shock.

"You don't need to pay us anymore."

"For how long?"

"For as long as Sophie is here."

"That could be fifteen or twenty years!"

"Even longer, possibly. *Hopefully* that is. Especially with the new care she'll be receiving. Let's just say that Mrs. Perlman has been a very good friend to the hospital, Mr. Abraham, and we appreciate her dedication."

Geoffrey had conducted enough deals and met enough of the right people to know when someone was considered a *friend*. He couldn't believe Ella had done this for them. She had no reason to—other than to do it out of the kindness of her heart.

"That does not surprise me, Dr. Glazer," Geoffrey admitted.

He watched as Albert ran his hand through Sophie's hair and kissed her cheeks, then clasped her hands in his and rocked back and forth, singing a familiar tune. He wasn't sure if it was a good idea to tell Albert the truth. In a way, he hoped Albert would be grateful that Sophie was in better care and leave it at that. But the opposing side of the issue was that Ella had interjected into the single most important area of his life. Whatever it was that kept Albert and Ella apart was something they needed to figure out.

Geoffrey knew his grandfather well, and he feared Ella's generous gift might divide the two further. Despite all the doubts he had about Ella's involvement, Geoffrey couldn't stop thinking about the one underlining fact of the matter. No matter how much was being spent, or what strings had to be pulled, his grandmother's life was better than it had been in six years. That was something they could all be grateful for.

17

Where Do I Start?

"Are you going to tell me?" Albert adjusted the heat vents in the car, aiming them toward him.

Geoffrey drummed the steering wheel with his fingers. "Tell ya what?"

"Geoffrey."

"Gramps."

"Tell me why your grandma was moved."

"It's just a better form of care, that's all."

"Geoffrey, be serious with me, please."

"I am."

"Son, I know you pay a lot of money to help your grandmother, and I will always be thankful for that, but why didn't you tell me you were moving her?" Albert seemed happy about the new arrangements, but confused nonetheless. "It's a nice gesture, but had I known I wouldn't have lost it back there. It was embarrassing."

This is going to be awkward. Geoffrey sighed, preparing himself, wondering if his grandfather could ever guess the answer on his own.

"Gramps, it wasn't me."

"David?"

"Please, you're kidding, right? No, not David."

"Then who?"

Geoffrey bit his bottom lip, and didn't answer.

"Geoffrey, tell me."

He stared ahead calmly, gripping the steering wheel, not wanting to see his grandfather's reaction when he told him.

"It was Ella."

"What?"

"Apparently your ol' pal knows some pretty influential people around the hospital. She made a call, and that was that."

"She did *what!* You knew about this?" Albert snapped. He sounded more disgusted than curious.

Geoffrey stammered. "No, Gramps, no . . . I didn't."

"You two planned this? You knew about this and you let me lash out at those people! I thought she was dead!" Albert pounded his fist into his hand.

"Gramps, I had no idea, I thought the same thing as you!"

"You went behind my back and you lied to me. You don't even know Ella! She does not run my life, and I do not need her handouts!" This time, he slammed his fist against the dashboard.

Geoffrey knew Albert was wrong, but couldn't take the badgering and relentless attacking. Without warning, he pulled onto the shoulder near the John Brown Coffee Shop, and the car dropped into the grass and came to a stop just short of the wooden fences lining the fields, jerking Albert's head forward.

Mud and water splashed across the side of Geoffrey's car as he tried to level out of the shallow ditch, and Albert's hat fell to the floor. As his grandfather reached to his feet, searching for his hat, Geoffrey turned the car off, flung his seatbelt behind him, got out, and slammed the door. He paced around the front of the car, hands on his hips.

Albert opened the door and peeked out. "What's a matter with you?" '

Geoffrey threw his hands in the air. "*Me?* What's wrong with me? That's a good one, Gramps, a really good one."

"Son, what is your problem?" Albert climbed out and approached him. "I should be the one pissed off, not you. You lied to me!"

Geoffrey looked up at the sky and shut his eyes tight. He shook his head from side to side, trying to dispel his negative thoughts regarding Albert's stubbornness. He put his hand in his pocket and pulled out his pillbox, emptying three small tablets and swallowing them fast. Just taking the pills brought a sense of ease to his body, even though they wouldn't take effect right away. He counted to ten under his breath before turning to his grandfather.

"Gramps, I am not a liar. *Never* call me a liar."

"I just wish you would have told me."

"You're not listening to me. I didn't know anything!" Geoffrey pointed at Albert accusingly. "I was just as freaked out as you were when you saw her empty bed. I had no idea what was going on either."

"You didn't?"

"No, Gramps, I didn't. I found out the same way you did. When you were with Grandma, Dr. Glazer told me the details. Ella made the call herself. I had nothing to do with it."

"Why would she do this?" Albert leaned against the bumper, crossing his arms over his chest. "This is none of her business. I never asked for this."

"Wait a second, are you mad at Ella now?"

"Hell yes, I am. It's not her place to butt into my life." He spoke as if Geoffrey should be feeling the same way.

"You really don't get it, do you? You are so far off the mark on this one." Geoffrey noticed he was getting a better handle on his temper, which meant the medication was kicking in.

"Get what, exactly?"

He leaned next to Albert on the front bumper, and tilted his head toward him. "Gramps, I don't know what your deal is with Ella, and until you're ready to chat, I guess I never will. But regardless of that, someone cares about you enough to make your life and your wife's life better. Do you understand how generous this is?"

"That's not the point."

Despite Geoffrey's meds, anger bubbled up once more. "No, that *is* the point. Put your feelings and your ego aside. Even if Ella dies tomorrow or something, Sophie's care will go on, do you know that? There are no strings attached. If anything, you should swallow your irrelevant pride, drive over to her house, and thank Ella right now!"

"It's not that simple, son." Albert turned away.

"Really? Seems pretty damn simple to me." He climbed into the driver's seat and shut the car door, then slumped with his head in his hands.

A moment later, Geoffrey thought he heard Albert say something. He opened the door, and leaned his head out. "What's that?"

"I will tell you!" he grumbled.

"You'll tell me *everything*?"

"What time do we have to pick up Layla?"

"Her riding lesson ends in two hours."

Albert turned back to the car, keeping his head down. He rubbed his cheek, scratching against scraggly facial hair, a week overdue for a shave. After climbing in, he looked out the window and watched as fallen leaves skipped across the deep green grass. The autumn air chilled the window, and he rested his head against the cool glass to soothe his migraine.

"Where do I start?" Albert asked.

Geoffrey put a hand on his shoulder. "Gramps, take your time. Wherever you would like to start is fine. I'm here for you. Never forget that," he said, hoping to soothe Albert's nerves.

18

Heavy Words

He started at the beginning of his life with Ella. It wasn't easy, and he often had to stop himself to hold back his tears. He told Geoffrey how they met, how they fell in love as teenagers, and the plans they made about marriage and their future.

He admitted Ella was his first love, and this seemed to catch Geoffrey off guard—perhaps because he wasn't used to hearing his grandfather talk about any woman other than Sophie.

They remained parked on the side of the road. Albert breathed in deep and let out a raspy breath to clear his lungs. Geoffrey handed him a bottle of water.

He paused longer this time and looked at Geoffrey, as if for answers.

"Gramps? What is it?"

"This may not be easy to hear."

"It's okay. I want to hear it."

***

Albert hurried to keep up with Collin's long-legged strides as he walked across the yard. They meandered past a large pile of fire wood, and closer to a grove of apple trees, surrounded on all sides by some of the most beautiful rose bushes in the county.

Collin didn't acknowledge Albert as he walked, his hands locked together behind his back. Collin finally stopped alongside his horse stables. With a single wave, he dismissed the stable manager who was tending to a group of horses grazing along the white wooden fence. Then he reached his hand over to one of his prize thoroughbreds, and rubbed the side of its face.

"Horses are such beautiful creatures," Collin said, his back to Albert.

"Yes sir, they are." Albert noted how similar Collin's large, thick frame was to that of his fine horses.

"Good boy, good boy," he said again, patting the horse sturdily on the shoulder. He then turned on his heel and spoke curtly.

"Albert, I think I know what you're going to ask me."

He almost breathed a sigh of relief as he tried to keep his legs from shaking. Collin would give him his blessing, and then welcome him into his family as his son.

"Yes sir?" Albert folded his hands in front of him and stood tall.

Collin turned to face him, but kept his gaze over Albert's shoulder rather than looking him in the face.

"I don't have much time, Albert, so I'll make this quick. My answer is no."

"What? Sir, I don't understand." His heart pounded as a cold sweat enveloped him, and he felt his stomach turn.

"What's not to understand, Albert?" Collin laughed. "You came to ask to marry Ella, correct?"

"Well, yes sir, I did."

"And my answer is no." Collin's expression showed no concern for Albert. He seemed more interested in observing the scenery than looking the young man in the eyes.

"But, sir, I don't understand . . ." Albert's hands trembled.

"You want me to spell it out for you?"

"Spell what out, sir?"

Collin turned to him and lowered his chin, meeting Albert's watery gaze.

"There ain't no way in hell I'm letting my daughter marry a damn *kike*."

Albert felt his chest cave in and the color rushed clear from his head, leaving a white glaze of confusion on his face. His legs went limp and it took every bit of strength to hold himself up.

This wasn't the first time he'd been called a kike, but this was a new side of Collin MacArthur he hadn't encountered until now. The word had caused Albert to get into dozens of fights in his youth, none of which he ever lost. Being called a kike was a trigger to his body—react, strike, fight.

"What did you just say, sir?"

"What, your kind doesn't like that word? It's better than saying Jew, if you ask me," Collin snapped. "I tolerated this teenage thing you two have but it's just that—*teenage*. It's not what a real relationship is like. It will never amount to anything, and frankly neither will you."

He paused, waiting for a response from Albert. When he said nothing, Collin checked his pocket watch, then placed it back in his vest pocket. He spoke with the ease and confidence of a man who was practiced at beating people down with words, as he'd done in the business world. To him, Albert was just another annoying obstacle, getting in the way of what he wanted. And what he wanted was a life for his daughter that Albert couldn't offer.

"Albert, Ella needs a man with a lineage, and a legacy. Someone with a good career planned out, goals, aspirations. A marriage is a business, Albert. There is nothing more important than merging two businesses together to make an even bigger one. And you, Albert, have no business in my family. Don't get me wrong, I don't mind watching you play baseball, but it's a game. A child's game, at that. Not a career. Or how you help out in the yard with my wife, or lug wood for the fire, but that's all you'll ever do. Jews don't have a place in our society, Albert. And they surely don't have a place in my family."

Collin had always been quiet, but Albert never thought he had any animosity toward him. He couldn't believe the words coming out of Collin's mouth. His foul, vulgar obscenities rendered Albert speechless.

"What, nothing, Albert? Well then, I guess we're on the same page." Collin slapped Albert on the side of his shoulder and started back to the house. "Good day, Albert."

Seeing Collin turn his back in such hatred and bigotry infuriated Albert. Weakness and fear were replaced with anger and vengeance. He never backed down from any fight, and never allowed anyone to talk to him that way. The last person who'd used those words against him ended up swallowing their teeth. Despite his love for Ella, Collin was about to do the same. Albert balled his fist and squeezed his hand until his knuckles turned white. His palms began to bleed as his fingernails dug into his flesh. Collin was only a few yards away.

"You can't stop us," Albert growled.

Collin rotated on one heel, hands in his pockets, and leaned back to laugh. "Really? Is that so? And what makes you think that, boy?"

"'Ella loves me, and that's all I need." Albert's eyes narrowed and his jaw flexed.

"Is that so?"

"It is."

"And what will you do?" Collin laughed again, as if the exchange was nothing more than an entertaining show.

"We'll leave and live together."

"Now that's absurd! That can't be what you really think will happen?" Collin walked toward Albert. He stood inches away from Albert's face, his tall frame two heads above him. Albert remained firm, only moving his gaze up to Collin.

"She will leave with me. I know it," Albert said, challenging him.

"Albert, you're a fool, a nobody, and just plain garbage!" Collin poked at his chest with every word. "You will never be anything in this world, just like the rest of your kind."

172

"Watch what you say, sir."

"And what do you suppose you're going to do?" Collin tipped Albert's chin up toward his face.

"Sir, I'm warning you." Albert knocked his hand away.

Collin took a step back, held his hands open, and leaned his chin into Albert's face.

"Hit me, Jew. Hit me with that Jew tail of yours, and then ram me with your damn horns!" Collin scowled. "I know you want to, so do it!"

Albert refused to flinch and kept his stance firm. "Your daughter loves me. She and I will be together, with or without your permission."

Collin stepped back and cackled. "Go ahead. Leave then, Albert."

"You will never see her again!" Albert shouted.

Collin rushed back to Albert's face, nearly knocking him down with his intense presence alone, but Albert remained upright.

"No, Albert! *You* will never see her again!" Collin jabbed his finger into Albert's chest. "You leave, and she is dead to me! She will never be welcomed back in this family or this house. Her mother, her sisters, her brother, aunts, uncles, hell, this whole damn state will ban her permanently! I have that power. I can make that happen, Albert. Do you hear me?"

"You're a fraud," Albert said, begging Collin to hit him first.

"If she leaves, I will find you, Albert. And even after I'm done with you, she still won't be allowed back here. Everyone she knows in her life will be gone. It will be as if she never existed at all! That's what you want? Huh? That's how much you love Ella? Tell me!"

"You're a liar!" Albert bent his elbows and balled his fists, ready to rise, ready to strike.

Collin glanced down at Albert's clenched fists. "Boy, you better hope you know how to use those. Because I sure as hell know how to use mine."

***

173

Albert and Geoffrey sat in silence for a long time. Albert had never told anyone that part of the story before. The version he usually stuck to was much simpler.

"We're just not right for each other," he'd said, over and over again, as if trying to convince himself as well.

Albert's head sank heavily on his shoulders. Anxiety and guilt weighed him down to a heap of emotions. Geoffrey stared impassively out the front window as cars rushed by in a blur. The temperature had dropped in the past hour, but neither bothered to turn on the heat.

"That's why you don't want to see her, isn't it?" Geoffrey finally asked, shifting his body toward Albert.

He nodded slowly.

"Ella has never heard this before, has she?"

Albert shook his head. "You are the first person I have ever told, Geoffrey."

"Not even Sophie?"

"No, not even her."

"What do you think Ella would say if you told her?"

He shrugged.

Geoffrey reached out and massaged Albert's neck with one hand. "Gramps, you have to tell her."

Albert looked at him, then turned away.

"You *have* to," Geoffrey insisted. "Gramps? She has to know the truth."

Albert pushed the window down. The afternoon chill quickly filled the car, adding a much needed relief, as if the crisp wind were washing away his worries and angst.

"Geoffrey, some things, especially like this, don't need to be repeated."

"But this is one of those things that does. All these years, she's held this against you or wondered about it, and you did nothing wrong. *Tell* her. She'll understand. She has a right to know."

Albert was growing impatient. He had replayed that last day with Collin over and over in his mind for decades. For a long time he wanted to do something, but ultimately knew nothing good would ever come out of it.

"You don't understand, Geoffrey. For Ella's entire life, she thought her father was the greatest man alive. He was—and his name is—a pillar of the community. If I tell her, it will erase all of that. With what little time she and I have left, I'm not going to ruin it. I can't do that her."

"Gramps, that's not the point. Fuck him!" Geoffrey hammered the steering wheel with his hand.

"Geoffrey!"

"Do you hear yourself? You don't want to ruin her father's *reputation*? That guy is a bigot! A piece of shit bigot! He should have been knocked on his ass years ago."

Albert wasn't used to Geoffrey cursing. In fact, he couldn't recall the last time he heard him say anything worse than *damn it*.

"Stop that! It's *over*! The past is over. I've moved on."

"You owe it to Ella." Geoffrey lowered his voice and let out a deep sigh. "And you owe it to yourself as well."

19

A Child's Eyes

They drove to Sagamore Farm where Layla had practice, and caught the last few minutes of her session. They rested their arms on the rugged wooden fence surrounding the horse track, and watched as Layla fed the horses with four other kids her age. A teacher instructed them on the importance of making sure horses ate right and got plenty of exercise. When she saw them, Layla waved excitedly.

Geoffrey elbowed Albert as the teacher spoke, as if Albert should take some notes on eating properly too. Albert rolled his eyes. They'd had a long day, and watching Layla was a good way for Albert to relax. Everything about her seemed to make every problem easier to handle. When she was around, both men felt euphoric.

The kids were dismissed, and all appeared disappointed. They could have stayed there all day if they were allowed. Layla hurried over to Albert and Geoffrey, giving them both big hugs.

"Daddy, can I sleep at Mackenzie's house after dinner? *Pleeeease!*"

"Sure, baby, I'll drop you off when we're done." He swept his hands through her hair, brushing sweaty strands out of her face.

Layla turned her friend. "He said yes!"

"You got her for a second, Gramps? I'm going to go talk to Mackenzie's mom real quick about tonight."

Layla grabbed Albert's hand and started swinging it with hers. "So, Zaide, where are we going tonight?"

"I don't know. Ella said it's a surprise."

"Zaide, can I ask you something?"

"Of course you can, sweetie, what is it?"

"Is Ella your girlfriend?"

Albert knew he had to be extra careful with Layla, knowing she was only six and probably assumed that anyone of the opposite sex seen together were probably dating, if not married.

"No, Layla. Ella is not my girlfriend. I'm married to Savta, remember?"

"Oh." Layla sounded somewhat defeated as she wrapped her arms around his waist.

"Why would you think that?" Albert gently tapped her back.

"I dunno, I just thought you were. She seems nice, that's all."

He rubbed the top of her back as Layla clung affectionately to his side. He looked out at the fields, scattered with horses and happy families walking around.

He could understand the connection Layla or any child would have with someone like Ella, and everything that came with knowing her. To Layla, Ella was cool and new, unlike other grandmothers who sat at home, knitting or playing checkers. She was unlike other mothers, for that matter. Plus, Ella gave Layla nice things. What child wouldn't like that?

The only person Layla could relate to as a grandmother—or *Savta*—was Ella. Even if she'd only just met her. Rose's parents weren't around, and when they were, they took little notice of Layla. And since Sophie had been in the hospital, Layla missed out on all the years she could have had with her. Albert knew this— and hated it.

"Layla, what do you know about Savta?"

"Daddy said she's sick."

"Well, that's true, Savta is sick, but you know Savta loves you very much?"

Layla looked down at her shoes as she shuffled her feet. "I know that. Daddy tells me all the time."

Albert always wished Layla and Sophie had more of a relationship, but he knew it was hard for a six-year-old to understand her condition. Old photos and movies could only do so much. He wanted Layla to be as excited about hearing Sophie's name as she was when she heard Ella's.

"Did I ever tell you that Savta was a champion Duckpin bowler?" Albert asked, raising his voice to increase her interest.

Layla pulled her head back and looked up at Albert. "Really? She was? I love Duckpin bowling! Remember my bowling party last year?"

"Of course I do!" Albert knelt to her level. "Actually, when Daddy and Uncle David were little, she used to take them with her to some of her games at the Pikesville Bowling Alley. They'd sit on the chairs at the little café and eat fries and chicken nuggets while she bowled."

"Really?" Layla giggled. "That does sound like something Daddy would do."

"And she won all kinds of awards and trophies," Albert said, making Layla's eyes light up. "How about this, when you come back to the house after your sleepover, we can go look at her trophies in the attic? You can have your pick of any of them. They're all yours."

"I've never had a trophy before!" Layla shouted, then reached out for a big hug. "Oh, thanks, Zaide! You're the best!"

"Not me, Layla, Savta is the best." Albert grinned as if he'd won a trophy himself.

"Zaide?" Layla tilted her head up to him.

"Yes, sweetie?"

"When Savta feels better, can she take me bowling?"

Albert's throat tightened. "Absolutely, Layla." He paused to brush a strand of hair from her face. "She would love to."

Geoffrey walked over and scooped Layla into his arms. She let out a playful scream as he bounced her over his shoulder. They loaded up the car and headed for home.

Albert thought about all the fun Sophie would've had with Layla, had she not fallen ill. Sophie was always involved with the boys' lives when they were little, and having a girl would have brought her a whole new life. A life she always wanted with Abigail, but was never able to have.

Geoffrey and Layla talked about practice and the upcoming trials for her class to advance to the next level. Layla changed topics often—from Sagamore Farm, to cartoons, to friends, to music on the radio, to the sleepover that night. She also talked about Ella, and with more enthusiasm than ever.

Albert said nothing, catching Geoffrey's gaze out of the corner of his eye.

20

The Check

Geoffrey looked himself over in the living room mirror, which hung next to a framed family photo from a family vacation to beach when Geoffrey was fourteen. He slicked back the sides of his hair with a wet hand and smoothed out his eyebrows, then buttoned and unbuttoned his shirt repeatedly, trying to figure out what looked best.

Layla was doing her hair in the bathroom, and Geoffrey knew what a mess that would be. He'd end up fixing it later. Albert had been in the attic for a half hour, going through loose boxes for trophies, as he'd promised Layla. He finally felt satisfied with his appearance for the evening after adjusting his belt one hole tighter.

"Am I losing weight?" he muttered to himself.

He shrugged off the thought, distracted by his phone. He'd been checking every five minutes to see if Rose had called, texted, or emailed, which she hadn't. He considered calling Brandon, to see if he'd heard from his wife, but knew he'd probably been instructed not to tell Geoffrey anything.

What he did receive was his confirmation email from The Inn at Perry Cabin, a famous hideaway in St. Michaels, Maryland, just outside of Annapolis. Nick had been raving about it, and Geoffrey thought it would be a great place to surprise Rose with when she got back. With any luck, it would ease the tension between them. Geoffrey fooled himself with fantasies of spending romantic evenings in the spa with his wife, but he knew it was just a feeble attempt to save their marriage.

Despite not being able to take his mind off Madilyn, he knew he had to work things out with Rose. Whatever issues they had could easily be fixed with expensive pampering, as usual. He made arrangements for Layla to stay at her friend's house that weekend, and had Nick on standby to visit the stores. Everything was covered. He just needed Rose to say yes.

Geoffrey checked his watch and saw that Ella would be there any minute.

"Okay, you guys! Let's go, Ella will be here is a few," Geoffrey shouted, as he once again adjusted his shirt, deciding to leave the top two buttons open.

Layla yelled out that she needed two more minutes, which always meant at least ten. Albert didn't answer. Geoffrey could still hear movement in the attic and was curious about what was distracting him.

He opened the narrow door tucked between two buffets in the dining room that led to the stuffy attic. The stairs were lined with old newspapers and spare tools that hadn't been used in years. Geoffrey felt like a giant stepping on the fragile wood, which seemed to cry out when he applied his weight.

His heart sped up when he realized he was spying on Albert, just as he had in the food store when he caught him talking to Ella. He called out, but Albert didn't answer. Geoffrey could still hear him rummaging through boxes. He called out again, and this time Albert grunted in reply.

"Gramps, I'm coming up!" Geoffrey shouted.

He made his way up the steps, fearing at any second he would fall through. Albert was on one knee tossing aside various items rolled up in newspaper. There were boxes everywhere, stacked higher than Albert. Geoffrey was always impressed by how organized Albert could be after all these years. Even though he rarely threw anything away, he was impeccable when it came to organization.

It was a room full of memorabilia, but he could find anything. Every box was labeled.

Clark Age 0–7, Clark High School, Clark College, Clark Wedding, Geoffrey and David Age 1–5, Geoffrey and David Age 6–10, Geoffrey and David Age 11–18, Geoffrey Graduation, David Graduation, Sophie, Newspapers, Magazines, Kid's Toys, Layla's Stuff, Navy, and so on.

The attic smelled moldy, mainly due to Albert's hoarding. Of all the boxes, Albert was focused on only one. Geoffrey watched as Albert dug through his hidden pile of treasures like Indiana Jones on some kind of adventure. Just like in the movies, Albert raised his hands in victory when he found his prize.

"I got it!" Albert said proudly, holding a four-inch rusted gold plated trophy of a woman wearing a skirt and holding a Duckpin bowling ball.

Geoffrey crept carefully toward Albert, so not to damage any of the boxes stacked up. Any subtle movement would send them crashing down.

"Gramps? You okay up here?"

Albert startled, clenching the trophy to his chest. "You almost gave me a heart attack, you idiot!"

"Sorry. I called your name like a million times," Geoffrey said, steadying him. "What the hell are you doing up here and why aren't you dressed? Damn it, Gramps!"

"What do you mean, I'm dressed just fine." Albert brushed the dust off his shirt and pants.

Geoffrey looked at his grandfather's dirty khakis, slightly stained white shirt, and mussed up hair, thinking he didn't look nice enough to pick up the mail, let alone go to dinner.

"Gramps, you'll have to wear a jacket to wherever we're going. Please change. I'll pick something out."

"Okay fine, whatever. This is more important. You see this?" Albert held up the small trophy in one hand, polishing it with his sleeve with the other.

"It's a trophy."

"This is one of Sophie's trophies from 1977, and I'm going to give it to Layla." Albert eyed the trophy as if it were made of real gold. Geoffrey doubted Layla would find it as fascinating as Albert did.

"That's great, Gramps, but let's go get ready, what do you say?" He held his elbow, trying to guide him along.

"Careful, Geoffrey, this place wasn't made for guys your size," Albert warned as they navigated the narrow pathway.

"Layla couldn't even fit in here," Geoffrey teased.

"I said *be careful*, Geoffrey," Albert repeated, as Geoffrey stumbled.

"I'm trying here, Gramps!"

Geoffrey took too big of a step, and fumbled, knocking over a well-aged cardboard box, causing letters to spill out. It was labeled Church Road—the name of the street Albert grew up on—and it was sandwiched under more recent decades.

Albert leaned over to pick up the letters, and Geoffrey tried to steady himself, pushing more letters out in the process. The box was already broken, and the slightest touch only made it worse. The letters were all sizes and tied together by string in large stacks. Albert slammed down to his knees and started to collect each bundle, seemingly in a panic.

Geoffrey knew Albert could be a neat freak, but this was absurd. Cleaning up old boxes and letters could wait. They had somewhere to be, and he was beginning to think Albert was just stalling.

"Gramps, just leave them. I'll clean them up later."

"No, I got it. I was looking through them the other day, and I need to clean it up anyway." He wrapped his hands around as many bundles as he could.

Geoffrey knelt down to help. "It's no big deal. Here, I'll help you."

"NO!" Albert lost his grip on a dozen stacks in his arms, and they overflowed onto the ground.

"Stop, don't be silly, I'll help you." Geoffrey frowned at him, confused, and reached to grab a stack of letters bound in red twine.

"No, Geoffrey!" Albert shouted, grabbing the letters.

"What's this one, Gramps?" Geoffrey asked, wondering why his grandfather was so frantic over that stack in particular.

"It's *mine*, that's what."

Geoffrey thumbed through the stack and pulled out the bottom letter, held in a weathered leather booklet, creased from the weight of being stored away for so many years, aged with mold spots. It was embossed with an *A* on the front in a curved font.

"What is this, Gramps?" Geoffrey whispered, even more curious than before.

Albert sat on the ground and cradled the letters in his lap. "These . . . these are letters."

"From who?"

Albert lowered his head.

"Wait, are those letters from the military?"

"Some."

"To Sophie? When? How many are there?"

"Hundreds, I suppose." Albert flipped through the stacks in his lap.

"Can I read them?"

"I'd rather you didn't."

Geoffrey looked inside the box. "Then can I see what's in this one?" He indicated the worn leather cover.

"Not now." Albert sounded hesitant.

"Why, Gramps? Why not this one?"

Albert reached out, and Geoffrey handed him the leather packet. It had been tucked at the very bottom of his letters, the oldest piece he had. Albert's hands brushed over the seal, and chips of ink fell off on his fingers.

"I haven't opened this in decades." Albert gasped, his eyes betraying unmistakable sorrow.

"What is it, Gramps?"

Albert said nothing.

"Gramps?"

Albert slowly opened the packet, no bigger than a standard nine-inch long envelope, and revealed a check inside. He looked up with sad eyes.

Geoffrey took the check from his hand. It was shedding loose strands on the edges. The ink was pale, but legible. Geoffrey squinted, trying to read the faded print.

"Collin MacArthur? Ella's father? Why did he write you a check for . . . What? Holy shit! *One hundred thousand dollars!*" Geoffrey showed it to Albert as if he'd never seen it before.

"I never told you the ending to what happened with Ella's father."

Geoffrey patted Albert's back. "It's okay, Gramps. We don't have to do this now."

"Now is fine, Geoffrey. I've taken you this far. You deserve to know the whole story."

21

The Choice

Albert could see it in his eyes; Collin was angry Albert wasn't backing down. The older man frowned and eyed him with increasing distaste, as if something had suddenly occurred to him that would fix everything.

"I have an idea, Albert. How about I make it worth your time?" He paused. "I know you Jews love money, right? So how about I buy you out?" Collin reached in the breast of his jacket and pulled out his checkbook and pen. "How does fifty dollars sound?"

"You can't buy me, Collin," Albert said firmly.

"*Collin?* What happened to *Sir?* Oh, Albert, you sure are a lousy businessman. I'll make it a hundred then."

"Your money means nothing to me," Albert growled, even though fifty dollars was more money than he'd ever seen at one time.

"Really? How about I add another zero to it. What about five hundred?" When Albert remained still, Collin continued baiting him. "One thousand? Ten thousand? Albert, look around you. There is nothing I can't afford."

Albert refused to back down.

"No, no, no, I forgot how greedy your kind is." Collin grinned wide. "This might rock you from your feet, boy . . . How about one hundred thousand dollars, Albert?" He leaned in close to Albert's face. "Now I dare you to tell me my daughter is worth more than that."

One hundred thousand dollars was life-changing money. Albert's parents had never made a tenth of that, and now he was being offered enough money to have whatever he wished. But what he wished for most was a life with Ella.

If Collin were another kid at school or on the street, this wouldn't have gotten past the initial name-calling. Albert was angry with himself for allowing it to go this far. He thought about Ella. He thought about how Collin would interpret the situation back to her. Without waiting for Albert's response, Collin signed the check, folded it, and placed it into Albert's shirt pocket.

"Take this, Albert, and go live your life somewhere else. That's enough money to set you up quite nice, just so long as it's far away from here. Be happy you have that now."

Albert stood with his hands clenched so tightly they were becoming numb. The conversation had just altered his entire life and future. He thought about the kiss goodbye he'd shared with Ella, when he dropped her off earlier, and now he realized it might be their last.

He looked at Collin—a man he'd once planned on calling his father-in-law— and could only think of punching him harder than he'd ever had hit anything before.

"Albert, hear me now, if you ever try to speak to Ella again, she will be dead to us forever. Even one word. If you love her, you'll let her live the life we have planned for her. I have already chosen who Ella will be with, and this man is not you. This man *laughs* at one hundred thousand dollar checks, he doesn't drool over them like you. His family has wealth beyond your comprehension. His parents and I have had this planned for a very long time, my boy. And once our families join together, I will be richer and more successful than I ever thought possible." Collin spread his arms, indicating the surrounding estate. "Look at this! Look at it, Albert! You think *this* is nice? You think this is *enough*? Well it ain't! And I want more.

187

It's business, Albert. Plain and simple. . . You wouldn't understand." Collin reached over and grabbed Albert by his shirt, yanking him like a dog by its collar. "And you will *not* get in the way of that. Never forget that, *kike!*"

Whatever limit Albert had for ignorance had been broken by Collin's remarks, and finally Albert couldn't take another moment of Collin treating him so poorly. He curled his right hand and swung for Collin, who effortlessly stopped him by clenching Albert's wrist with his incredible grasp. Albert screamed in pain, as he felt his wrist slowly snapping from the pressure, but he tried again with his other hand. Collin caught that one as well, after letting go of his shirt and his other arm. Collin pulled Albert forward by his hands, then rammed his thick forehead onto the bridge of Albert's nose, shattering it. Blood shot out from Albert's nostrils, then Collin threw him to the ground.

He landed face first in the tough earth, brushing up dirt into his eyes. His arms and nose throbbed, making it hard to form fists or breathe properly, let alone push himself up to his feet to defend himself. He thought his right wrist might be broken, snapped like a twig from Collin's grip alone. He was just too big and powerful for Albert to fight, but as he tried to get to one knee, Collin punted his legs out from under him and jammed his boot into Albert's ribs repeatedly.

Albert rolled in the dirt with every impact, throwing his body around with each blow. He wrapped his arms around his ribs, probably fractured by now, yet Collin didn't let up. He leaned a knee on Albert's chest, pulled his head up with one hand for a better angle, and slammed into his face with his colossal granite-like fists, over and over.

When Albert was nearly unconscious, Collin stood over him, wiping the blood off his hands with his handkerchief and straightening his jacket and tie.

"*Now* do you understand me, Albert? Take the money, and never come back. If I see you again, I will not be so generous. You'll leave tonight." Collin dug the toe of his boot on Albert's right arm, as if he were stamping out a cigarette in the dirt. "And if you come back . . . I *will* kill you."

***

Albert's head wobbled from side to side. He felt dizzy, as if he was going to pass out. He put his hands on his head and held them against his temples, then squinted and mumbled something.

"Gramps? *Gramps!*" Geoffrey had one knee behind Albert's back and the other on the ground. He rubbed his chest and wiped his forehead. "You there, Gramps? Stay with me!"

It took him a moment to compose himself. The dizziness passed, and he shook his head as if to clear it. He turned and looked at Geoffrey, then wiped his dirty hands on his pants.

A few more moments passed, and Geoffrey asked, "Gramps, he tried to *bribe* you and nearly killed you?"

Albert nodded.

"I can't believe that," he mumbled.

"I . . . I feel okay now. I . . . I should change, you're right. I should change, son." He said it over and over, unable to return to the present. It was as though he was back there again, lying broken on the ground, watching Collin walk away as if nothing had happened.

"You have to show this to Ella," Geoffrey said as he supported Albert.

"I don't know."

"She needs to see this. She needs to see what her own father thought of her."

Albert stopped and placed his hand on Geoffrey's shoulder. "Not now, please."

"Of course, Gramps."

***

Geoffrey took a deep breath as they made their way down to the living room. They changed their tones for Layla's sake upon leaving the attic. Geoffrey could hear Layla watching television in the other room.

"Now, are the Abrahams ready to go all fancy tonight or what?" Geoffrey said, still holding Albert tight. He whispered in his ear, "I got ya, Gramps."

Albert tilted his head toward his grandson, and they touched foreheads gently as a sign of affection. He could always count on Geoffrey.

Layla skipped out of the living room, and they were both surprised to see her hair was in decent shape.

"Daddy, you look so nice!"

"Thank you, my dear. And I think you're the prettiest girl in the world," Geoffrey said.

"Can I have my necklace now?"

Geoffrey grabbed the box from the dining room table, and opened it for Layla. "Of course you can, sweetie. The night wouldn't be complete without some *bling*, as you little kids say."

She lifted her hair up so her father could put the necklace around her neck. Geoffrey couldn't help but think how much this moment reminded him of Rose. Layla had seen Rose put on countless pieces of jewelry over the years, and now it was her turn.

The large gold pendant gently slid against her skin and sat perfectly on her chest. Layla cupped it with her hand in awe of the jewels and decorations, even though she had no idea what she was wearing. The size of a quarter, it was worth far more than any piece of jewelry she would ever own.

Her favorite color was green, so the emerald necklace was even more special to her. The ivory casing around the jewel laced the gold pendant like cable rope securing an anchor to a ship, braided tightly into curls, nestling the jewels with care. Geoffrey had never seen anything so eye-catching and mesmerizing in his life, and he had been around the block when it came to expensive jewelry. One day, Layla might understand what the necklace truly meant—both emotionally *and* financially.

If only she knew she's wearing what I'll end up spending on her first semester of college.

"I feel like a princess!" She spun around in a circle.

"You are," Geoffrey said when she turned to face him. Albert was watching with obvious interest.

She grinned, bobbing the charm in the palm of her hand. When she turned it over after feeling a rough spot on the back, she held it close to her face.

"Daddy?"

"Yes, Layla?" Geoffrey asked as he flattened out the wrinkles on his shirt with his hands.

"What does this say?" Layla asked, holding out the charm.

He knelt down in the light so he could see it better. "It says *Hope Makes the Heart Beat.* That's very pretty."

"What does it mean?"

"I don't know. Maybe it's a poem or song or something?"

"I'll just ask Ella," Layla said, then ran back into the living room.

Geoffrey heard a loud crash from behind, and turned to see Albert gasp loudly as he tried to catch himself on the edge of the dining room table before falling to the floor.

"Gramps!"

Geoffrey wasn't sure why, but as he helped his grandfather to his feet, Albert looked as if he was going to pass out again.

"Gramps, what's wrong?"

He shook his head and mumbled nonsense, just as he had upstairs. Geoffrey put his arms around him to hold him upright.

"I got ya, Gramps. I got ya. You're okay."

"I can't believe she wrote that."

"What's wrong with what she wrote?"

"I can't believe Ella wrote that on Layla's charm." His voice was gravely and dry.

"Why? What does it mean?"

"I can't believe she even remembered that."

"What? What does that *mean?*" Geoffrey pressed.

Albert gave his hand to Geoffrey to steady him, then balanced himself against a chair, breathing slowly and trying to calm down. Those past few days had done a number on his body, and it felt as if every time he had a break, something new hit him with a jolt.

Once again, it was because of Ella. He looked up at him, finding the words to explain.

"Those were the last words I ever said to Ella."

***

Ella's arms were wrapped tightly around Albert's waist as the wind rushed through her long, damp hair. The hour-long ride home on Albert's motorcycle was sometimes more adventurous than their days spent at Cunningham Falls.

Albert sped faster down the open stretch of Camden Road, a flat paved five-mile drive of pure motorcycle bliss, which led to Ella's house. He revved the engine harder and faster, making Ella scream in playful fear of falling off. She clung to him even tighter.

Albert laughed, then shouted over his shoulder. "Hold on, El!"

"Faster, Albey! *Faster!*"

"You got me, baby?" Albert kicked the bike into full speed, whipping around the curves and swinging them down the road.

Albert felt her hands move up his chest, squeezing him closer, as she rested her head against his back. Albert touched her hands with one of his, brought them to his lips, and kissed just as firmly as she held on, as Ella leaned in closer and whispered "I love you" in his ear.

Whether they took Ella's car or Albert's old motorcycle, she would still hold onto him as if every moment was their last.

When they arrived at Ella's house, her mother was waiting on the steps, fixing the flowers that lined their porch. She waved to them, and Albert turned the engine off. The couple held hands as they reached the edge of her driveway.

"Thank you for today, Albey."

"Tomorrow we can go again if you like," Albert said, brushing her wind-dried hair behind her ears.

"I can't wait until tomorrow, Albey. Let's go again tonight."

"Soon Ella, we'll have every day, every *minute* together," Albert promised.

"It can't come soon enough. Will I see you later, after I get home from going into town?"

"I will be here when you get back from shopping with your mother. We can go for another drive. I'll bring the blanket. It should be a nice night for star gazing."

Ella titled her head into Albert's chest. "Albey, how did I get so lucky?"

"Ella, *I'm* the lucky one." He lifted her chin up.

She brought his hand to her chest and held it there gently. Her heart was beating rapidly. "Do you feel that? That's my heart speaking to you. I hope to see you tonight, Albey."

Albert looked at his hand on her chest. Soon he'd ask for the same hand in marriage, and they'd be together forever. He could feel her heart beating faster. His fingers tingled with excitement. He kissed her delicately and with more emotion than ever before. He pulled her in closer by the small of her back, and looked into her eyes.

"Hope, Ella . . . *Hope* makes the heart beat."

They kissed again, neither wanting to stop.

Her mother called her from the steps. They let go of each other, and she rushed back to the house, turning around as she ran, making sure Albert was still watching, which—as always—he was.

***

"Gramps?" Geoffrey said, tapping his arms.

Albert had been silent for several minutes, staring off through the window, lost in thought.

"I'm calling for help right now."

Finally, he turned and put his hand on Geoffrey's phone. "No, son, I'm fine."

Albert slouched over the dining room table on his elbows, his heavy mind weighing his body down. Geoffrey pulled up a chair next to him and leaned in close, putting his arm over his shoulder for support.

"Gramps, you stopped talking. You were about to say something about the inscription."

"It's nothing, son."

"You know, in the past week, every time you say *it's nothing* it tends to be *something*. You nearly went comatose for a couple of minutes. I was seconds away from calling an ambulance."

Albert shook his head.

"Gramps?"

Albert wiped his eyes with his hands.

"What does that saying mean?" Geoffrey asked softly.

Albert lifted his head as if weights were tied to his back and were being cut loose one by one. He parted his lips, exhaling deep. "I can't believe she remembered that."

22

A Rooftop Gala

Layla's excited scream interrupted them, and Geoffrey leapt to his feet when he heard his daughter's name being called from the front door.

Albert was still collecting himself.

When Geoffrey stepped into the living room, he saw Ella at the door and Layla dancing around in excitement as she ushered her inside the house.

"Ella! Ella! Ella!" she shouted, hugging her waist.

Ella bent down to kiss her cheeks. "Well, hello dear, that surely is a nice welcoming."

"I'm wearing your necklace, Ella. Look!" She tilted her chin up to show her the charm.

"Well, I'll be. That looks even better on you than it did on the model in the picture. You *are* a star!"

Geoffrey walked over to greet Ella with a kiss. "Ella, so great to see you. Where's Walter?"

"Oh, he's outside—in the limo." Ella raised her eyebrows at Layla.

"A limo! *Awesome!*" Layla bolted out the door and ran to the car where Walter stood waiting.

The glistening black limousine could easily hold twelve people, and it was so long it dipped over the edge of the driveway into the street. Everything on the car was shining, and it was obvious it was only used for special occasions. The tires hardly looked used, the tread thick and sturdy. Walter opened the back double doors, grinning at Layla's excitement for the big night. He cleared a path for her, allowing her to dive right in. Her voice echoed through the car, and they heard her from the front door.

"A TV, soda, cookies! Daddy, you have to come see this!"

Geoffrey and Ella watched as Walter leaned into the car.

"Did you see the Xbox too?" Walter asked. "Here, check this out."

Suddenly loud pop music was blasting from the impressive sound system.

Ella winked at Geoffrey. "Not exactly Sinatra, but she likes it, right?"

"I don't think she'll want to come out." Geoffrey laughed.

Ella peered around Geoffrey's side to see where Albert was. Geoffrey couldn't help but notice her large diamond encrusted earrings, with her pearl and Safire necklace, matched her dress perfectly. Again, she'd dressed as if she were going to a wedding. For all Geoffrey knew, they might be. In fact, she hadn't told them where they were going at all.

"Where's the elder Abraham this evening?"

Geoffrey turned around, expecting to see Albert behind him in the chair as he was before. "Just freshening up," he guessed. "Here, have a seat and I'll go check on him."

She handed him her sparkling purse, and he carefully placed it on the table. He held her hand as she lowered herself into Albert's couch in the living room, her finery a stark contrast to the shabbiness of the furniture. She rested her manicured fingers over the duct tape that hid the holes in the couch, and waited.

"Ella, I want to thank you for what you did at Cedarmere," Geoffrey said.

"That was nothing." She grinned up at him.

"Seriously Ella, it's hardly nothing. I don't know where to begin to thank you."

"Geoffrey, I am honored to do it."

"Still—"

"Norman and I have donated more money to that place than any other donor ever has. It was about time I cashed in all those good-deed points."

"You're a real character, Ella Perlman." Geoffrey leaned down to kiss her cheek again. "I owe you more than you can imagine."

Ella kissed him back.

"My grandma would be grateful too," Geoffrey said in a soft whisper.

"You don't owe me anything. Your friendship is more than enough, my love."

He patted her on the hand and walked over to Albert's room. Before he could turn the knob, Albert emerged. He had cleaned up and put on the sport coat Geoffrey had laid out. He'd even changed his pants, and his hair was nice and parted. Albert was even clean shaven, which was a milestone in Geoffrey's eyes. For the first time in a long time, Geoffrey saw Albert *dressed up*.

He held his arms out. "Is this good enough?"

"You look great, Gramps! Hold on, I need to get a picture of this." Geoffrey took out his iPhone and added, "Smile!"

"Don't be absurd. Let's go," Albert grumbled, the wrinkles in his face deepening as he grimaced.

They walked into the living room and found Ella flipping through an old photo album Albert kept on the coffee table. She had a wide grin on her face as she delicately turned each page.

She stopped to cough heavily into her handkerchief, then turned back to the album. Both Albert and Geoffrey thought the cough sounded bad, but Ella seemed to treat it as if it were nothing.

Albert cleared his throat.

Ella set the album down. She turned and gasped, her eyes wide. "My-my, Albey, you do look handsome. Like you just walked off the cover of *GQ*!"

"Hardly," Albert said, glancing down at his outfit.

For a moment, Geoffrey thought they resembled a couple of school kids on their first date. "Okay, well," he began, disrupting the moment, "we're all here, so let's go take that puppy for a spin."

"I hope y'all are ready. Walter's been preparing the car all day."

There was a loud, long honk from the car, and then they heard Layla shout, "Daddy, Zaide! Let's go!"

"She's the boss," Geoffrey said, ushering them out of the house. Once Ella had walked ahead of them and was far enough out of earshot, Geoffrey whispered in Albert's ear, "Damn, Gramps, you could have at least hugged her hello."

***

Ella watched as Layla pressed every button she could find and surfed through the channels on the television. Walter humored her with an answer for every question she threw at him.

"Walter, do you always drive this car? Walter, what does this button do? Walter, do you have a limo in pink? Walter, what's your favorite color?"

Geoffrey unsuccessfully tried to wrestle her back into her seat.

Ella sat across from Albert and Geoffrey, bobbing her foot against the floor rapidly—annoyed.

"Albey?"

He turned and looked at her.

"Albey, do you remember when you came over for dinner?"

"Yes."

"Do you remember when I lost my temper slightly?" Ella spoke in a firm voice, not hiding her irritation.

"Yes, I remember."

Geoffrey kept quiet so as not to interrupt them, and Layla occupied herself lowering and raising the windows with the automatic button.

Ella leaned toward Albert, her elbows resting on her knees. She pointed a long bony finger at his face, motioning him closer. "Now, I don't want another episode like that. You hear me?"

"I hear you," he said, slowly leaning back in his seat.

"Good now!" Ella winked, perking up. "I thought so." She pressed the button on the call box by her seat. "Walter, dear, we're almost there, correct?"

"Yes, Mrs. Perlman. Pulling in now," Walter replied over the speaker.

"Good-good-good. I hope y'all like the world's greatest food, because I have a very special night planned for us." Ella rubbed her hands together.

Geoffrey adjusted his sleeves and smoothed out his hair. "Ella, where are we?" he asked, looking out the window at a dark parking garage.

"Well, I'd rather keep you guessing for a bit longer."

Walter opened their doors and held his hands out for Layla and Ella. Their footsteps echoed in the empty garage.

"This way, boys." Ella motioned to Albert and Geoffrey as she walked hand in hand with Layla.

"What the hell is this, son?" Albert tugged on Geoffrey's arm.

"You got me, Gramps."

They entered an elevator and Ella asks Layla to push the button for the eighty-first floor. The doors shut and the elevator rattled up the cables. Albert, somewhat claustrophobic, braced the walls. Geoffrey tapped his hand to keep him calm.

"Oh, Albey, stop your belly aching, you ain't afraid of heights. We used to jump off the old Loch Raven Reservoir bridge all the time," Ella said, rolling her eyes.

Layla laughed into her hands.

The elevator stopped gently, announcing, *"Now entering the rooftop."*

When the door opened, the whipping wind crossed their faces and blew Ella's dress to the side. She caught it with her hands.

"Don't worry, fellas, it's just a small breeze. I got us heat lamps for the evening."

Ella led the way, nodding to Walter, who waited outside the elevator.

When Albert, Geoffrey, and Layla stepped out of the elevator, a bright light blocked their vision momentarily. They could hear the sounds of horns, string instruments, and a piano. The smell of food was overwhelmingly delightful. Old Bay seasoning filled the air, thanks to the crab cakes waiting for them, along with the smoky smell of fresh sirloin to go with it. Ella pushed aside silky white curtains and presented them with the night she had planned.

Albert and Geoffrey gaped when the curtain rooftop finally came into view. An elaborate seven-piece orchestra stood on a stage, ready to begin at a moment's notice. A thick wooden dance floor was in the middle, large enough for thirty people. A man on a unicycle appeared out of nowhere juggling three balls, then hopped off to give Layla a flower he pulled out of his sleeve.

Waiters approached them one by one presenting mini crab cakes, pieces of steak, chicken, fish, sushi, and even small chicken fingers for Layla. The heat from the food was intense—as if it had just came out of the oven the second they arrived. Seasoned to perfection, and not missing an ounce of detail in the presentation, the appetizers were far better than any entrée Albert had in years. Fresh, salty popcorn overflowed from a vintage 1950s movie theater style machine, with a young woman dressed as an usher ready to dish out the treat. Next to her was a vibrant display of colors and flavors flowing from a cotton candy machine with a male attendant dressed to match. The two ushers simultaneously tipped their hats to Layla who broke free of Geoffrey and ran over.

"Now this is a party!" Ella exclaimed. "Right, y'all?"

Geoffrey put his arm around Albert. "This could be the wildest party I've ever been to, Gramps. Where are we, Ella? *Oz?*"

"Oh no, my dear, this is no fairytale, this is actually happening. We are on the very top of the Ritz-Carlton. They don't usually hold such events like this, but . . ."

"Let me guess, you know someone?" Geoffrey said.

"You're picking up a pattern on how I work, huh?" Ella winked.

Albert passed on the fish, steak, and chicken but finally obliged on the crab cakes. He walked slowly through the maze of staff who moved to their stations on the edge of the roof, waiting for Ella's instructions. For a small party of four, Ella had over a dozen staff, plus musicians.

"Gentleman, I hope you like the best food in the world, with the greatest view in the city. Because that's what we've got tonight." She curtsied, then turned her back and waved to an imaginary crowd, as if being applauded by thousands.

"Bravo, bravo, Ella! This is incredible." Geoffrey turned to Albert and slapped him on the back. "Look at this place!" He wrapped his arms around Ella, and she hugged him tighter.

Ella stepped back and looked up at him. "Geoffrey, dear, did you try the steak yet? It's the finest cut of Kobe you'll ever have. I had it flown in this morning."

"I'm on it, Ella. I will never turn down good steak," Geoffrey said, as a waiter swiftly approached with a full plate. Layla dashed over and pulled him to the popcorn machine before he had a chance to dig in.

Ella watched as Albert sunk his hands deep into his pockets as usual and let his gaze skip across the evening skyline.

"I hope you like this, Albey." She held out her hand, but he didn't even look at her.

Despite their past, fate had allowed them to come together once again. She'd been nothing but nice to him and his family, and she couldn't understand why he wouldn't open up. She'd saved his wife's life, given his great-granddaughter a necklace that most people would kill for, and she'd thrown a party in his honor. Ella's confusion deepened as she felt the effects of her six decade long heartbreak.

"Do you like what I've done, Albey?"

He managed a small smile. "Yes, it's very nice."

"Just *nice*?"

"What do you want me to say?"

Her frustration took over and she was losing her temper, quicker than she'd expected. She placed her hands on her hips, and although she didn't raise her voice, she kept her tone direct.

"What now, Albey? Why is it always two steps back with you?"

"I'm sorry, Ella. That's not what I meant."

"Then take my hand." As she reached out, the city lights ricocheted off her diamond rings.

Albert took a step closer but didn't take her hand.

"Well now, at least we're getting somewhere," Ella said. "I won't bite."

Then he reached out with a bent arm, elbow first. Ella walked closer and looped her hand through.

"All right then, I'll take that. Now, let's go try some good food, shall we?"

They tasted at different stations, each waiter approaching them before they could get close enough. Albert took a small piece and immediately his eyebrows rose.

"Albey, you like it don't you?"

"Yes, I do. This is incredible." He dove in for another bite.

"I knew you would." She gently patted his arm. "Albey?"

"Yes." He spoke between bites.

"I was wondering . . . would you like to dance with me?"

He stopped chewing as if he'd just bit down on a bone.

"No . . . I mean, not right now," he stammered.

"But maybe later? Just one dance, Albey?" She rubbed his arms gently, almost too afraid to touch him.

"I, uh, I'm not a very good dancer."

Ella thought back to the photo album at his house. In one of the photos, he'd looked so happy dancing with Sophie. She wanted to know what that was like, if only for a moment.

"Oh, it's okay, I don't mind. Just one dance. Please?"

He looked over her shoulder at Geoffrey and Layla dancing in front of the band. She stood on Geoffrey's shoes as he held her hands and moved his feet to the music. She laughed as she tried to keep her balance and when Geoffrey lifted her high in the air for a spin, she let out a rowdy laugh.

"Daddy, higher!"

"Maybe," Albert finally mumbled.

"Well, that's better than a no." Ella smirked.

She heard someone coming from behind and when she turned, she saw it was Madilyn. "Maddy! Oh, Maddy, I'm so glad you could make it!"

She wrapped her arms around her, then stepped back to admire Madilyn's long black dress. It was cut low on her chest, but modestly worn, and brushed close to her toned body.

"Oh, Maddy, you look lovely."

"Thank you, Grandma." The wind tucked Madilyn's smooth brown hair against her wide smile.

Ella and Madilyn hugged again, swaying side to side. Ella kissed her cheeks over and over again.

"Grandma, cut it out," Madilyn joked.

"Oh, don't think just because you are all grown up I can't kiss you!" Ella laughed. "Come, I want to show you off." She pulled her granddaughter by the hand, and they approached Albert.

"So great to see you again, Albert," Madilyn said, hugging him.

"Maddy, I've been trying to get Albey to hug me for a week now and *nothing*! I guess you like 'em young, Albey," she said, trying to get a rise out of him.

"Grandma, come on, you're going to embarrass him. You look quite dapper tonight, Albert," Madilyn said, rubbing the side of his arm. She turned to Ella. "You really outdid yourself."

"If you're not trying to outdo yourself every day, than you're simply wasting your time. That's my motto. Plus, I'll do whatever I gotta do to get this big lug to give me some of his time." Ella bumped his side with her hip. "Ain't that right, Prince Charming?"

Albert nodded uncomfortably and managed a small smile out the corner of his mouth.

***

Geoffrey and Layla heard the commotion, and when they turned to see what was going on, Geoffrey nearly tripped over his own feet when he saw Madilyn.

"Daddy, who is that?"

"That's Ella's granddaughter." He almost let go of Layla's hands, as the whole world around him seemed to disappear. "Would you like to say hi?"

Before Layla could answer, Ella waved them over.

"Geoffrey Abraham, this is my lovely granddaughter Madilyn."

Holding Layla on his left side, he reached out with his right hand. A shiver passed over him when his fingers touched Madilyn's.

"Yes, we've met actually. At your store one day," Geoffrey said.

"It's good to see you again." Madilyn blushed.

"Well, well . . . looks like y'all can catch up again." Ella winked.

Layla reached out her hand the same way Ella had for Albert—arm straight and wrist bent. "I'm Layla!"

"It is a pleasure to meet such a pretty lady with such a *very* nice necklace . . . *Grandmother?*" Madilyn looked over at Ella again.

"I'm sorry, boys, I didn't tell you before, but I wanted Madilyn to be a surprise," Ella said, ignoring the comment about the necklace.

"Yes! Surprised. Very nice to see you again," Geoffrey said nervously as he set down Layla.

"Geoffrey." Albert lightly smacked his arm.

Layla reached over and grabbed a hold of Madilyn's dress. "Madilyn, do you like cotton candy?"

"Who doesn't?"

"Good. Follow me!"

"Don't mind us!" Madilyn called behind her as she ran off with Layla.

"She's gorgeous, isn't she?" Ella said quietly to Geoffrey.

"I, uh . . . *Wow*." Geoffrey ran his hands through his choppy hair.

They watched as Layla and Madilyn giggled while they fed each other gobs of cotton candy and popcorn. Madilyn glanced back at Geoffrey, then knelt down to talk to Layla.

Geoffrey turned when he heard Walter's voice.

"I'm so sorry to bother you, Mrs. Perlman, but you have a call."

"A call?"

"From your *colleague*." He leaned into her ear to whisper.

"Oh *yes*, the call I've been waiting for. Must be my overseas distributors, they are always calling at odd hours. It's probably breakfast in Hong Kong. Geoffrey, Albert, go enjoy the food and festivities, and I'll be right back."

Walter put his arm around Ella and escorted her out through the curtains.

Geoffrey checked his phone but no one aside from Nick had called him.

"Nothing?" Albert asked.

"I was just checking about a deal coming through."

"Sure, son."

"I should go let Madilyn enjoy herself and relieve her from Layla."

"Oh, shut up, Geoffrey. I got her. Go talk to Madilyn and try not let your tongue hit the ground this time."

"What are you talking about?" Geoffrey snapped, knowing full well what he meant.

He pulled out his phone again and walked to the edge of the rooftop, on the opposite end of the band, where it was quiet. He looked out at the skyline of downtown Baltimore and felt guilty for forgetting how majestic the city was this time of year.

The Domino Sugar Factory sign illuminated the harbor, its neon reflection dancing across the water. Small motorboats zipped across the dark water, alongside the taxi boats that bounced between Fell's Point and Harbor Place. Music could be heard from various venues all around, as hundreds of people flocked to the harbor's shops and restaurants like sea gulls taking a break from the still waters of the Chesapeake Bay.

Growing up, his father and grandfather would take Geoffrey and David to the harbor for hotdogs and gourmet sweets, like homemade fudge from the famous Fudge Factory. Geoffrey could still remember the taste, and even recalled the variety of flavors he'd chosen from. All four of them would pile into paddleboats, and tour around the bay. Then they'd walk to Federal Hill and have a picnic at the top where Geoffrey and his brother could use the playground for hours on end. It was their routine, and they'd loved it.

As he reminisced, Geoffrey dialed Rose's number, hoping to catch her before she headed out for wherever she might be going that night. Wherever she was, Rose was certainly going out for the night. For quite some time he had accepted her lack of interest in him, but her recent behavior was bothering him more than ever.

No worries, all can be saved, he reassured himself. *She'll love the weekend I have planned.*

Rose's phone went right to voice mail, and he wondered where she was. She never skipped out like that—not so fast anyway. He usually heard from her.

"Rose, hey, it's Geoff. Listen, I'm just wondering how you're doing, and really *what* you're doing too? But you wouldn't believe where I am right now. It's a long story that I'm sure you'll love to hear! Call me soon, please. I have a surprise for you. I love you, Rose. Call me." The phone beeped—*end of message.*

"Is everything all right?"

Geoffrey turned on his heel, his phone in his hand. "Madilyn. Hi there. I had a call from one of my partners. Just checking in." He slipped the phone back into his pocket, admiring her appearance. *Simply gorgeous.*

"You have a very nice family, Geoffrey." She smiled, glancing over her shoulder at Albert and Layla.

"Thank you. Sorry about Layla dragging you around."

Madilyn giggled, her green eyes shining like the stars over the harbor. "She's a sweetheart, and a lot fun. I don't mind at all."

Geoffrey smiled knowingly.

"Okay if I join you?" she asked, motioning to a spot near the ledge.

"Oh yes, of course!"

They leaned on the edge in silence for moment, gazing out at the city.

"Can I ask you something?" Geoffrey said.

"Anything."

"This evening . . . Is this something your grandmother does often?"

"Well, for just five people, I guess it's a bit overboard, but it doesn't surprise me."

"She's very generous."

"Always has been," Madilyn agreed. "When I was ten years old, my softball team had an end of the year party. We were supposed to have it at her house, since everyone loved it there, with the normal kids things like pizza, soda, and stuff like that. But when we all arrived, this giant bus, like what rock stars travel in, pulled up, and she told us all to pile in. Next thing we knew, we were at Camden Yards. We had a picnic and got to run around for hours. Hands down, one of the best days of my life. I mean, we were ten! Who gets to do that?"

"That's amazing. What's more remarkable is that with a single call, I think she might have extended my grandmother's life for an extra fifteen years." Geoffrey sipped his wine, not bothering to explain.

"Wow. That does sound like something she would do," Madilyn said.

"All in a day's work, right?"

Madilyn turned around and leaned her back against the brick ledge, as she sipped her red wine, then curled the glass to her chest. "Okay. My turn. I have a question for you."

"Shoot."

"Remember our homework? Turns out your grandfather really broke my grandmother's heart over sixty years ago. Why?"

"It's complicated."

"So he told you? We had a deal, Geoffrey."

"I know. I just found out myself."

"I hope he tells my grandmother."

"I do as well."

They watched Albert and Layla feed each other pieces of chocolate cake from the dessert table as the music continued to play in the background.

Madilyn tilted her head to the side and put her glass down on the ledge. "Geoffrey, do you dance?"

A tremor passed through him. *Those magical green eyes.* How could he say no?

"Not at all." Geoffrey winked. "But I don't care if you don't."

207

He took Madilyn's hand and they walked in the middle of the dance floor, past Albert and Layla. The band played a soft ballad with subtle horns and light strings. As if they'd danced a thousand times before, Geoffrey and Madilyn fell into one another effortlessly. Madilyn draped her delicate arm around Geoffrey's neck, and he wrapped his hands around her waist, running one hand up her back, then back down to her waist. The tips of her fingers gently skated across his neck. They had only known each other for a few days, but something internal told them both this was meant to be something more than friendship.

Despite their closeness, they both knew he was a married man—unattainable. They held each other close affectionately, but refused to move beyond that. Still, their eyes met, and without words exchanged, their connection was secure. Sometimes the eyes said more than a mouth ever could.

***

Albert couldn't help but watch them dance together. He liked Madilyn very much. She seemed familiar to him, and he knew why. Madilyn was just as breathtaking as Ella had been when Albert first met her. He remembered telling his friends he was in love after only one date. They kidded him, but anyone who knew Ella fell in love with her. Now, for the first time in a long time, he saw Geoffrey with a woman who appreciated him—Madilyn.

"Well, look at this couple! Take a picture, Albey," Ella shouted, making a grand entrance. "Oh never mind, I'm sure you don't have a camera anyway, but I have one on my BlackBerry." The image of Geoffrey and Madilyn holding one another was framed on her cell phone screen before she took the picture. "It's like something out of a magazine, Albey, wouldn't you say? I know the editor of Baltimore Bride Magazine. I can make a call, hold a spot for them."

Albert rolled his eyes, thinking of Ella's many contacts she kept at her disposal. "I don't think that's necessary."

"Oh, good Lord, Albey, I was just joking with you. But, let's be honest, they do make a good couple."

Albert couldn't disagree there.

"Layla, if your Zaide won't dance with me, will you?" Ella asked.

"Let's go!" She bounced up and down on a sugar rush from the cotton candy and chocolate.

Ella walked Layla onto the dance floor and ordered the band to "turn it up". She bent down, holding Layla's hands and swinging them side to side. Geoffrey and Madilyn separated and attempt a swing dance, sliding each other around, scooting across the floor the best they could.

"Come on, Gramps!" Geoffrey yelled over the music, still holding Madilyn's hand.

They all motioned for Albert to come onto the floor, but he was more comfortable by the dessert bar.

"Come on, Zaide! Zaide, dance!"

Albert smiled but only shook his head.

Layla ran over and pulled Albert grudgingly onto the dance floor. "Zaide, dance with us."

Albert followed her, but didn't dance so much as he stood and watched. Geoffrey managed a couple of moves, but it was clear his focus was on Madilyn. She danced next to Albert, getting him to move at least a little bit. The band blasted through another fast song, a New Orleans infused jazz piece.

Suddenly Ella stepped backward as if she was going to fall, and Geoffrey caught her quickly from behind.

"Ella, are you okay?" Geoffrey asked, catching his breath.

"Oh dear, are you trying to put a move on me, Geoffrey?" Ella fanned herself, but it was clear she was a little dizzy.

"Grandma, why don't you sit down?" Madilyn offered.

There were droplets of blood on Ella's bottom lip.

"Sit? Now? Not a chance. Albey was just getting ready to ask me to dance." Ella steadied herself and wiped her mouth. "Fellas, play us something a little calmer now," she told the band.

Albert waved his hands. "No. I'm not a good dancer, Ella."

"Albey, what did we talk about in the car?"

Albert pressed his lips firm and took tiny hesitant steps toward the middle of the floor. Ella stood with her arm extended, waiting for him. Geoffrey, Madilyn, and Layla watched as Albert moved slowly toward her, his palms sweating.

The last time he'd danced with Ella, he was seventeen at his cousin's wedding. Ella looked stunning that night. But that was a different time and Albert was much older and more fragile—both physically and emotionally. These days he didn't dance. Without Sophie, there was no reason.

Geoffrey nudged him along.

"See, that isn't any trouble now is it?" Ella placed her hands behind his neck. Albert's reflexes caused him to bring his neck down and forward in a quick jerk, just from her touch alone. "It's okay, Albey. I won't bite."

Albert wiped his brow and rubbed his hands dry on his shirt before stepping on Ella's toes as he approached. "I'm sorry. I don't know if I can do this." He was too afraid to meet Ella's gaze.

"Just come on in, you can." She reached out. "I'll just hold your hands in mine."

Albert jumped back, covering his mouth. "No. No, I can't do this."

"Gramps, it's cool," Geoffrey said.

"No, this isn't right." Albert stared at the ground, then looked back at Geoffrey and Ella. He hurried through the curtain, toward the exit.

Albert leaned up against the elevators—his only source of escape—and closed his eyes. Small tears fell from the corners of his eyes.

"Sophie. I'm so sorry, Sophie."

"Albert? Can I come through?" Ella called out from the other side of the curtain.

"I'm fine. I'll be out in a bit." He spoke hoarsely, trying to hide his anguish.

"I didn't mean to upset you, Albey. I was wrong. I shouldn't have forced you to dance."

Albert turned his back to Ella and balled his fists, embarrassed and frustrated. Ella was being so generous, and he couldn't thank her enough. He couldn't thank her until he was completely honest with her.

"Albey, is it okay if I come in? I need to see your face."

Albert still couldn't gather the strength to allow her in.

"Albey, please . . ." She walked through the curtain and approached him. "Albey, please turn around."

His head was down, chin tucked to his chest. "I appreciate everything you did for Sophie, Ella. Please understand that."

"I was happy to."

"It isn't necessary."

"But it's done and I would do it again heartbeat. I'd do anything for you and your family."

Heartbeat. The word stormed through his mind.

"And the necklace." He shook his head. "It's way too much."

Ella chuckled. "Honestly, Albey, *that* really wasn't too much. Well, not for me anyway."

He tilted his head upward.

"Albey, what is it?"

"Do you want to know why I left?"

And there it was, dropped like the thousand pound weight that had rested on his shoulders for six decades. The topic Ella had wanted to discuss for more than half her life. Now she would find out. Now she would have her answers.

"More than anything, Albey. More than anything ever! Please turn around."

"I can't do that. But I will tell you."

"Do I need to sit down?"

Albert breathed in and out slow and heavy. "Ella, the last day I saw you, when I dropped you off, I wanted to ask you something. I'm sure you know what it was. We talked about it that day. But I wanted to wait, to do it properly and ask your father." He paused, then bent at his waist and rose back up again, breathing in deep. "So I went back to your house, while you were in town with your mother."

"You went there for what, Albey?"

"Ella, I needed to ask your father for his blessing. His blessing that I could marry you."

"Oh, dear. I *do* need to sit down." She leaned against the wall by the curtains.

He turned slowly to face her. *No more holding back*, he told himself. For this, he had to face her. He owed that to her. His eyes were brimming with tears, red and swollen. His hands were folded in front of his belly.

"When I asked your father, he said 'no'. He didn't even give it a thought."

"That doesn't sound like him, Albey. He always liked you. What did he really say? His *words*."

Albert made sure to look directly into Ella's eyes this time. "Ella . . . This is so hard. Your father offered me one hundred thousand dollars to leave you and never see you again."

"What?"

"He tried to buy me out of your life," he explained, choking up again.

"What in the world, Albey? You must be kidding me!"

He held his hand up and walked closer to Ella. "Please. Let me finish. I didn't want it. I didn't spend it. Ever. That wasn't the issue."

"*One hundred thousand dollars*? Back then? That's like a million now! My father would not have offered you that much money just to leave me. He knew how much you meant to me."

"I told him to keep the money, that no money could ever make me leave you. But he said if I ever came back to your house and saw you again, he would cut you out of the family. You would be—" He feared this part would be most difficult for her to accept. "You would be *dead* to him if I returned." Albert lowered his head.

She crossed her hands over her chest. "That is absurd, my own father would never speak like that. Cut me out of the family? That's outrageous!"

"It's true, Ella."

"A father would not do that to his daughter."

"He called me a *kike*."

"He did what?"

"He said he would never allow you to marry a *kike*. It's a derogatory term--"

"I know what the word means, Albey!" Ella said cutting him off. "But he would never say such a thing!"

"He taunted me, he belittled me. He made me feel like less than a man. Like I wasn't worthy of anything. It's *true*." He begged Ella to believe him.

She refused. "It can't be true. My father never had a problem with you being Jewish."

Albert dropped his hands, his face empty and pale. He had finally opened up, and she would have none of it. This was what he had feared most.

"You have to understand how much I loved you. I was just as shocked as you are. He called me names. He told me I had *horns* and a *tail,* that Jews only like money, and that's why he was paying me to leave."

She turned her back and tapped her foot fast and hard. She coughed into her handkerchief harsher than before, leaning one hand against the wall for support. Albert reached for her to steady her, but she pulled away, leaned over, and coughed louder.

"Ella, this is why I didn't want to tell you. That's why I left. I did it for *you*!" He opened his hands to her, offering himself to her for the time.

Ella whipped around, her eyes running with tears, makeup collecting in dots on her face, blood smeared on her chin from the cough.

"*This* is how you make up for leaving me? To make up some bullshit story about my father being a *racist?*"

"Ella, please, you have to believe me!"

"If you didn't love me, if you didn't want to marry me, then you should have just said so!"

"Ella, he beat me! He beat me to the point of unconsciousness. With his bare hands, he broke my eye socket and my nose. He took his boots and rammed them into my ribs until they cracked in half. He broke my wrist. He was relentless, Ella. I couldn't even defend myself!"

"Stop it, Albert."

"I was in the hospital for a month and on bed rest for three!"

"You're lying to me, Albert. That couldn't have happened," Ella shouted.

"You have to believe me!" Albert screamed, tears in his eyes, nearly out of breath.

"Wow, Albert, that's quite the story." Ella dried her eyes with her bloody handkerchief, shaking her head in total shock and disbelief. "Over sixty *Goddamned* years I waited and wondered about where you were and why you never came back. I thought you were dead!"

"Ella, please, I had no choice," Albert begged, reaching out to her.

She pulled away, pacing back and forth. "Oh, you had a choice! You could have written. You could have called. If you wanted me to keep it a secret, I would have. But you lied!"

Albert could feel his blood pressure rising. He tried to do his breathing exercises but his heart was racing too fast to settle down. "Your father said he wouldn't have allowed it, Ella. It was the hardest decision I've ever had to make. Please, you must understand."

"You want to call my dead father a bigot, all because you couldn't tell me you just never loved me in the first place?"

That hurt Albert the most. "Never loved you? Ella, that's crazy. You can't really think that, can you?"

"I don't know what to believe, Albert. I guess I never knew who you were. I should have never tried to get to know you now, either." Her voice was tinged with blatant disgust.

Geoffrey's voice came from the other side of the curtain. "I'm coming in, you two, no funny stuff. I hope you're decent, Gramps!"

Ella waved him off. "Don't you worry, Geoffrey. Nothing is going on here. I'm done. I'm going to find Walter. I'd like to go home now."

Albert reached for her hand. "Ella, please don't do this."

She pulled away, then smoothed her dress and quickly patted her face dry with a silk napkin she had in her purse. She caught Geoffrey's gaze.

"I think it might be best if we call it a night." Ella's best attempt to appear as if nothing had happened was lost. She pulled Geoffrey's face to hers to kiss him on the cheek. "Geoffrey, I hope you had a fun time tonight, and always know you can call on me for anything."

"Ella, I'm sorry. But I think Gramps isn't explaining—"

Ella patted his chest. "He's said enough, Geoffrey. He's said enough." Ella looked over at Albert who stood quiet, ashamed, with his head down and hands out, still waiting for her. "Goodbye, Albert. I'm sorry for trying to involve myself in your life. Clearly, I was wrong."

She walked through the curtain and disappeared into the dark night.

Geoffrey rushed over to Albert. "Gramps, what happened?"

"Exactly what I figured would happen." He watched the silk curtain waver in the wind and brush away the memories of Ella one last time, knowing he would never see her again after this.

"Did you tell her about the check?"

"Yes."

"And?"

"And *what,* son? Look what happened!"

"She wasn't pissed off about it?"

"I told you she wouldn't believe me, Geoffrey."

"But did you tell her you'd show it to her?"

"Geoffrey, it doesn't matter anymore."

"Come on, you have to do *something.* She'll believe you if you show it to her."

"It's over! I told you this is a bad idea. I told you, and you didn't want to listen."

"Gramps, you can't leave things like this."

Albert charged forward, and yanked on his grandson's shirt. "Drop it! *Look!* Look at what happened!"

Geoffrey pulled back in shock, then told him to wait while he got Layla and excused himself for the evening. Ella was standing close to the ledge by the band that had now begun packing up. Her back was turned as Geoffrey watched her. He saw her hand rise to her face and lower again as she sobbed.

Madilyn walked over with Layla, after Layla hugged Ella goodbye. "Well, this ended up being a rather interesting evening," Madilyn said, raising her eyebrows in confusion.

"Please tell Ella I'm sorry. And Gramps is sorry too."

"Don't worry, Geoffrey, I'll talk to her. We'll work this out."

Geoffrey picked up Layla, and she wrapped her arms and legs around him as he rubbed her back. "You ready to go, kiddo?" Layla nodded yes, her head tucked against his neck. The sugar rush had died down and she was sleepy.

"Madilyn, listen I uh . . . I hope I'll see you again. I mean, I think we have a lot to talk about." Geoffrey tilted his chin toward Ella, whose shoulders rose and fell slowly, still visibly shaken.

Madilyn reached in for a hug. "Yes, I would like that very much."

When Madilyn pulled back, Geoffrey stared at her again. He didn't speak, he just watched her. She didn't move either. Their eyes locked. She smiled the way Geoffrey wished Rose would smile at him.

"Daddy, can we go now?"

"Yes, baby. We're leaving. Goodbye, Madilyn."

"Goodbye, Geoffrey," she said, before going to Ella. Geoffrey watched as she put her arm around her grandmother, pulling her close. Ella turned into Madilyn's chest and continued to cry. Geoffrey saw her reactions first hand and found it hard to believe that after everything, after the past Ella and Albert shared, all was lost again.

***

Walter met Albert by the elevators and offered to drive them home, but Albert insisted on a taxi. The ride home was quiet. He rested his head against the window, motionless. Layla slept on Geoffrey's lap. The taxi rolled up Albert's house, and he climbed out without preamble, slamming the door hard. He shuffled through the rocks in the driveway, kicking up dust in front of him. Geoffrey paid the driver and held Layla against his chest.

"Gramps, I'm going to drop Layla off at Mackenzie's house, I'll be back in a half hour."

Albert nodded his head as he took his keys out to open the door, when a voice called out to Geoffrey.

"Geoffrey Abraham?"

Geoffrey blocked the car's bright lights with his hand as he turned around. A narrow silhouette appeared through the blinding glare.

"Are you Geoffrey Abraham?"

"Yeah. Who are you?" Geoffrey replied, unsure why the man was there late at night.

The man approached Geoffrey, and handed him a manila envelope.

"Mr. Abraham, you've been served."

23

Now It's Your Turn

For the first night in a long time, there were no nightmares, no bathroom breaks—just sleep. When he finally opened his eyes, he realized the picture of Sophie from his nightstand was face up on the bed next to him, on *her* side of the bed. He remembered clutching it to his chest as he fell asleep. Then he thought of last night.

The evening was a disaster and went the way he figured it would go if he ever told Ella about her father. Albert recalled arguing with Geoffrey, and then coming home to see him being handed papers by a mysterious man. He was either being sued or getting a divorce. He hoped for the latter. Geoffrey didn't say much afterward, but when Albert said goodnight to him, he was sitting on the couch, staring at the envelope in his lap.

Albert climbed out of bed still fully dressed from the night before. He looked at his sweats on the floor, and thought, *why bother?*

He was more concerned with Geoffrey. But knowing his grandson, he was probably on the phone with his team of lawyers, three coffees deep, preparing for the day. But when Albert left his room, there was only the aroma of his stale house—not the smell of European coffee he had anticipated.

The newspapers weren't laid out on the table and there was no sign in the kitchen that Geoffrey had been cooking anything. When he reached the living room, he found Geoffrey sitting there as he had been the night before, staring out the window in front of him, the envelope still in his lap. *Has he even slept?*

"Son, you okay?"

"Yeah, Gramps," Geoffrey mumbled, his lips hardly moving.

"Have you been up all night?"

"Yup."

"Geoffrey, you're wearing the same thing you had on last night? Have you moved at all?"

"Paced for a bit . . . but after that, I've pretty much been doing this for the entire time. Well, actually, it's been eight hours and twenty-seven minutes of doing *just* this. I've been counting." He remained motionless, his arms resting on the pillows beside him for support, as if the softest breeze would push him over.

Albert lowered himself onto the couch beside him. He sat on something hard, and when he pulled the object out, he found a pillbox.

"Son, tell me what this really is," Albert said, holding it out. "Geoffrey, what did you take?"

His grandson shook his head. His lips began to quiver but he remained focused on the window.

"Geoffrey, look at me."

He turned his head. His eyes were bloodshot, and heavy bags hung beneath them. He'd never looked so gaunt before.

Albert grabbed his face in his hands. "Geoffrey?"

No answer, just a blank stare.

"Geoffrey!"

Again, nothing.

"I'm calling 911!" Albert reached for the phone, but before he could get to it, Geoffrey caught his arm.

"It's okay, Gramps. I didn't take anything. *Today,* that is. Or last night."

"What?"

"You were honest with me, I'll be honest with you."

Albert leaned back into the couch. "Okay, son. Okay."

"Gramps?"

"Yes, Geoffrey."

"You want to go for a drive?"

***

Albert drove this time, which was a definite change of pace. He felt awkward in the large SUV, worried he may wreck it. But Geoffrey adjusted the seat and told him where all the buttons were.

When they stopped at the railroad tracks on Warren Road for the Light Rail train, Albert called Cedarmere with Geoffrey's hands-free phone that spoke out of the car's stereo system. He couldn't help but yell as if the hospital was at the cusp of a mountaintop and he was far below.

"Gramps, they can hear you fine," Geoffrey assured him. "Just talk normally."

As they hoped, Sophie was well. She was sleeping well, and she was about to get a massage. Her new situation was bittersweet. They were worried that after last night Ella might've made some calls to have Sophie moved back, but she hadn't. As they drove past Ella's house, neither said a word or looked in her direction. Geoffrey navigated, and Albert obeyed.

"Do you want to start, son?"

"The envelope from last night—"

"They're divorce papers, aren't they?"

Geoffrey nodded.

"I'm sorry to hear that, son." Albert tried to keep his eyes on the road, but wanted to look at him as he spoke.

His grandson chuckled. "Who are we kidding, Gramps? You and I both knew it was coming. I tried to ignore it, but I knew. I'm such a fool."

"Geoffrey, go easy on yourself. A fool wouldn't have a clue."

220

"No, Gramps, a fool is someone who tries to convince themselves that what they see isn't real. My therapist told me that."

"So what were you trying to convince yourself?"

"That she wasn't cheating on me." Geoffrey kept his eyes on the scenery passing by. Albert felt his shame, but wanted to keep him talking.

"Earlier this year, I hired a P.I. that David uses for his cases. I told David it was for a business deal that went south. Kind of the truth." Geoffrey breathed in deep and let out a sigh. "The guy came back with a folder full of pictures of Rose and this douchebag she works with. Even then, I didn't want to believe it, but a photo is worth a thousand words, right? Well, I was speechless to say the least. He said he would keep following her, but I had already seen enough."

"How long did this go on?"

"I don't know, a month? A year? Maybe our whole marriage. I confronted her, but she denied it. Of course she would."

Albert turned down a side road to avoid heavy traffic along 83 South. "Why didn't you show her the photos?"

"Why didn't you show Ella the check?" Geoffrey retorted.

Albert didn't respond. He kept his eyes forward and focused on the road.

"Sorry, Gramps. I don't know why. I wanted to see if she would try to tell me the truth. She didn't though." He was quiet for a moment, then wiped his eyes.

"Son, you okay?"

"Yeah." Geoffrey's voice cracked. "I was willing to make it work, Gramps, for Layla's sake. I'm almost forty years old, and I'm the only one of my friends who isn't divorced yet. The only one. You know that? I mean, all these wealthy guys just threw money at their problems and it didn't work. But me? I thought we could be part of the small percentage of people who remember their vows."

"Geoffrey, divorce is not the end of the world." Albert patted his leg with a gentle hand.

"I know. But how the hell do I explain it to Layla? Rose is going to take her away from me, Gramps."

"We won't let that happen."

Geoffrey dragged his finger across the frigid window, making waves through the frost.

Albert watched a tear fall from his chin, which Geoffrey didn't bother to catch. He knew his grandson was vulnerable but he still had questions. He still had concerns.

"And the pills, Geoffrey?"

"They're prescription."

"You have a very generous doctor."

His grandson grinned in reply.

Albert drove past an old coffee shop that sat off the side of York Road, heading north into southern Pennsylvania. He cut right down Phoenix Road. He needed privacy and knew that was the only way to get Geoffrey to open up about his drug use.

"It's not what you think, Gramps."

"Seems pretty evident to me."

"I'm not a drug addict." His voice was calm and even.

"Are you sure?"

"I don't think I am, at least. Not in the way you probably think." Geoffrey took off his sunglasses and placed them in the cup holder. "You know, before yesterday, I took ten to twelve pills a day."

"That sounds like an addiction to me."

"It's fine, really," Geoffrey said, rubbing his knees. "But the oddest thing happened. Last night when I got the papers, I didn't take any. The entire night, I didn't take *one* pill. I *wanted* to. I should have. *Normally*, I would. But I didn't."

Albert wasn't sure he believed him. *How can a person go from a dozen pills a day, to none at all?*

"Geoffrey, why did you come to my house to stay rather than go to your other homes or even a hotel?"

"I thought you'd like it."

"I did, and I do. But you could have easily just visited during the day. My house is the size of your bedroom at the beach house, and as you so nicely pointed out, my food is hardly up to par with the hotels you usually stay in. Let alone you don't even fit on my couch."

Geoffrey raised his eyebrows. "Well, that's true."

"So why?"

Geoffrey stared out the window and said nothing.

Albert continued heading toward an old fishing spot along the North Country Railroad stream, where he used to take Clark and the boys when they were little. He parked the car and rolled down the window, then closed his eyes, taking in the symphony of the shallow waters lazily washing over the small rocks. When his eyelids fluttered open, he watched leaves float down the stream in an elaborate display of autumn in motion, sweeping past frost-chilled bushes.

"Geez. I haven't been to this spot in years," Geoffrey said.

"You never answered my question."

"Come on, Gramps."

"Stop it, stop it! You can't do this anymore. You're almost forty years old. You said it yourself."

"Exactly."

"Meaning?"

"Gramps, you don't understand."

"Try me."

Geoffrey leaned his head back. "Everything I've ever wanted in life, I have. Money, family, homes, cars. Well, I *had* it. Now? Now only half of it will be mine. And I knew it was going away, even before Rose made it official. I tried to get away for a couple of days a month ago, just to see what it would be like. You know? Just to see if I could handle what would most likely happen to me any day now. I lasted an hour before wanted to go mad! It was the *emptiness*, the *silence*. I was scared. I was depressed. I didn't want to go at it alone. And I know you can't be alone any more, either. I'd take that small, beat up couch over a penthouse any day of the week."

"Throw them out," Albert said softly.

"What?"

"The pills in your pocket. Get rid of them."

"Gramps, that's not what this is about."

"Over there, into the water, Geoffrey. Now!" he insisted, challenging his claim of sobriety.

"What are you trying to prove?"

"If you can be so cavalier about not needing those pills, and not being an addict, then this shouldn't be a problem." Albert reached over his lap and pushed the door open. "Go."

"It's not that simple, Gramps."

"Oh?"

"The feeling from last night, it felt new and comfortable but—"

"What, son? You said you're not an addict. Prove it!"

"It's not that easy."

"It's a start. You need a new start."

Geoffrey ran his fingers over the bottle nestled in the deep pockets of his heavy wool coat. Albert knew it was a comfort for him, one he depended on too much. He seemed to think about it for a long time, as if considering whether or not he could really give up something he was so attached to.

Despite Geoffrey's incredible wealth, and glamorous exterior, he seemed so ragged inside. Albert couldn't understand it. Part of him felt guilty for putting him so blindly on a pedestal of success that it made him forget his grandson was just as flawed as anyone else.

After a long silence, Geoffrey looked back from the window and said, "Fine. I'll do it."

***

Geoffrey adjusted his jacket, holding it shut with one hand as he stepped out of the car. Albert remained inside. He hesitated by the water, and dug his heels into the rocky shore. Water covered his boots and Geoffrey could feel his feet getting colder. He looked overhead and saw the clouds hanging in the pale blue sky. He squinted his eyes, letting a brief sense of warmth from the sun cover his face. Then he emptied the bottle into his palm. Cupping the pills between both hands, he shook them like a rattle, then took a deep breath in and let the air out slowly. Looking at the pills, he shook his head.

No more, he told himself.

Then he grit his teeth with years of anger and regret, leaned back, and threw hard, thrusting them into the air. They seemed to hang midair for a moment, like fireworks falling in the sky, before tumbling one by one into the water.

Geoffrey watched them float and disappear downstream. He ran his long fingers through his hair as if shaking the memories away for good, then smiled wanly at his new sense of freedom.

He felt relieved. Open. Renewed.

He turned to Albert and bowed gracefully, waving to an imaginary crowd as if this was his final performance. And in a way, it was. Albert applauded in his seat as Geoffrey walked back to the car.

"I'm very proud of you, son."

Geoffrey nodded.

"I think you should talk to someone about this, though. But I want you to know I'm always here for you." Albert reached over and rubbed his back.

Geoffrey lifted his head. "And I'll always be here for you, Gramps."

24

The Connection

"Layla, you got Zaide, right?" Geoffrey said, putting on his jacket.

"That's right, Zaide, I'm in charge." She lifted her head up from her coloring books and glanced toward her great-grandfather, who was reclining in his chair.

"You're the boss, kiddo," Albert said, humoring her.

"Gramps, I'll be back in a bit." Geoffrey tapped the manila envelope in his hand.

"Take your time."

He got into his car and tossed the papers carelessly in the passenger seat. He'd signed them the night before and agreed to all of Rose's terms; half the bank account, the main house, the cars, the vacation house, furniture, practically everything. They would share custody with Layla. Geoffrey's only request was that he could see her whenever he wanted to. He hoped settling on the other issues would allow that go through. If she disputed that, he'd fight harder. Everything else was replaceable. Layla was the only thing he needed. After he mailed the envelope, his net worth would drop more than seventy-five percent, but he didn't care. He was better off than most, and he needed to start over anyway. In fact, he was looking forward to it. He'd started his businesses without Rose, he could do it again.

Clean slate, clean head, clean start.

He told Albert he was meeting with his lawyer that morning, but didn't tell him about his other plans. Geoffrey felt as if he was betraying his grandfather as he glanced down at the leather packet with the embossed *A* on the outside that now sat on the passenger seat. The packet held Collin's check to Albert, which he'd taken from the attic while Albert was asleep. He had to show it to Ella. She had to see it for herself.

***

Walter greeted him warmly when he arrived. He'd called ahead and begged Walter not to tell Ella he was coming, even filling in him on the reason. Walter couldn't say no. Geoffrey grabbed the envelope in one hand, then knocked on Ella's front door. The door opened. To his pleasant surprise, Madilyn was standing there.

"Geoffrey?"

"Madilyn! Hi, I didn't know you'd be here." He leaned in for a hug, holding her close, breathing in the sweet scent of her perfume.

"I was going to go for a swim. Please, come in." She held the door open and stepped aside.

"I was actually hoping to see Ella. Not that you're *not* a wonderful surprise."

"She's at the new Rockville store for the afternoon, but is there something I can help you with?" Madilyn asked, shutting the door behind them.

Geoffrey pulled out the leather bound packet holding Collin's check, and handed it to her. "I think Ella should see this."

"Care to fill me in over some coffee?"

"You read my mind."

They sat on the large plush couches in the den, where volumes of encyclopedias and books lined the dark wooden shelves. Pictures of Madilyn and her cousins sandwiched between Ella and Norman filled the room. There were framed magazine covers from *Forbes, Inc., Money Magazine* and *The New York Times* with articles on Norman inside. Awards of every shape and size hung on the walls, and stood next to books on the shelves.

Geoffrey rested his cup on the coffee table in front of them, and began to tell Madilyn everything Albert had told him in the car and at the house. She found it hard to believe. He hadn't believed it either—until he saw the check.

"I didn't really know my great-grandfather, but everyone always spoke so highly of him. He's a legend around here." She started at the check in her hands. "This piece of paper. It's so fragile, but what it implies, the story it tells—I can't believe it. I can't believe this."

She sat with her legs curled underneath her, inclining against the tall back of the couch. Her hair fell around her face, framing her lips and eyes, like a work of art. Geoffrey couldn't help but be captivated by her.

The words *classically beautiful* came to mind as the best way to describe her. She needed no makeup or fancy clothes. Today she'd settled for a tight blue t-shirt, held snug against her body, revealing just enough cleavage for Geoffrey to feel lightheaded. The color complimented her eyes and well-worn dark jeans, and the slight tear in the knee seemed to show her casual approach to life.

Absolutely gorgeous.

"I don't know what to say, Geoffrey." Madilyn took her gaze away from the check, but still held it carefully between her fingers.

"I felt the same way when I saw it."

"I don't get it, though—why a check? If he was trying to buy him off, it would have made more sense to give Albert a stack of cash to leave town."

"I've thought about that same thing, and I'm pretty sure I'm right with my theory. Collin wanted to make sure there was no doubt Albert would use the money. Proof that he took it. If it was just cash, he could spend it, hide it, invest it, throw it in the frickin' Chesapeake Bay, and there was no way to trace it. In the end it would be Albert's word against his. But with a check, there was a trail." Geoffrey took another sip of his coffee before continuing.

"If Ella ever did find out, he wanted her to know Albert not only *took* the check but also cashed or deposited it. Then Collin could see the date of when he cashed it, hoping he could show Ella how quick Albert was willing to benefit from leaving her forever. It's clever, really. Sick as all hell, but clever. Still, Albert was better than that." He watched her expression as she peered down at the check again. "I hope this doesn't hurt you, Madilyn. Please understand that isn't my goal." He placed a gentle hand on her knee.

"Oh God no, Geoffrey." She patted his thigh. "I would never think that." When Geoffrey looked down at her hand, Madilyn pulled it away. "Sorry. Am I being too forward again?"

"No, not at all."

"I can tell you care a lot about your grandfather and your daughter, Geoffrey." Madilyn glanced down, hiding her eyes. "Your wife is very lucky."

Geoffrey raised his eyebrows sarcastically. "Really? Well I don't think she would agree with you." He took a sip of his coffee and frowned.

"Gosh, did I just do it again?" Madilyn playfully slapped herself on the head.

"No, not at all. In fact, according to my FedEx tracking receipt, I will no longer have to worry how she feels about me as of tomorrow before noon, Eastern Standard Time, that is."

"I'm so sorry, Geoffrey."

"Nah, please, don't be." Geoffrey took another sip, then set his mug on the table. "It's a long story, but it was a long time coming."

"These things happen."

"You speak from experience, and I could use that knowledge."

She shrugged. "Well, when you're ready, you can tell me more about what's going on, and I can guide you through it if you like. I find a nice glass of red wine works as a great addition to calm the nerves."

Geoffrey leaned in closer, wanting to make sure she knew he was listening. Just in case his body language wasn't enough. "What happened in your case?"

"Let's just say my ex and I wanted different things," Madilyn began, stirring her coffee by moving her cup in tiny circular motions.

"Like?"

"Like, I wanted him to love me."

"And he . . . ?"

"And he did not," she added with a nervous laugh.

They clung to their mugs, toasting their humorous take on self-pity.

"I wish we'd met earlier, Madilyn." Geoffrey noticed her staring at him, but she'd glanced away, blushing.

"Me too. I wish a lot of things would have happened earlier."

Geoffrey reached for her hands and slid his fingers on top of hers, her skin smooth and gentle. As if her body was craving his touch, her fingers wrapped around his, returning the gesture. Geoffrey tugged at her hand softly to bring her closer. Their eyes met, this time with more meaning, more concentration, and more passion than before. Neither said a word.

Geoffrey couldn't stop thinking about the bizarre irony of his situation. Six decades ago, their grandparents were lovers who'd planned to marry. Now he and Madilyn were sitting in the same room, two divorcees, with nothing but optimism when they look at one another. Despite everything around them going wrong, they couldn't help but feel incredibly safe in each other's embrace.

As Madilyn moved closer, her legs brushed against Geoffrey.

"Madilyn?" Geoffrey asked

"Yes, Geoffrey." Her mouth was only inches from his face.

"Kiss me."

Just as their lips were about to touch, Madilyn's phone rang and Geoffrey backed away as she apologized for interruption.

"Hold that thought," she said, winking. She caught her phone on the third ring. "Hi, this is Madilyn." She mouthed to Geoffrey, "*My aunt.*" Then she rolled her eyes, obviously thinking this would be a long conversation. Suddenly she stood up, pressing a hand to her mouth.

"Wait, slow down . . . What? She's *where?*" Her face turned pale. "I'm on my way. Stay there, I'll be there in fifteen minutes."

Geoffrey leapt to his feet. "What's wrong, Madilyn?"

"It's Grandma." She fell against Geoffrey's chest.

"It's okay, it's okay. Here, come with me. I'll drive you."

25

You Have My Word

Geoffrey stepped into the elevator at Cedarmere he'd ridden so many times before. Now he was there for a different reason. The smell was still there. The clanking of the cables hadn't been fixed. Geoffrey's mouth had gone dry, and his temperature rose in the humid, enclosed space. Today's visit brought on *fear*, and he prayed Ella would be all right. Albert was on his way, and Layla was with a neighbor.

He tried to take a deep breath, but the elevator was too confining. He remembered his pills, and how he'd thrown them away. A part of him wished he had them back. He panicked, fighting the urge as he did the night before. It wasn't easy, but he was doing it. He heard Albert's voice in his head, repeating what he told him by the stream—*a new start*. A strange thought to have as he rushed to see Ella who might be in her last moments.

When the elevator doors opened, there were crowds of people surrounding the nurses' station. Jill was working the desk, and greeted Geoffrey when he walked up.

"Hi, Jill, I'm looking for Ella Perlman's room."

"You and the rest of the city." She indicated the groups of people gathered everywhere in the narrow halls.

"All these people are here to see Ella?"

"She's pretty popular around here, as you know."

"And Sophie, she's doing okay today?" Geoffrey asked.

"Perfect. But I'll go check again for you." Jill smiled warmly.

"Actually, can you wait for my grandfather? He should be here any minute. And just send him to Ella's room when he gets here."

She agreed and directed Geoffrey down the hall to the opposite wing where Sophie lived. People with tears in their eyes lined the corridors.

Dr. Glazer was outside her room, discussing her vitals with a staff of nurses. He walked up to Geoffrey with his hand out.

"Mr. Abraham, so nice to see you. But Sophie's room is the other wing. Would you like me to show you?"

"Thank you, but I'm here to see Ella."

"By all means, please come with me." Dr. Glazer put a hand on Geoffrey's back and led him toward Ella's room.

Madilyn and four other family members were inside, standing over Ella's bed and adjusting her blankets. Wires ran from her body to machines that blinked different lights with printouts from all ends. Various doctors walk over to read them, and conversed quietly about her status. The atmosphere wasn't fast paced, but there was a definite sense of urgency.

Doctors came and went with blank expressions on their faces, nodding curtly to one another. It didn't take a medical degree to understand that Ella's life might be coming to an end. Geoffrey knocked on the door softly so as not to alarm anyone.

Madilyn turned around, her eyes watery and lips shaking. She wiped her eyes the best she could, but it was like trying to put a piece of Scotch tape over a burst dam. She struggled for a slight smile that quickly faded back into sorrow. Geoffrey hung his head, not wanting Madilyn to see him cry through the glass window of the door that separated them. She walked over to Geoffrey and he opened his arms for her. When she pressed her face into his chest, he kissed her on the head, supporting her body with his. She was weakened and tired. She seemed so frail; he held her closer.

"I'm here for you," he whispered.

Madilyn broke down in his arms, sobbing against him. "Geoffrey, I . . . can't . . . I can't watch this . . ."

Geoffrey watched Ella through the window. It hurt him to see her laying their motionless, her eyes closed, breathing tubes running from her nose. Her hair was tangled and frayed. It seemed as if she'd aged twenty years over night. From afar, she was hardly recognizable.

"Here, come with me," Geoffrey urged, walking Madilyn away from the room.

Family members met them outside. Geoffrey passed Madilyn off to her uncle, then found Dr. Glazer having a quiet discussion with one of the nurses. Geoffrey tapped him on the shoulder.

"Dr. Glazer, tell me . . . how bad is it?"

"Do you really want to know, Mr. Abraham?

"Yes."

Dr. Glazer pulled him aside, away from the family. "Mrs. Perlman has been battling emphysema along with heart disease for most of her life. I've been treating her personally for about eight years. Two months ago, we found a tumor in her lungs. It's spread much more rapidly than we had anticipated. The other night, we called her to let her know that the most recent tests didn't come back the way we'd hoped. Usually we don't call our patients that late at night, but she insisted on knowing right away."

"Last night?" Geoffrey remembered Walter telling her she had a call while they were on the rooftop.

"Yes, like I said, Mrs. Perlman insisted. Earlier today, I think her body just *gave up*. To be blunt, you may want to say your goodbyes and make peace with the situation. Right now we're just trying to make her last moments as *comfortable* as possible."

"Oh my God." Geoffrey looked through the window and thought of the last interaction he'd had with Ella. It pained him to know the last memory she had of him and Albert was pain and sadness. He wanted to take that last moment back but knew he couldn't.

"Mr. Abraham, understand we're doing everything we can and have been for some time now. Not many people in her condition even make it *this* long."

Geoffrey turned to look at Ella through the window. "She's a fighter."

"To the very last bell, Mr. Abraham."

"Can I have a moment with her?"

"It's only supposed to be family, but I know you've gotten quite close. She told me. Yes, go right ahead. Again, I'll warn you, it's very severe."

Geoffrey carefully opened the door and walked into the room as if any noise might awaken her. A small-wheeled stool sat next to Ella's bedside. He pulled it closer, and Ella's eyes blinked open. She grabbed helplessly at her face, trying to pull her breathing tube off.

Geoffrey gently took her hand. "Ella, no, no . . . you *need* that."

She gazed at Geoffrey, as if looking through him.

"Albert? Oh my sweet Albey." Ella gasped for air.

"No, Ella, it's me, Geoffrey."

"Oh dear . . . I could have sworn you were him." She took a deep, shaky breath. "Your face, Geoffrey. Your face is *his*."

"I'm so sorry, Ella . . . for everything," Geoffrey said, his eyes brimming with tears. Her hand was cool and fragile as he held it between both of his.

Ella rubbed his hand tenderly. "No, dear, I should apologize. I know what happened. I should have believed him."

He lifted his head, tears streaming down his face.

Ella shifted her head slightly. The motion caused her to press her eyes shut tightly and squeeze her fists. When the pain seemed to settle, she continued. "Madilyn told me about the check, Geoffrey. She wanted to make sure I knew about it." She covered her eyes with her hands as she wept. "I can't believe he had to go through that for me. I'm so embarrassed for my family. I sat up all night thinking about Albert sitting their hurt and wounded, all because of what my father did to him. And I can't believe I said those things to him last night."

"Ella, it's okay."

"Geoffrey, I need to see him."

"He will be here shortly, Ella. I promise."

"I can't die like this, Geoffrey. I can't die without seeing him again."

"Don't say that, Ella. Don't talk like that. You're *not* going anywhere. He will be here. You have my word."

"Geoffrey?"

"Yes?"

"Madilyn. Please take care of her."

"*That* I will promise as well."

Geoffrey let his chin sink to his chest, then he lifted Ella's hand and kissed it. She placed her other hand on his head and ran her fingers through his hair.

"I'm just going to step outside and find Gramps, okay?"

Geoffrey stood up, still holding her hand. He didn't want to let it go, fearing he might never be able to hold her hand again. His whole body trembled and his stomach turned. Ella smiled and closed her eyes again. Geoffrey looked back at her before leaving.

"I'll never forget you, Ella."

He hoped she would still be there when Albert arrived. He stalked down the hall to the nurses' station and placed his large hands on the counter, looking earnestly at the girl who sat behind the desk.

"Did my grandfather come by yet?"

"Yes, he's with Sophie," Jill replied.

"Thank you," Geoffrey said, gritting his teeth.

Geoffrey went to the other end of the hospital, and found Albert beside Sophie, wiping her forehead with a cool, moist towel and rubbing her arm affectionately.

"Gramps?" Geoffrey called from the doorway.

"Yes, son?" Albert didn't take his eyes off Sophie.

"She looks good, Gramps," Geoffrey said, stepping inside to kiss Sophie on the cheek.

"Her temperature is up a degree and half. I told Jill." Albert patted her face with the towel.

"It's okay, I just checked with them, and they're on it."

"Well *they* are not here, so it seems like it's not being *checked*."

"Gramps?"

Albert didn't answer, focusing more on Sophie.

"*Gramps.*" Geoffrey snatched the cloth from Albert's hand. Albert's nostrils flared and he reached out to clutch it, but Geoffrey pulled it away. "I need you to come with me to see Ella."

"I have nothing to say to her and I don't think she does to me either."

"Gramps, she's dying." Geoffrey hoped being blunt and direct would get his attention. "She won't make it much longer."

Albert paused as if thinking it over. "She probably has fifty of the nation's greatest doctors tending to her every wish."

Geoffrey walked around the bed. "*Minutes.* In *minutes,* she will be dead."

Albert looked back down at Sophie.

"Gramps?"

"Stop it, Geoffrey."

"Did you hear me?" Geoffrey pulled Albert away from the bed. He tried to fight it, but Geoffrey's grip was too firm.

"Get off of me!" Albert shouted.

"No! You will come with me or I will drag you there myself. If Ella's last vision of you is with me hanging you upside down by your ankles, then so be it. But I promised her on her deathbed that I would bring you to see her, and I *will* keep that promise!"

Albert looked up begrudgingly, but there was a hint of something else in his eyes that Geoffrey couldn't name. "Minutes?" he asked.

26

One More Dance

The walk toward Ella's room was quiet, tranquil, and cold. The skywalk connecting her wing to Sophie's had a breeze coming through the glass enclosure's vents and Albert shivered. Geoffrey put an arm around him, rubbing his sides. More people had gathered already, making the pack of family members twice as deep. Everything seemed to move in slow motion around them. People's mouths moved, but their voices fell silent. Albert could feel his heart beat harder and faster. The *fear* was creeping back into his body. He couldn't believe how many people were there to see Ella. Madilyn was talking to Dr. Glazer, her arms wrapped around her body either to console herself or fight off the chill, Albert wasn't sure.

When she saw Albert, she called out to him, smiling through her tears. She gasped, hurrying to him, and he embraced her.

"I'm very sorry, Madilyn."

"I'm sorry too, Albert. For any harm my family may have caused you."

"Excuse me?"

"Geoffrey showed me the check."

Albert looked back at Geoffrey to reprimand him, but Madilyn touched his arm and brought his attention back to her.

"Don't be mad at Geoffrey. It was the right thing to do." Her eyes were full of tears. Her hands fell to her sides, her body limp and exhausted.

"Honey, it's nothing," Albert soothed. "It was a long time ago."

"That doesn't make it okay, Albert." Her voice was heavy with sorrow and regret. She reached for Albert's hand. "Come with me, please. She's waiting for you."

She walked him into the room before he had a moment to think about it. Albert looked back for Geoffrey, needing his support. He wasn't ready. He didn't want to do this. It was too fast.

"Albert." Madilyn kissed his cheek. "We'll be outside. Take your time." Then she opened the door, ushering him inside.

He froze.

He could see it in her face, in her body language, and he didn't feel right being there. He needed more time. He couldn't do this now. He backed up to the door, reaching for the knob. He couldn't look away from Ella, but it was killing him to see her this way. He twisted the knob.

"Where do you think you're going, Albey?" Ella muttered, her eyes shut, her body motionless.

"I . . . I . . ." Albert stammered.

A soft smile spread across her pale face, but she didn't open her eyes. "Albey, are you all tongue-tied around me?"

He didn't want to admit that he was now, as he always had been.

She opened her eyes and moved her head to the side, then patted the bed next to her, inviting him to sit down. Albert's feet felt as if they were trapped in quicksand, sinking farther and farther into unfamiliar ground, with nothing to pull him out.

In his long life, he'd had the unfortunate opportunity to witness many people close to him pass away in hospitals. It got harder every time. Children, friends, siblings. Once Sophie went into the hospital all those years back, he knew the day would come when he would have to be there by her bedside to say goodbye. When he disappeared from Ella's life decades ago, he never imagined he would be there when she passed.

He had never stopped thinking about her and their life together, despite his reluctance over the past week. It had been buried in the back of his mind and never discussed. No one had known about his life with Ella, not even Sophie. When he and Sophie met, his life started over—his world changed—and he'd liked it.

Ella leaned forward and coughed heavily. Her body jerked and twitched with every exhale. She laid her head back and tried to soften her breathing.

"Don't make a dying woman get out of bed," Ella mumbled.

He took a small step forward and then stopped.

"Albey, please." She held out her hand. Her long frail fingers were bandaged with medical tape.

He took another small step, then another, finally reaching her side.

Her eyelids fluttered. "I'm sorry I didn't have time to put makeup on."

"Ella, stop . . ."

"Albey, *shhh*." She smiled softly. "Let me speak." She took a deep breath and dabbed her eyes with a tissue. "I'm sorry, Albert. I wish I would have known . . . I wish for so many things . . . I'm sorry. I'm so very, very sorry."

"I should have told you. I shouldn't have left like that."

"But you came back."

"I was wrong."

"No, you weren't. You were right. *We* were right. It was out of our hands, Albey."

"Ella—"

"At least we had our time together at last. This past week has been one of the greatest times of my life."

There was so much he wanted to tell her, he just didn't know where to start. He had to open up. If not now, when?

"Ella, there's something I never told you. I wanted to earlier but I didn't like talking about it."

239

"Don't . . . I understand. It's fine. Let's just enjoy our time now."

"No, I think you need to hear this." Albert paused and looked away, squinting, forcing the words out. "I had a daughter before Clark." His eyes began to swell just from thinking of her. "She died at birth." His hands shook and his mouth trembled. Ella reached out to him. He covered his mouth, barely comprehending what he was about to say. He placed his hands on his lap. "Her name was Abigail."

"Abigail?" Ella's eyes widened.

Albert nodded as tears rushed down his face, landing in heavy drops on his hands.

"My middle name," Ella said, her eyelids flicking tears aside.

"You kept asking me if I ever thought about you. And I want you to know, I never stopped thinking about you, *ever*." The words stung him even harder than he imagined they would.

He put his hands together, elbows resting on the bedside and brought them to his mouth. He tried to stop crying but it was useless. She reached up and cupped his face in her hand. On instinct, he turned his face into her palm and kissed it gently. He hadn't kissed her or even hugged her since they'd met again after all those years. Now, in her last minutes of life, Albert lowered his guard. It was time.

He took her hands tenderly, looking at her, imagining her when they were teens with their dreams at their fingertips. He knew she needed him to be the man he was then, now. Slowly, he moved his fingers around Ella's and laced them between his own, feeling the same familiarity he had when they were younger. He remembered what Ella had said: *Our hands are made to be together.* And so they were.

"Laced fingers." Tears rested on his lips.

"Albey, I hope you didn't forget what that means."

Her chest moved up and down with the beating of her tears. Albert swallowed a mouthful of emotion and years of remorse before placing his hand over her heart. She placed hers on top.

"I hope this isn't goodbye, Albey."

"I hope not, Ella."

"Do you feel my heart?"

Albert smiled. He did.

It had taken them decades to find one another but now their eyes met the same way they had when they were teenagers in love. It was as if they were sleeping on the hot summer rocks by the falls again, looking at the stars, dreaming. There was no hospital room, no machines, no distractions—just hope. The same hope Ella held onto for six decades. He didn't have to dig deep now to find the right words. They'd been in the back of his mind, like the photographs he kept of her in his attic.

He shifted forward, still holding her hand. As if each one of the millions of stars she'd wished on every night since he left granted all her desires at once, he brought his lips to her own.

They kissed.

He gently held her close. She pulled him as close as her power could allow. Neither of them wanted to let go. Not just from the feeling, but of time as well.

Albert placed his hand on her heart and whispered into Ella's ear the words she'd waited to hear since he disappeared from her life long ago.

"Hope, Ella," Albert began, "hope makes the heart beat."

In over sixty years he hadn't shown any ounce of affection toward another woman but Sophie, and even when she went into Cedarmere and Geoffrey begged him to "get out there" he didn't listen.

He had no desire to hold anyone's hand other than Sophie's. But he didn't see this moment as betrayal. He was saying farewell to a long time friend he'd let go of too soon. They'd lived as strangers for the better part of their lives, but Ella and Albert still had a bond. She'd opened her heart and her life to him and he shut it down. She paid Cedarmere a generous donation to move Sophie to a better unit and increase her care. She'd given Layla a necklace that could very well pay for her college. And most of all she showed Geoffrey what it meant to live life to the fullest.

Ella did not have to do any of this but she wanted to. It had taken Albert too long to realize her generosity was based around connecting with him and wanting nothing more than to be in his life when she knew hers was ending soon.

Fate didn't always happen when you wanted it to. It didn't always appear in the form you expected, or present itself in the situation you felt it should. Fate, in essence, was what you made of it. Albert was well aware of his situation now, and it was up to him to make the best of it before it vanished. He owed her this time, and he owed it to himself.

He looked over his shoulder. "You have a lot of people waiting for you, Ella. I should probably let them see you." He hadn't let go of her hand.

Her eyes, now more glazed, focused on him.

He started to stand, then paused and smiled out of the corner of his mouth. "Ella, I'll see you tomorrow at six o'clock, right?"

"Is that so?" Her hand shook slightly.

"I thought we could go dancing."

"Really?"

"I always loved dancing with you."

"I'll make sure to wear something nice," Ella said, struggling to keep her breath.

Albert kissed the back of her hand. "Then it's a date."

They smiled at each other, knowing it might be the last time, but wishing they could make it to tomorrow night. Their gazes magnetic, bonded, he released her hands and backed away from her bed. Albert stopped before the door and looked back at her one last time. Ella was still watching him, her arm still extended in his direction.

"See you soon, my love."

Outside the window, Geoffrey crossed his arms over his chest and raised his hands to his mouth to hide his crying. Madilyn wrapped her arm around his waist and pulled him close.

Albert opened the door to the sea of visitors. He didn't want to face them. He didn't want to talk. Madilyn and Geoffrey parted, and she went with her relatives while Geoffrey walked over to him, where he was leaning up against the wall gasping for air.

"You okay, Gramps?"

He didn't answer.

"I'm proud of you." Geoffrey put his arm around him.

He swayed side to side, trying to find his balance.

"Come on, we should go now," Geoffrey said, holding him firmly, almost carrying him as they headed back down the hall.

Friends and family waved to them. Any friend of Ella's was a friend of theirs. They walked through the glass corridor to the lobby. Albert shivered, and Geoffrey pulled him closer.

As they approached the nurses' station, phones began ringing and nurses hopped up to answer. Jill shouted to other staff and they bolted past Geoffrey and Albert. Doctors with stethoscopes whipping around their necks yelled to one another, "Hurry up!"

Albert lifted his head but Geoffrey placed his hand on top, keeping his eyes forward.

"Don't, Gramps," Geoffrey begged, knowing why they were rushing, not wanting Albert to look back.

Screams and crying echoed down the hallway behind them. People shouted and crowds emptied out of the lobby toward her room.

Albert pulled Geoffrey's shirt to his face, gripping it with every bit of strength he had left, burying his tears and screams into Geoffrey's chest.

"It's okay, Gramps, I've got you . . . I will always have you."

The End

CPSIA information can be obtained at www.ICGtesting.com
Printed in the USA
BVOW02s1704210814

363412BV00001B/3/P